D0018725

3 1336 09105 1657

Down the Mysterly River

BILL WILLINGHAM

Illustrations by
Mark Buckingham

STARSCAPE

A TOM DOHERTY ASSOCIATES BOOK
New York

This story is dedicated specifically to the men and boys of Boy Scout Troop 496, Chief Seattle Council, Renton, Washington, 1967 through 1973. It's also dedicated generally to all of the BSA, yesterday and today. Steady on against the storm, boys.

NOTE: If you purchased this book without a cover, you should be aware that this book is stolen property. It was reported as "unsold and destroyed" to the publisher, and neither the author nor the publisher has received any payment for this "stripped book."

This is a work of fiction. All of the characters, organizations, and events portrayed in this novel are either products of the author's imagination or are used fictitiously.

DOWN THE MYSTERLY RIVER

Copyright © 2011 by William T. Willingham

Illustrations copyright © 2011 by Mark Buckingham

All rights reserved.

Map by Mark Buckingham

A Starscape Book
Published by Tom Doherty Associates, LLC
175 Fifth Avenue
New York, NY 10010

www.tor-forge.com

ISBN 978-0-7653-6634-4

First Edition: September 2011
First Mass Market Edition: October 2012

Printed in the United States of America

0 9 8 7 6 5 4 3 2 1

WITHDRAWN

Adventure awaits . . .

Down the Mysterly River

Finally they came to a break in the trees where they could get their first unobstructed look at the vast forest valley below them. Far below they could see the silver ribbon of a great river that split the great wooded valley as it wound its way to some unknown destination.

"A river that big has to have a name," Max said, looking at McTavish.

"So?" McTavish said.

"Well, you've been here the longest. Did you happen to hear if it was called anything? Or, more important, if it leads to anywhere civilized?"

"It's a mysterly to me," McTavish said.

"Mysterly?" Banderbrock said.

"Yes," McTavish said. "As in something unknown, or mysterlious.

"What's so funny all of a sudden with you two? I'm not a backwoods hick like you guys. I was born civilized in a real barn, around educated animals that belonged to a man who had his own actual book. It's true. I saw it once through the farmhouse window. If you got yourself an education, you might develop a rich and varied vocabulary like mine.

"Stop that grinning right now, both of you! I'm starting to get mad again!"

"I'm sorry, Mister McTavish," Max said. "I didn't mean to be insulting. Sometimes us educationally underprivileged types become envious of our more advantaged friends, and attempt to cover it with humor. Please forgive us."

CONTENTS

Book One
CUT AND RUN

CONTENTS

Book Two
ROAD AND RIVER

CONTENTS

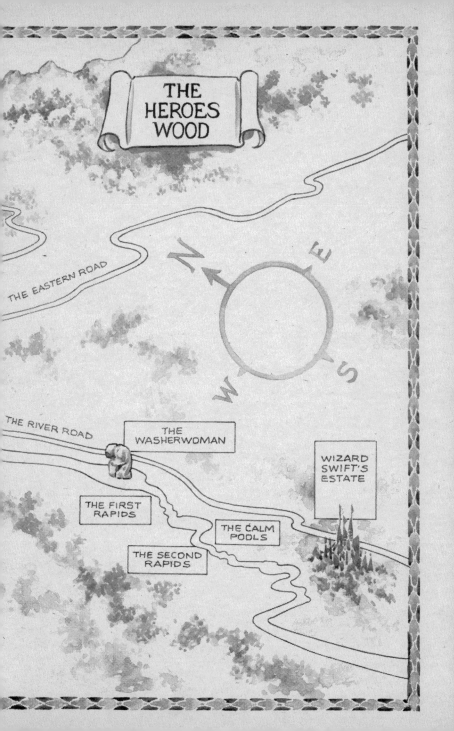

Book One

CUT AND RUN

Wolves and Badgers and Thrilling Boy Detective Stories

1 Max the Wolf was a wolf in exactly the same way that foothills are made up of real feet and a tiger shark is part tiger, which is to say, not at all. Max was in fact a boy, between twelve and thirteen years old, and entirely human. He was dressed in a Boy Scout uniform. His loose cotton shirt and shorts were a light greenish tan in color, as were the knee-high stockings that rose out of the weathered brown leather hiking boots he wore. Many brightly colored cloth badges, of every odd shape and size, were sewn onto the front of his shirt. More badges were sewn onto the breasts and back of the dusty red jacket he wore zippered halfway up over his shirt. A blue and white triangle of cloth was draped around his neck, its tightly rolled end points connected in front by a neckerchief slide, deftly hand-carved into the shape of a gray wolf's head, its fierce jaws open to reveal white fangs.

Max had blue eyes and fair skin, lightly dusted with freckles. He had a wild mop of brown hair that he frequently had to brush out of his eyes. Usually his hair was restrained by his cap, but he seemed to have lost his cap recently, though he couldn't exactly recall where.

Now that Max thought about it, not only could he not remember how he'd lost his cap, he couldn't recall where he was or how he'd arrived there. This was troubling for many reasons. In all the years he'd been a member of Troop 496, Chief Seattle Council, in the countless hikes and camping trips he'd enjoyed, and the many adventures he'd had, Max the Wolf had never once been lost. He was a wizard with map and compass and had earned his Orienteering merit badge while still a Tenderfoot Scout. And he'd never suffered a loss of memory, nor even the briefest moment of blackout.

And yet here he found himself walking down the slope of a hill, in the midst of a great forest of mixed broadleaf and evergreen, or so at least it appeared from his limited vantage place. As he walked he passed in and out of the shade of the leafy canopy high overhead. To any observer, and there was at least one, the infrequent pockets of undiluted golden sunlight made Max seem to suddenly shine brightly, like a character in a painting, before he stepped once more into the subdued, heavily filtered light of deep green shadow. The enclosed world was alive with the usual sounds of a forest. Birds sang and bugs chattered to each other from their many hidden enclaves. Many foresty scents drifted on the cool, soft breeze.

"Well, Max, it seems you've landed yourself in another adventure," the boy said out loud, even though there didn't appear to be anyone on hand to talk to.

"At the beginning of the mystery," he continued, "the best way to isolate what you don't know is to first take stock of everything you do know." This was one of Max's five most important rules of detection. Reciting it helped him to order his thoughts and prepare his mind for the coming investigation. "First, I am in the middle of a forest I don't recognize, though it is so much like the familiar forests of the Pacific Northwest, I'll assume I'm still in that general area, until evidence suggests otherwise. Second, I don't know how I got here." He ticked each point off on his fingers as he mentioned it.

"Judging by what I can see of the sky," he said, counting a third finger, "it's about midday and not likely to rain any time soon, so I'm in no immediate danger of exposure.

I can't hear traffic sounds, so I must be at least a few miles from any well-traveled road."

Now that he was back in a detecting frame of mind, the uneasiness brought about by his initial confusion began to fade. Max was seldom if ever fearful, not even during the Mystery of the Gruesome Grizzly, but he'd never suffered a loss of his mental faculties before. No matter what, he'd always been able to trust his ability to reason, until now. Talking out loud in such an odd situation comforted him just enough to help keep the unfamiliar traces of panic at bay.

"I must have been involved in some Scouting activity," he continued as he strolled downhill, "because I'm in uniform. If our Troop was on a camping trip I'd have a backpack, or at least a canteen for a day hike. But I could've lost those along with my hat."

As soon as he thought of his possibly missing backpack, Max checked his pockets for his Lost Kit, which an experienced Scout always carried apart from his backpack, just in case he ever became separated from the rest of his gear in the wild. He found his Lost Kit in his left front pants pocket, exactly where it was supposed to be. Inside a small watertight cylinder were a dozen strike-anywhere matches, a candle, a roll of fishing line with two hooks, a few bandages in sterile wrappings, and a needle and thread. A length of heavier twine was wrapped around the outside of the plastic cylinder, since it didn't need to be protected from the elements.

Along with his Boy Scout knife, which he discovered safely in his right front pants pocket, he had the minimum basic tools necessary for a resourceful Scout to survive in all but the most extreme sort of wilderness. Since he was in the habit of carrying his knife and Lost Kit during all Scouting activities, even those which took place in the middle of civilization, their presence in his pockets shed no light on the unresolved question of whether or not he was on a day hike or overnight camping trip prior to his memory loss.

The bandages in his Lost Kit reminded him that most cases of memory loss were caused by injury, or some other serious trauma. So, mentally criticizing himself for not thinking of it sooner, he stopped walking long enough to give himself as thorough a physical examination as his situation allowed. It didn't take long. His head seemed free of lumps, cuts, or tender spots. He suffered no headache or dizziness. Moving down his body, he discovered no broken bones, or serious cuts. In fact he couldn't even find superficial cuts, scrapes, or the kind of minor scratches and insect bites anyone picks up after spending a reasonable amount of time in the woods. "So the evidence suggests," he said, "wherever I am, I haven't been here long.

"If I was on a hike and became separated from my Troop, there's a pretty good chance some of them might be nearby, looking for me." Standing still and quiet in the great woods, he listened for human sounds. Any search party would be blowing on loud whistles or actively calling out his name, not only to find him, but also to aid themselves in not becoming separated from each other. Losing additional members of the search party was always the greatest danger in any rescue operation. He decided to put off calling out himself. For now, he reasoned, it was more important to listen.

He could hear all manner of birdsong, but failed to recognize any. Identifying individual birdcalls was never his strong point; not like his patrol mate Danny Underbrink, who could tell a hundred different birds by their song alone. Max did better with plants. Unfortunately the many varieties of tree and shrub he could immediately identify were common to all western forests.

After a few minutes of more thorough investigation, he found some mushrooms nestled in the shady roots of a large spruce tree. He recognized them as a type called Bulbous Cort, which were common to the mountainous forests of the Pacific Northwest, though not entirely exclusive to them. It was enough though to add support to his original theory that he wasn't far from the woodlands regularly explored by his Troop.

As bad off as he was, at least it was unlikely he'd been spirited away to some remote corner of the world. In the adventure he called the Mystery of the Cautious Kidnappers, he and Taffy Clark had been taken as far as Canada's remote Northern Territories before he could effect their escape.

Because the Bulbous Cort mushroom ripened only between September and October, Max was able to deduce what time of year it was, which suddenly struck him as the strangest aspect of the mystery so far. No matter how much he'd forgotten of recent events, he should still be able to remember the month, or at least the general time of year.

"You can't blank out entire seasons, can you?" Try as he may, he couldn't even pin down what his last specific memory was. Though he could recall just about every detail of each one of his adventures, and even fit them in the right chronological order, there seemed to be a big blank between the end of his last adventure and the moment he realized he was walking through these woods.

At this point the panicky feeling threatened to well up inside him again, and it was only by a great effort of will he was able to force it back into submission. It was time, he thought, to quit worrying and go back to solving specific problems. "Figure out enough of the small details, and the big mystery will solve itself." That was another of his famous first five rules of detection.

Even though the sun was still high in the sky, promising that there were still several hours of reliable daylight left, Max decided to make some plans, in case it turned out he truly was on his own, and he'd be spending the night in the woods. He turned slowly in place, in two complete circles, looking up and down, from the forest floor to the branches high above him. He could detect no break in the trees and underbrush that might indicate a possible clearing, where he could expect to find a less obstructed view of his location. The next best thing was to head back up the hill he'd been walking down, until he found a clearing or reached the hilltop, where he could climb one of the taller trees to see what he could see.

The disadvantage of going uphill, beyond the obvious fact that it was harder than walking downhill, was that he'd tend to be walking away from most sources of fresh water. He'd need to find some water before he settled down for the night, but he had some time before that became the first priority. He'd listen while he hiked. On hillsides any water would tend to be in motion, and moving water made noise.

Having decided on his immediate objective, Max removed his jacket and, draping it over one shoulder, set out at a brisk pace up the steep slope of the hillside. Before he had gone very far, while passing through a particularly dense area of underbrush between two black cottonwood trees, he was surprised by a gruff voice from under a leafy bush.

"I don't think either of us would like it if you stepped on me," the voice said.

Startled, Max stepped back a couple of paces, until he was well clear of the bushes. In almost no time at all a squat and furry form came out from under the very same bush, waddling a bit from side to side as it walked on four short legs. The stout creature was nearly twenty inches from nose to tail, and, except for its elongated snout, it was almost as wide as it was long. In a mostly white face, two dark stripes of fur ran from its black nose, one across each eye, to taper off just beyond the back of its head. An additional dark patch of fur colored each cheek. In a very striking pattern, the dark and white lines flowed back along its coat, gradually shading into a uniform gray along the way, turning brownish just before the bristly fur entirely ran out of creature to cover. Max recognized it instantly as a very large example of the species *Taxidea taxus,* or in plain language, a badger.

Max looked back and forth between the badger and the bush it had just emerged from, hoping to get a look at who'd spoken, all the while wondering what odd sort of fellow would share space under a bush with a badger.

"You might want to be a touch more careful to look where you're going," the badger said, provoking a yawlp of astonishment from Max. It was the same gruff voice he'd just heard. There was no one else in the bush.

"You talked!" Max said. He backed another full step down the hill, careful not to take his eyes off the impossible creature.

"Well, why shouldn't I?" the badger said. "You were already talking so much, it seemed impolite not to join the conversation." The creature shuffled forward a little bit as he talked. As he did, Max stepped back each time, keeping a uniform distance between them.

"But badgers can't talk!" Max said.

"Of course we can. We talk all the time. Back in my old sett it was everything I could do to get my wife and cubs to shut up long enough to hear myself think. Of course, this is the first time one of you fire callers ever answered back. For all of your endless jabbering, this is the only time one of you said anything I can understand."

This time the badger didn't shuffle forward on his stubby legs, perhaps because in doing so he would have backed the poor fire caller right into a tangle of devil's club behind him. Their multitudes of two-inch needles were bad enough on a badger's thick coat. Against a fire caller's soft unfurred hide they'd be torture. Instead the creature huffed and snorted and rocked from side to side all the while clawing absentmindedly at the dirt in front of him. It seemed to Max a very badgerly thing to do.

Suddenly all evidence of surprise and fear at such an unusual encounter vanished from Max's face, to be replaced by a wide grin that burped out several solitary chuckles, before they connected into a more proper and delighted stream of laughter that lasted for some moments. Max didn't back up any more. In fact he boldly knelt down in the spongy carpet of dead leaves and pine needles to get a better look at his new companion.

"Do badgers amuse you, fella, or are you just some sort of kook?"

"Neither," Max said, once he was able to get control of

his laughter. "I'm simply relieved to have finally solved this particular mystery. I should have suspected it before. The clues were all there. Not knowing what time of year it is should have been a dead giveaway. But the sensations of my environment were so detailed and consistent with reality, the obvious answer never occurred to me, until now. I'm in the middle of a very enjoyable dream. I'm going to regret waking up from this one."

"I hate to interrupt your good mood," the badger said, "and Brock knows I've had some crazy dreams of my own, but I don't think this is one of them."

"Of course you wouldn't think so," Max replied, "because you aren't the one dreaming. You're just a character in mine."

"Nope," the badger said. "I doubt that very much. Though you and I have both landed in a strange place, I don't think it's the land of dreams. I know the smell of that country like I know the scent of my own beloved missus in the dark of our den, and this ain't it. This land smells all wrong. Not in a bad way, precisely, but foreign-like."

"Where are we then?" Max said, his broad smile fading only a little.

"I think we're in the afterlife, young fire caller," the badger said in a voice gone quiet and sober. "My best guess is that you and me are stone-cold dead."

Flights and Fights and Campfire Tales

2 McTavish the Monster was on the run again. Given the darkness of the night and the density of the woods, with all of its myriad hidey-holes, he could easily have escaped the hunter, if the hunter were on his own. Humans, for all their amazing tools and other wonders, were dull things and easy to outwit. But the two black hounds were another story. Dogs could sniff anyone out of even the most hidden lair, so the only way for McTavish to escape this time was to run and dodge and run some more.

McTavish was getting tired though. If it were only a single dog on his tail, he would have turned to fight long ago. Killing a big bad dog wasn't so hard as all that, even a well-trained hunting dog. More than one hound's ghost was currently whimpering in some foul canine Hell because it had been foolhardy enough to pick a fight with him. But a dog and its master were impossible for even a crafty old fighter like McTavish to beat. And when the hunter had two dogs? Well, that was nothing short of unfair.

So McTavish ran for his life, followed closely by the hounds that howled and yipped and bellowed to their master following far behind them as best he could. This was not an occasion for stealth. All four of them, hunters and hunted, crashed headlong through the bramble, with not a care for how much noise they made. From time to time as he fled, McTavish yowled his own vulgar protests to the heavens, and whatever warrior gods there were who'd decided to stack the deck so completely against him.

He was an old yellow tomcat, of the species most commonly referred to as a Domestic or House Cat. But to attempt to describe McTavish by either of those names would be seriously misleading. He'd never been inside of any house, and in all of his thirteen hard years of life, no one had been able to domesticate him. He was feral through and through, and bigger than any cat of his variety had a right to be. He weighed at least thirty pounds of pure meanness, spit, and bile, and there was not a jot of fat on him. His ratty, ungroomed fur—where there wasn't so much scar tissue that it still grew—was of a sickly yellow color, except for one white sock on his right hind leg and a splash of unusually lustrous white fur under his chin.

Once, in the process of murdering his second dog, he'd had his throat ripped open. The dog—a giant of a Shepherd-Golden Lab mix, with more daring than sense—had partially torn away a great bloody flap of flesh, from his chin down to his chest. As McTavish lay bleeding into the dust of the barnyard, preparing to join his adversary in death, the leather-skinned old man who owned the farm found him.

Normally the farmer was wise enough to avoid the evil old barn cat, but McTavish was too weak by then to resist him. The old man carried the dying animal into the barn, and set him on a workbench to see if he wasn't beyond all help. It wasn't done for love. The old man hated the foul creature, but a good mouser was worth its weight in gold on a farm. In addition to everything else it destroyed, McTavish killed a pile of rats and mice every day of the week. That alone made him worth saving, if it were possible.

Carefully the old man washed out the wound and shaved all the areas around it. Then he set the ragged flap of McTavish's skin back in place and stitched it with a normal household sewing needle and the length of extra-thick neon pink thread that he had no other use for, since his wife had passed on. He didn't have extra money to waste on animal doctors, so that was as much as he could do for the thing. He laid McTavish in a bed of dry straw and went back about his business, leaving the cat to decide for himself whether he would live or die.

It took some time, and things looked dicey for a while, but McTavish lived, eventually recovering the full measure of his health and general meanness. "Too evil to die," the old farmer said.

What's remarkable though is that the fur under the old cat's chin, where he'd been so severely wounded, grew back silky and white, as fine and lovely as the fur of the most pampered house cat, and in stark contrast to that which covered the rest of his great, battle-scarred form. It was as if some invisible hand had pinned a gleaming medal on his breast, an award for fierceness and courage in war.

The patch of glorious white only showed how ugly and ill-used the rest of him looked. Countless scars from countless battles covered his ancient body. One eye had been clawed out years past and the hole it left had healed badly. His ragged tail had a kink in it, from where it was once bitten nearly in two, and was missing the last inch, from another opponent's slightly more successful attempt to bite through it. One of his teeth had broken off in the hipbone of a plow horse who'd been too slow getting out of his way.

In the inky dark of night under the trees of the strange forest, McTavish continued to scamper just out of reach of the hunting dogs' fangs. A great boulder suddenly loomed out of the darkness, directly in his path. He was going too fast to avoid it, so instead he jumped into the sky, meeting the vertical rock face at the top of his arc, and frantically clawed his way to its top, scrambling in a wild blur of churning feet over the slick wet moss that crowned it. The dog immediately behind him wasn't quite so lucky. All of his attention had been on his intended prey. He never saw the boulder, not even when he crashed headfirst into it at full speed. Teeth broke and blood splashed with the ugly collision. The dog's cry of pain pierced the night so as to make every sort of creature shiver in its den. The other dog was more fortunate. He avoided hitting the rock face by smashing instead into his injured brother's backside, pushing his ruined muzzle back into the rock a second time.

Above them, McTavish pranced and strutted on top of the boulder, reveling in his brief moment of victory. He would have liked to hurl insults at the two hounds, but was so out of breath he couldn't speak. So, instead, he lifted one hind leg and whizzed down the face of the rock, more or less in the direction of his injured and disheartened pursuers. "That's as much poetry as you can understand anyway," he said, when he'd recovered enough wind to speak.

Then McTavish took a look around him from his vantage point at the top of the huge rock. He wouldn't have time for more than a quick look before the dogs recovered enough to continue the chase, but that was all he needed. Far off in the darkness, up the slope of the wooded hillside, he could see the flickering light of a campfire. The rudiments of a plan formed in the old cat's mind and he acted on it without hesitation. He bounded off the other side of the mossy rock and once again sped into the night.

L ord Ander fought to draw breath into his tortured lungs as he ran through the darkened forest, following the loud baying of his hunting dogs. He was dressed in muted grays, browns, and greens that blended in with his surroundings. Over his tunic and leggings he wore a long wool cloak that seemed to catch on every hidden branch in his path, as he crashed and stumbled along in pursuit of his dogs and their prey. In the frequent rains that visited the territory the heavy wool cloak was good for bleeding off water, keeping him dry and comfortable underneath, but in a nighttime chase it was just another hindrance. With every step the scabbard of his sword slapped hard against his thigh. Unseen branches whipsawed his face.

He was able to catch a brief moment of rest when he came across his hounds, who'd suffered a mishap. One of them—Caradoc, he thought, but it was hard to be sure in the dark—had injured itself by running into a boulder. But the dog recovered quickly enough and seemed eager to press on, so the chase resumed. Judging by the sounds they made, they'd had no trouble picking up their quarry's trail again.

The demonic creature had led them all on a merry chase, up and down the hillside, through the thickest parts of the forest. It led them, it seemed, through every hazard the night-dark woods could offer. Despite his thick protective clothing, Ander had already suffered numerous cuts and bruises, and a painful twist to one ankle that he'd likely not be able to walk on in the morning. Once they caught it, he'd enjoy cutting every evil thing out of the beast, until it no longer remotely resembled its present form.

Max and his newfound badger companion sat near the comforting warmth of the fire he'd built. To be accurate, Max seemed to be the only one that derived any comfort from the fire. The badger, true to its wild nature, continued to be wary of flame and would only approach it cautiously, ready to bolt at any provocation.

Earlier that afternoon, after his first startling pronouncement about death and the afterlife, the badger had complained about being hungry and suggested putting off any further conversation until they'd found food and water. Max couldn't do anything but agree. An actual talking badger was strange enough, but one who insisted they were both dead was especially disturbing. Though he was still convinced he was dreaming, doubts began to weaken his certainty. Too many details were unlike dreams he'd had in the past. He felt real pain when he pinched himself, and real hunger when the badger suggested they seek out dinner. That didn't happen in dreams.

Time and again, on past Scouting trips, Max had proved his skills at finding edible plants in the wilderness. He had little trouble finding some mushrooms, roots, and tubers that could sustain him, even if they wouldn't be exactly tasty. But where Max was merely competent, the badger was an expert. In the hours it took Max to find his few edible items, the badger had located enough for a feast. He gorged on wild strawberries, blueberries, and raspberries, then dug up squirming bundles of fat, juicy earthworms and greedily slurped them down. After that he spent some time rooting tasty, crunchy nuts out from under the wet carpet of matted dead leaves and pine needles that covered most of the forest floor.

When he was so full he couldn't eat another bite, he found a cool mountain stream to ease his thirst. Then the newly contented badger waddled off to see how the young fire caller had fared. He found the boy looking forlornly at the small pile of edible plants and fungi he'd been able to gather.

"Is that all you're going to eat?" the badger asked in his low grumbling voice. "Aren't you very hungry?"

"Oh, I'm plenty hungry," Max said, "but this is all I could find so far." Talking to an animal hadn't become any more normal over the intervening hours since their first encounter. But one of his rules of detection directed that, "A detective can't solve a mystery simply by picking and choosing the evidence that suits him." So, for the time being, he decided to accept the fact that a badger could talk, until he woke up, or some better explanation presented itself.

"Then I guess you're just particular about what you eat," the badger said. "Because you walked right past a bunch of fat, sweet berries to get at those twisted little roots you dug up."

"Really?" Max said. "I never noticed. I don't suppose you'd be willing to show me?"

"Of course. It would be bad manners not to."

"Speaking of manners," Max said. "I suspect that it's time we got around to introducing ourselves to each other. I'd have suggested it sooner, but discovering the world's first talking badger sort of threw me off balance."

"Yes," the badger answered. "Trading names is a good thing to do, but I didn't know what the custom was for you fire callers. Some folk think giving their name to a stranger is a good way to get a black curse put on them. Never ask a goose his name, if you want to save your eardrums. But we're more enlightened than geese. Badgerkind isn't burdened with such superstitions. Trading names is fine with me.

"I'm called Banderbrock, hero of the Great War of the Thrumbly Hares. My name means 'one who follows the ways of the first badger,' and that is the code I live by."

"I'm very pleased to meet you, Mister Banderbrock. I'm called Max the Wolf."

"Oh, I'm terribly sorry to hear that," Banderbrock said. "Did you get your head bopped in, or fall down a steep hill when you were a cub, or what?"

"I don't understand," Max said.

"Yes, that's evident. But do you know what happened to get you that way, or is that particular memory part of what's broken in your mind?"

"No," Max said, quite confused by this point. "I don't understand why you think I'm injured in my head. My head is fine, as far as I know."

"Well, I'm sorry to be the one to bring you bad news," Banderbrock said, "but something has you confused, because you aren't a wolf."

"Oh, I understand now," Max said with a grin of visible relief. "I didn't mean to suggest I'm a real wolf. That's just a nickname I have. Everyone calls me Max the Wolf because I'm the leader of the Wolf Patrol in my Scout Troop."

"Oh, you're a hunter of wolves," Banderbrock said.

"No, not exactly," Max said. "Although I did have to hunt a wolf once during the Mystery of the Silver Moon. But as a general rule I don't do that. We're called the Wolf Patrol because . . . Well, it's actually sort of complicated. The wolf is a symbol for us, almost like a totem. Don't your kind take nicknames?"

"Not like that," Banderbrock said. "If I were to take the wolf's name he might come to get it back someday. I've had to fight wolves a time or two before, but always for a better reason than taking a fancy to his name. You fire callers have odd ways."

"Yes, I suppose we do. I don't imagine we can go find those berries now?"

"We can indeed," Banderbrock said, and then started off through a stand of blackthorn trees. "Follow me."

Once Banderbrock had directed Max to the various bushes, shrubs, and patches where all manner of delectable berry could be found, Max's mood improved considerably. He picked and ate, while the badger napped in the sun, snoring quietly.

He woke up about an hour later to find Max sitting in his own slowly fading patch of sun, licking the ripe juices of the last strawberry off his fingers.

"Did that fill you up?" Banderbrock murmured sleepily, while scratching his big belly with his long digger claws. "Or would you like some meat to go with that? I'd be happy to dig you up a mess of fresh worms."

"No, thank you," Max said. "I never developed a taste for worms, but if you happen to know where to find a plump chicken . . ."

"I doubt we'll find any chickens this far from a farmstead, but would a rabbit do?" the badger asked.

"Seriously?"

Not much more than an hour later a skinned and cleaned rabbit slowly cooked on a wooden spit, over the fire Max had built while the badger hunted. They'd made their camp near the splashing waters of the small stream Banderbrock had found earlier in the day. The sun had set behind the crest of a far hill and darkness settled in quickly behind it. The fire popped and crackled as juices from the cooking rabbit dripped into it.

"Are you sure you want to burn it like that?" Banderbrock asked.

"We fire callers prefer our meat this way," Max said. "It will take some time to cook, so maybe this would be a good opportunity to pick up our discussion on why you think we're dead."

"There's many reasons that occur to me," Banderbrock answered from the edge of the firelight. "One is that I've never talked to a fire caller before. Such miracles are to be expected in the great beyond, don't you think?"

"I guess that makes a degree of sense," Max answered, in a noncommittal voice.

"But the most compelling reason is I remember dying," Banderbrock continued. "I was in the lair of a great and evil dragon, destroying its monstrous offspring as they hatched. One of the dragon cubs got its fangs into me and I was paralyzed by its poison. It took some time to die from it, and I was still awake when more of the creatures hatched and began to eat me up. Then there was the expected darkness, and then I found myself here on this hillside in this forest, under vasty mountains that had never existed in my earthly home. I expect to find the Great Sett somewhere around here."

"What is that?" Max asked.

"The Great Sett is the endless communal badger warren where every good and honorable badger lives in the afterlife. All my friends who died bravely in any of our wars are there, waiting to welcome me."

"And does this look like the sort of place you'd expect to find the Great Sett?" Max said.

"Yes, it does," Banderbrock said. "Though I expect it's a bit farther down the hill where the bones of the earth aren't so close to the surface and the trees aren't so thick together. Tomorrow I'll head down into the valley to find it."

They continued to talk as the night grew older, trading tales of their many adventures. Max ate the rabbit when it was done. He offered a bite to Banderbrock, who didn't like the burned taste of it. Then, after another trip to the stream, they settled in to sleep. Max built the fire up first, because the night was cold and breezy, and he only had his thin red jacket to act as a blanket. Banderbrock had his fine fur coat, so didn't need the fire's warmth. He moved off to find a comfy notch under a fallen log in which to make his bed.

The First Night, the Battle, and
What Was Learned as a Result

3 Before Max and Banderbrock had been asleep for very long, they were wakened by the sounds of barking and howling dogs not too far off in the distance. Added to that were the intermittent screams of some other sort of creature.

"What do you suppose that is?" Max asked of the fruggerdly old badger, as he shivered and snorted himself into wakefulness. Max was surprised to be woken by dogs barking in the night, but he was more surprised to still find himself in strange woods in the company of a talking badger. He'd fully expected to wake up quite badgerless in his own bed in the suburbs of Renton, Washington. His theory that he was only dreaming was getting harder and harder to support.

"Hunting hounds are on the scent of some quarry," Banderbrock said. Then, after shushing Max so he could listen, and then snuffling at the air for a time, he said, "There are two dogs, and someone of your kind behind them, I think. I don't know what sort of thing it is they're chasing, but we're likely to find out soon. They're coming this way."

"What should we do?" Max asked.

"It's too late to snuff your fire. You called up too much of it. So we should expect their arrival. I wouldn't count on night hunters to be among the friendly sort, so we'd best prepare for a fight. Now would be a good time to pull out that portable claw you carry in your pocket."

Banderbrock referred to Max's Boy Scout knife, with its various blades, which he'd seen in use earlier. The badger seemed fascinated by the thing, but couldn't understand why anyone would find advantage in a claw that one could put away, and possibly lose. "The only good place to keep your claws is on the end of your paws, always out and ready for business," he'd said earlier in the evening. He'd also wondered whether fire callers also made their teeth removable. He didn't quite believe Max when he admitted that they sometimes did, but usually only their eldest.

"Do you really think we'll have to fight?" Max said, listening to the hounds come closer.

"It's better to prepare for what could happen, than what you hope will happen," Banderbrock said. "I'll need your help if it is a fight we're facing. On my own I can beat at least two of anything, but three or more isn't as certain."

Max did take out his knife, and opened the longest cutting blade. He'd never had to stab anyone before, and didn't relish the thought of doing it now. But his companion's words made sense, and Max wouldn't leave a friend to face danger alone. He gripped the knife firmly in his right fist, but didn't hold it out in a threatening way. If there were going to be violence, he wouldn't be the first to start it. He turned to face the sound of the oncoming dogs, and whatever screeching, wailing thing they were chasing.

Just then there was a crashing of leaves, and a frightening yellow shape flew out of the darkness and landed almost in the fire, skidding against the hot stones Max had placed around it.

"I'd run or hide if I were you," the bizarre apparition said. Then it streaked off into the night again, in the opposite direction from where it appeared.

Max didn't have time to decide what it was he'd just seen, because by then two large black hounds trotted out of the circle of darkness surrounding their camp. Their eyes seemed to glow with demonic fire. A mere reflection of the firelight, Max had to remind himself.

The dogs paced and growled at the edge of the light, slipping into and out of shadows, like beastly ghosts. Max had to turn every which way to keep them in sight as they circled the barrier of light, which they seemed in no hurry to enter. Banderbrock was nowhere to be seen. Max hadn't heard him leave the camp area. He was alone against whatever danger the hounds represented.

"Hello the camp," a voice said from out of the darkness. "I'm alone, and master of these hounds. May I come forward?"

"Come ahead," Max called.

Within moments there was a soft rustling of underbrush and then a tall man, quite human in appearance, stepped into the circle of firelight. As he approached, he whispered some sharp command to the dogs, who stopped their pacing and growling, but remained back in the shadows, twin statues of impending danger.

The man wore a long, hooded gray cloak. The hood was lowered at the moment and Max could see that he was somewhere either side of thirty years old. He had long dark brown hair that was tied behind him in a curly ponytail. He also wore a short beard and mustache in good trim.

"I'm surprised to find a young man alone in these dangerous woods at night," the stranger said, with a slight and not very comforting smile. "I'm Lord Ander, of the Fellowship of Justice. Also called the Clarifiers or the Ring of Truth. Who might you be?"

"Max of the Wolf Patrol," Max said. He'd only intended to say "Max," but the rest slipped out unbidden. Maybe he wanted this man to think he wasn't necessarily as alone as he looked. It seemed to do the job, because suddenly the man looked impressed.

"Do I understand that you're the one called Max the Wolf?" Ander said.

"Yeah, do you know me?" Max said. This was an unexpected surprise. "Have you been looking for me?"

"Not me," Ander said. "But some of my companions have been. You're not where you were supposed to be. You arrived in the wrong part of the Heroes Wood. I'll be happy to take you to them though."

"I'm sure that will be fine," Max said. "But there are lots of things I don't understand, so I'd like to have some questions answered first."

"That wouldn't be practical, young man. Why should I bother loading you up with a lot of information we'd just have to cut out of you later?" As he said this, Ander reached inside his cloak and drew a menacing sword out of a leather scabbard belted to his left hip. The sword had a relatively short blade, only eighteen inches at most, but it was of an eerie blue metal that shined with the reflected light of the campfire.

"You'd best drop that little knife you have clutched in your sweating paw," Ander continued, as he advanced toward Max, one pace, then another. "You won't be able to hurt me with it, but I'll get angry if you try." Ander's subtle smile had broadened considerably, but there was still no warmth in it.

As he stepped forward, Max stepped backward. He raised his small knife defensively and, as he did so, Ander spoke a sharp command that had both dogs growling and on the move again. The three of them together advanced toward Max, who had no chance of escape.

Then there was an ear-piercing screech of animal rage, and something small but terrifying in its violence dropped out of the sky, between the two dogs. It was Banderbrock, and he was instantly locked in battle with both dogs. The three beasts fell into a howling tumble of twisting, biting fury. They moved with blurring speed, kicking up a small whirlwind of dust and loam. The sounds they made were horrifying in their ferocity. Max could see nothing more coherent than an occasional flash of tooth and claw.

He looked back at the swordsman, to discover that he'd also been distracted by Banderbrock's arrival. Max wasted no more time, and aimed a vicious kick between the man's legs. Either it was badly aimed, or Lord Ander moved, because it didn't quite land where Max had intended. Instead it struck Ander's right thigh, but it connected hard, and Ander grunted in pain. In return, Ander slashed at Max with his sword, but his leg buckled slightly under him and the blow fell short. The cut aimed at Max hit low across the trunk of an ash tree instead, and the tree—at least ten inches thick—was severed clean through where the blade cut it. An impossibility! Max thought.

Impossible or not, it happened, and it saved Max's life. The bulk of the tree came crashing down between them, just as Ander was about to strike again with the miracle blade. A flurry of ash leaves and branches hid the two opponents from each other long enough for Max to run out of the circle of firelight, into the darkness of the woods. From behind a thick tree trunk Max watched as Lord Ander forced his way through the branches of the fallen ash tree, only to find that Max had disappeared.

The fight between Banderbrock and the dogs raged on, but by now there were as many yelps of pain as there were screams of fury. Max wanted to run deeper into the protective night and keep going, but that would leave the badger alone to eventually face that terrible sword. Max decided he had to stay and do his part, no matter how frightened he was of Ander and his deadly weapon. But he had no plans to get within its reach again. He folded the blade of his knife and put it away. Then, as quietly as he could, he crouched down and felt around the damp ground for rocks of good throwing size. Ander paused at the edge of the firelight, peering in every direction. Max searched more frantically. If he didn't act before Ander left the lighted area, he'd have no chance of hitting him.

When Max had six usable stones, he put four in his jacket pockets and held one in each hand. Then he stepped out from behind the tree, but still well within the concealing darkness, and threw the first stone at Ander with all his might. He aimed for the man's head. His body would make a better target, but a hit there wouldn't do the damage Max needed to inflict. The first stone missed, going too high and wide to the left of its target. Ander flinched from the missile, but then rushed the area where it looked to have come from. He was angling slightly off from Max's location, but Max moved to place himself squarely in the man's path. It wasn't due to courage, or any foolhardy sense of fair play on Max's part. He needed to keep Ander positioned between him and the firelight in order to have any hope of a clear target to throw at. Ander's bold advance gave Max time for only one more shot, before the man would be on him again.

Max held his ground and waited, letting Ander come as close as he dared. Then he threw the second stone. It impacted Ander's forehead with a sickening thump. Max watched the man's firelight-haloed silhouette as it stood still for a long moment. Then it seemed to fold in on itself and crumple to the ground.

Max didn't approach the fallen swordsman right away. He waited to see if there was any movement from him, but there was none that he could detect. Max approached him tentatively, ready to run back again at the first sign of renewed menace. The man was still except for the rhythmic twitching of his fingers that kept closing and relaxing. His head was painted in a dark splash of blood, almost black in the dim light.

Max felt for his own knife in his pants pocket. It would be easy to cut the man's throat now, and it was probably the sensible thing to do. But Max didn't have it in him to kill a helpless man, no matter what his crimes, or what danger he might offer in the future. Still, mercy only went so far. Max knelt next to the man and gingerly picked up his sword from where it had fallen near him. He carefully handled it only by the grip. He wasn't about to touch the strange blue metal of its blade.

Standing again, with Lord Ander's sword in his hand, he twirled the blade three times over his head and then threw the deadly thing far into the darkness. It crashed once among unseen leaves and made no further sound.

Next, with a bit of fumbling about, Max stripped the heavy wool cloak off the unconscious and disarmed swordsman. The fight between Banderbrock and the dogs continued, and he had the notion of throwing the heavy cloak over one of the dogs to entangle him, leaving his courageous partner with only one foe to fight.

Max walked back toward the light of the campfire, holding the cloak spread out before him in both hands, like a net. He walked around the fire to the spot on the other side of it where the other battle still raged unabated. Then Max heard a whisper of sound behind him. He turned in time to see Ander, back on his feet and staggering toward him, blood flowing copiously down his face, spreading out in a gruesome river delta before it soaked into his wet sticky beard.

Ander stumbled into Max and the two of them went down together. Even unarmed and injured, the man outweighed Max by as much as a hundred pounds, so when he landed on him, all the air rushed out of Max's chest in a single painful whoosh.

Ander threw his arms around Max in a clumsy bear hug, pinning them together face to face. One of Ander's eyes was covered in blood and useless for the moment. Max tried to work one hand free to claw at the other. But, even weakened with his injury, Ander was too strong and both of Max's arms remained trapped.

They rolled over and over in their ungraceful struggle until Max's shoulder smacked against the sharp edge of one of the large rocks surrounding the fire, which still blazed away. The impact sent a wave of pain through him, and his right arm lost all sensation. They had come to rest with Ander back on top of him, a look of uncontained madness in his one visible eye.

Ander released his grasp on Max, but remained sitting on the boy, pinning him with his body weight. With no thought for the pain it must have caused him, Ander grabbed one of the large, hot rocks surrounding the fire, and brought it up high over his head in both hands. At least my death will be instant, Max thought.

Then Ander just let the stone fall out of his hands. It fell to one side of Max's head, into the fire, sending an explosion of sparks into the night sky, as if every fallen star that had ever hit the earth had all at once decided to return burning back into the heavens. Something had caused Ander to drop the stone, rather than crush Max's head with it. Whatever it was that had saved Max, it made a lot of noise, like the wail of a hundred tortured ghosts.

Ander rolled off Max, frantically batting at his own head, desperately trying to dislodge a yellow, clawing thing that had attached itself there. There was a short moment of rolling and screaming, and then Ander was back on his feet, free of the terrible thing that had finally fallen away from him. Now Max could see the beast, which had landed inside the circle of firelight, on four splayed-out legs. It was just a big yellow tomcat.

With no further glance at any of the combatants, Ander ran drunkenly out of the camp, calling his dogs to come with him. Only one dog followed him back into the darkness of the forest, favoring one deeply gashed leg as it went. The other dog lay still and ragged in the churned earth.

At some point during his second struggle with Lord Ander, the fight between Banderbrock and the dogs had ended. Banderbrock stood over the fallen dog, a wild look in his eyes, his breath heaving in and out of his chest like a blacksmith's bellows. Most of the badger was coated in dark blood. Max had no immediate way of knowing whose blood it was.

"That is absolutely the first and last time I ever climb a tree," Banderbrock gasped out in the spaces between labored breaths. "I got no higher than the lowest branch, but it was enough to nearly scare the pellets right out of me."

"I was wondering where you'd gotten to," Max said, failing to sound nonchalant. For all his past adventures, he was still only a boy. Tears began to bead at his eyes, but he swore to himself that he wouldn't start crying.

"I wanted to be able to come at them from a direction they'd never suspect," Banderbrock said. He was beginning to get control over his breathing.

"Well, you certainly accomplished that," Max said. "Your arrival from above surprised all of us. Are you okay?"

Max didn't feel okay. His arm was still dead numb and he was beginning to get the cold shakes from the recent adrenaline surge.

"Of course," Banderbrock said. "It wasn't even a fair fight. One of the dogs was already injured before it began."

"Is that one dead?" Max asked, indicating the dog lying under the badger's front paws.

"I sure hope so," Banderbrock said. "That was my intention, anyway."

Banderbrock bounced up and down on the dog's bloodied ribs a few times with his front end, sinking his long claws back into the dog's chest each time. There wasn't so much as a twitch of response from the creature.

"I would say he is definitely dead," Banderbrock said. "His brother should have been too, but I couldn't concentrate properly on my work. I kept getting distracted by what you and the dogs' master were doing. I wanted to help you out, but these damned mutts didn't know enough to quit."

"That's okay, Banderbrock," Max said. He was trying to rub some life back into his arm. "I was rescued at the last second by that thing."

That's when Banderbrock and Max saw the huge cat clearly for the first time. It sat placidly in front of the fire, grooming bits of Lord Ander's face and neck out from between its claws. To Max it looked at best like a grotesque parody of a real cat, in much the same way that Frankenstein's monster resembled a real human.

"I was wondering how long you two were going to ignore me, without so much as a thank-you," McTavish said.

A Company of Fugitives

4 "I never expected you to fight my battles for me," McTavish said, in the dying light of the campfire. "The best I hoped for was that the hunter and his dogs would have to scatter for a while, chasing more than one trail, before they figured out which was which."

After the battle, the giant malformed tomcat had introduced himself with a number of names and titles: Lord Mousebane, Boss Cat, King of the Barn, Dogkiller, and of course, McTavish the Monster. Banderbrock seemed unimpressed for the most part. "I've never needed so many names to remind myself who I am and what I can do," he'd said. That had earned the badger a long evil stare from the wild cat.

Banderbrock's only response to that was to turn his back on the cat and go down to the small stream to wash the blood off himself, to find out if enough of it was his to merit any concern. He'd received a few cuts, but only one bite of note. Luckily the teeth had only punctured him and not torn. The bleeding from the bite had already begun to scab over. Afterward they gathered back at the fire to decide what to do next.

"That man knew who I am," Max said. "He said his friends were out looking for me, but I wasn't where they expected to find me."

"Which is lucky for you," Banderbrock said. "I didn't get the impression whatever plans they had for you would have been to your liking." Turning to the cat, he said, "What can you tell us about him?"

"Not much," McTavish said. "That one and a couple of his buddies have been chasing me off and on over the entire six or seven days I've been in this strange land, but I never paused long enough to ask them why. A porky-pine I ran into down by some big waterfall called them the Blue Cutters. She said they hunt down any creature that arrives here from other lands, but she doesn't know why they do that any more than I do."

"Do you think they'll give up, now that we beat one of them so badly?" Max said.

"We can't count on that," Banderbrock said. "If he has friends, there's a good chance he's on his way to get them now. We should smother this fire and then move far away from here."

"Which way?" Max said.

"Downhill's as good as any other direction," Banderbrock said. "We'll cover more ground that way, and we can walk inside the stream for a few miles, to throw the dogs off our scent."

"Good luck then," McTavish said. "But I won't be joining you."

"Why not?" Max said.

"Because McTavish does not get wet," McTavish said. "Walking in a stream isn't something I'm ever going to do, not in this life. You and Banderblock can enjoy the swim without me."

"It's Banderbrock, not Block," the badger said. "And we won't regret the loss of your company."

"I disagree," Max said, cutting off whatever foul retort the cat was about to make. "There's safety in numbers, and McTavish saved my life."

"Only after he put it at risk," Banderbrock said. "He didn't fix anything he didn't cause in the first place."

"But, if what he's told us about these Blue Cutter people is true, they would have been after you and me sooner or later," Max said. "By causing us some trouble tonight, he probably saved us from much greater danger later on, when we might have unwittingly run into a much larger group of them."

"Yeah, the kid's right," McTavish said. "I'm the hero in this adventure, and there's no denying it. But none of that matters. I won't be going with you, if you're determined to walk down the stream, because McTavish does—not—get—wet!"

"You can still come with us," Max said. "I can carry you."

"No, you can't," McTavish said. "You're hardly bigger than I am, and I've never been able to understand how your kind can stay up on your hind legs, or why you'd want to. You may trust yourself wobbling around like that, but I won't."

"He seems to be steadfast in his decision," Banderbrock said. "We should respect it and be on our way."

"No," Max said. "I'm adamant on this. It's simply not logical to divide our resources in the face of unknown dangers. Banderbrock, you're a war veteran; isn't it a basic strategy in warfare to try to divide your enemy's forces and pick them off one by one?"

"Yes," Banderbrock said, "but . . ."

"Then why should we do our enemy's work for him?" Max said.

Banderbrock didn't have an immediate answer to that,

and Max didn't wait for him to think of anything. "We aren't budging from this spot until I convince you of the undeniable logic of staying together, even if it means risking an unwanted bath."

In the end McTavish relented. Only, he claimed, because Max seemed capable of talking until the universe in its entirety spun down into dust and decay. But the cat wouldn't be carried. He insisted on riding on Max's shoulder, so that he could leap to the nearby riverbank anytime it looked like Max was about to fall over. This made Max's work twice as hard as it should have been. McTavish was too heavy to ride on one shoulder without overbalancing him, so the cat's back end rode on his shoulder, while his front end was perched up on his head.

To make matters worse, McTavish constantly shifted around, causing Max to have to keep readjusting to the shifting weight distribution. And when McTavish got nervous, which was often, he dug his claws into whatever parts of Max he was holding on to at the time. It hurt a lot, causing Max to wince, which in turn caused McTavish to sink his claws deeper, while screaming that Max was about to dump them both into the poisonous drink.

Max carried the hunter's cloak rolled up under one arm. For all his arguments about logic earlier, he'd failed to consider the best use for it. The cloak could have provided some padding between his flesh and McTavish's claws. There was no way to fix it now without moving the cat off his head and shoulders. So Max suffered things the way they were, and blamed only himself for his misery.

The water was cold and Max was barefoot. His hiking boots hung looped around his neck by their laces. He'd considered the merits of the improved traction keeping his boots on would give him, but in the end decided to risk the less steady footing over the slippery rocks of the stream bed, in exchange for having dry footwear at the end of their river walk.

It was slow going. Any touching of either riverbank might give hunting dogs a trail to follow. By the time they'd gone a mile, the morning's sun was beginning to peek over the crest of the mountain behind them. Banderbrock insisted they keep to the stream for at least another mile, arguing that with each step they decreased the chance that the hunters' dogs might pick them up again. He spoke truly, but didn't mention that he also wanted to continue on in the water because he enjoyed watching the comedic dance of Max and McTavish, as they fought each other every step of the way.

Banderbrock had no trouble splashing his way down the shallow stream. By the time they left it, just short of two miles away from their camp by Max's reckoning, the sun was high enough in the sky to quickly dry the badger's soaked coat. Both Max and McTavish breathed a sigh of relief once the cat was free to jump down to solid earth.

"Never again," McTavish swore.

"We may need to," Max said. "You never know."

"Never, I say. One trip down treacherous river rapids, balanced on a boy's head, makes for an interesting story to tell the ladies. But no one needs two such stories to tell."

"Treacherous river rapids?" Max said. "It was a tiny brook."

"When you do tell such a tale," Banderbrock said, "don't rely too heavily on words like 'grace' and 'balance' to describe your efforts to stay high and dry. From what I could see, your abilities weren't much to brag about."

"You have a smart mouth on you, for someone who's not much more than an obese squirrel," McTavish said. "You should be cautious not to anger me."

The two animals turned to face each other, circling a few feet apart. The cat hissed, arching his back, causing the matted fur along his spine to spread out in spiky bristles. The badger huffed and barked short growled warnings, and clawed at the dirt as he circled.

"The only worry I have about you is how bad you'd taste with my teeth buried in your throat, and how little sport you'd provide before your corpse lay rotting under my claws," Banderbrock said.

"You think so?" McTavish said. "I've killed enough kinds of everything to populate a bigger afterlife than this land could hold. On my worst day, blind in both eyes, with three broken legs, busted teeth, and a bad case of runny-butt from eating too much rotting carrion, I could still beat a pretty-boy like you, all the while sparing enough attention to compose love songs for each of my three dozen mistresses."

"So you say," Banderbrock said, "and yet I can't help but notice that you're doing a lot of prancing and hissing, but no actual fighting. Would it help if I take a nap while you see if you can work up your courage to actually do something?"

"Stop it, both of you!" Max finally interrupted. "You're both acting ridiculous! If all you want to do is fight each other, we might as well turn around and surrender ourselves to these Cutter people. Then you can impress each other with how quickly they chop each of you apart!"

"He started it," McTavish said.

"Not another word!" Max said. "What was the use of taking a long walk in the cold water, if you were just going to give us away by making all this noise?"

"Well, to be fair," Banderbrock said, "in a strict volume sense of the word, you're the one making most of the noise."

Max couldn't think of anything reasonable to say to that, so he said nothing further. His efforts to break up the imminent fight between his two companions seemed to have worked, and there was no use in assigning blame.

After everyone calmed down, and Max pulled his socks and boots back on, the small company of fugitives moved into the woods, away from the stream, until they could no longer hear it. Then they listened quietly for the sounds of pursuit. The one good thing about hunting dogs—to the hunted at least—is that they did everything loudly. No one heard anything doglike. Provided the group stayed reasonably quiet as they walked, they'd have plenty of advance warning of danger from the so-called Blue Cutters.

Through the wind-whispering trees, they moved downhill as the morning wore into the afternoon. When there were berries or nuts they could gather without too much effort, they stopped and ate. At such times McTavish dashed off in search of a mouse, or some other sort of small game. "I eat meat, or nothing," the cat said. "Sure, I chew grass from time to time, but only because it helps me expectorate hairballs."

The forest didn't thin out as they moved downhill, but hemlock, pine, and red cedar began to gradually give way to stands of aspen and oak. They helped each other over giant deadfalls and boulders as massive as buildings, while cottonwoods filled the air with a false snowfall of floating white.

Finally they came out to a break in the trees, at the top of a high cliff, where they could get their first unobstructed look at the vast forest valley below them. They were still high in the foothills of a range of tall snowcapped mountains Max could see by holding on to a tree branch, leaning out over the cliff, and looking up behind them. Both McTavish and Banderbrock agreed that it was a stupid risk to take, just to enjoy some scenery. Far below they could see the silver ribbon of a great river that split the vast wooded valley as it wound its way to some unknown destination.

"A river that big has to have a name," Max said, looking at McTavish.

"So?" McTavish said.

"Well, you've been here the longest. Did you happen to hear if it was called anything? Or, more important, if it leads to anywhere civilized?"

"It's a mysterly to me," McTavish said.

"Mysterly?" Banderbrock said.

"Yes," McTavish said. "As in something unknown, or mysterlious.

"What's so funny all of a sudden with you two? I'm not a backwoods hick like you guys. I was born civilized in a real barn, around educated animals that belonged to a man who had his own actual book. It's true. I saw it once through the farmhouse window. If you got yourself an education, you might develop a rich and varied vocabulary like mine.

"Stop that grinning right now, both of you! I'm starting to get mad again!"

"I'm sorry, Mr. McTavish," Max said. "I didn't mean to be insulting. Sometimes us educationally underprivileged types become envious of our more advantaged friends, and attempt to cover it with humor. Please forgive us."

"I guess I don't blame you so much," McTavish said, after first making sure that the last traces of smiles had disappeared from both of his companions. "I should try not to flaunt my better upbringing in front of my new friends."

"Now that that's settled," Max said, "I propose that, as our goal, we make our way down to our recently christened Mysterly River and follow it downstream to any settlement we might find. If there are answers to be gotten about our unknown enemies and general situation, we're most likely to find them there."

"If there's settlements, there'll be farms," McTavish said. "I wouldn't mind finding my way to another farm. It wouldn't take me but a minute or two to kill whatever mewling barn cat thinks he's in charge there and take his place. Once I'm king of the barn, we'd be set for life."

"What about searching for the Great Sett?" Banderbrock said.

"Of course, if we find any word of the Great Sett, we would first divert there," Max said. "Reuniting Banderbrock with his lost comrades-in-arms would be a task well worth the delay in finding our way to a town."

After more discussion, which mostly involved McTavish listing all the things he'd do first, once he had a kingdom to rule again, the company of friends—for they had, albeit reluctantly in part, become friends sometime over the last hours—agreed to Max's plan. They set off along the top of the cliff, walking eastward, because that direction looked to have a slightly better chance of sloping downward than the westward direction did. They walked for most of an hour before each of them gradually became aware that they'd been hearing the faint sounds of dogs barking for some unknown length of time. The sounds came from high above them in the hills, and it was impossible at that point to tell if they were getting closer.

"There's a lot more than two hounds in that pack," Banderbrock said.

Blue Cutters, Their Ways, and the Green Man

 Just before dawn, Lord Ander buried Caradoc in a meadow higher up the same hill on which he'd lost the fight with Max the Wolf and his allies. The badger had mortally wounded the dog, but it was testament to its strength and will that it lived long enough to follow its master as far as it did, before finally collapsing. With no other tools available to him, Ander had to scoop the grave out with his hands, after first using the pointed end of a

stick to loosen the earth. It was a shallow grave, but the best he could do under the circumstances.

Ander bathed his wounds in the icy-cold water of a small subalpine lake that probably fed the same stream the company of fugitives walked in down below. He had a severe cut to his head from Max's thrown rock. Though it had stopped bleeding some time ago, he suffered from a terrible headache and frequent bouts of dizziness. The scratches inflicted by the demonic cat were mostly superficial, but so abundant his face looked like a fright mask when he saw his reflection in the water's surface.

When he'd finished washing, he continued his slow climb uphill, until he emerged above the tree line. By then he could see his destination, still a good ways above and ahead of him. Clinging to the side of Sentinel Mountain, which rose stark and forbidding out of the green foothills, was Fort Dare, the Fellowship chapterhouse that controlled this part of the Heroes Wood. Informally they called it Cutters Keep. He needed to report his failure to Lady Kerris and the rest of the Fellowship as soon as possible. But he was delayed by the frequent need to stop and rest when he became too dizzy to go on. Without his cloak, the alpine breeze chilled him. Worse, without his sword, he'd be shamed before his brothers and sisters when he faced them.

Unknown to him, Ander was being watched from back

down in the wood line he'd recently left. The man in the woods was dressed all in green. He had dark hair and gray eyes. He carried a longbow made of yew, but he didn't nock an arrow. He wasn't there to kill one of the Blue Cutters—at least not yet—but to observe their comings and goings from the fortress above.

By the time Max and his companions had finally abandoned the stream for dry land, Ander had met up with a small troop of Blue Cutters coming down from the keep. Lady Diana, who was in charge of the troop, sent Lord Hywel running back to the chapterhouse to rouse the master of the hounds, then call everyone in residence to the Hall of Council. Then she led the others in helping Ander back up the hill, which was much steeper than he'd remembered.

Shortly afterward, all of the lords and ladies in residence were gathered in the Hall of Council, within the great stone keep. The dressed stone walls of the hall ended in a vaulted ceiling high above their heads. Torches burned in iron sconces, spaced evenly along the walls. Between the torches, long tapestries hung. Each one of them depicted the heroic deeds and exploits of some famous Cutter from long ago.

More than thirty Cutters had gathered in the great room. Except for Lady Kerris, who presided over the chapterhouse, each of them had come dressed in their traveling clothes, and already had their blue swords buckled around their waists. Ander was helped into the room and, in deference to his injuries, given a chair to sit in, though it was customary for councils to be conducted with all but Lady Kerris standing. Ander was painfully aware that everyone had a sword but him. Even Kerris kept her blue sword nearby—in its scabbard, resting across her lap—as a reminder to everyone of her rank and status.

At Kerris's instruction, Ander told the complete story of his recent misadventure. No one interrupted him and, when he'd finished, no criticisms were directed at him. He knew they would come later, in private conversations.

"We must act quickly," Kerris said, after she had questioned Ander on some of the details of his story. "If the three of them have banded together, we can assume they've already heard about the sanctuaries, and are even now attempting to reach one of them. Needless to say, we must prevent that. How certain are we of their identities?" She directed the question to Lord Robert, who consulted his master schedule.

"McTavish we've already identified," Robert said, after studying his journal for a time. "He arrived in the Setting more than a week ago, but has been successful in eluding us so far. The badger is probably Banderbrock, who we've been expecting to arrive sometime in the last day or two.

Lord Kelvin is currently out searching for him. As for the boy called Max the Wolf, he obviously wasn't on our schedule, but most of us should be familiar with him just the same."

A wave of low murmuring rippled through the room at the mention of Max. His name appeared often in *The Book of Better Creation,* as someone in need of deep and detailed cutting. Max the Wolf believed in too many wrong ideas, adhered to the wrong principles and codes, and had accomplished much in his life that was contrary to the current way things should be done. He was much too set in his ideas about right and wrong, and always deliberate in achieving his goals. Today's more enlightened standards called for less intractable dogma and more openness to outside guidance. Self-confidence too easily became overconfidence. Max had a well-documented history of working alone, ignoring the advice of his elders and, worst of all, being overly prideful at the results.

"What's he doing in our territory?" Kerris said. "Our chapter of the Fellowship is concerned with rescuing beasts. We shouldn't be distracted from our work by such an improbable character as this ridiculous so-called boy detective."

"My best guess is that someone made a clerical error, due to his unfortunate choice of nickname," Robert said. "It's rare, but not unprecedented. You weren't here at the time, Lady, but those of us who were should remember when Virginia Raven ended up here, and the trouble it took to sort out that mess."

"Do we have enough information on Max the Wolf to redeem him ourselves?" Kerris said. "If it's at all possible, I'd like to avoid bringing in agents from other chapters to meddle in our business."

"I'm familiar enough with the particulars of his case, Lady," Robert said.

"Then you'll lead one of the teams to capture these creatures," Kerris said. "Lady Diana will lead the other group. Diana, you'll take the hounds—all of them this time—down to their campsite and pick up their trail, if you can. If you succeed, simply run them down and take them. If not, fan out and keep driving them south, down into the valley where they're headed anyway. Robert's team will go on horseback to get in front of them. Cut over to the mountain road and follow it down to the crossroads where it joins the eastern and river roads. Get there quickly enough and Diana will drive them right into your arms."

There was some business deciding who would be part of which teams, arranging for supplies and such, but none of it took very long. The Blue Cutters moved quickly once they'd determined a course of action. Within the hour the gates of Cutters Keep were thrown open and the two gray-cloaked groups, one on horseback and one on foot surrounded by howling dogs, thundered out to the hunt.

* * *

When the council was ended, Lord Hywel helped Ander to his rooms. As the lords and ladies departed the great hall, others moved in, servants to clean and maintain the place. Some of the servants had once been Cutters themselves.

"That's my fate," Ander said, limping from the great room, leaning heavily on Hywel.

"Excuse me?" Hywel said.

"I'm going to end up one of the servants here," Ander said, "scrubbing floors and toilets for my betters. That's the fate of anyone who loses his sword. I'm done for. Disgraced."

"Maybe not," Hywel said. "You can appeal to Lady Kerris for a formal hearing, and if the judges conclude that you weren't at fault, or there was some justifying mitigation, then Kerris might let you take a pilgrimage back through the many lands, to the First Setting, where you can enter the Origin Cave and petition the great and terrible Blue Guarding Stone for another sword."

"If! If! If!" Ander snapped. "It's all too unlikely. I failed, and did so miserably. Shamefully. I didn't lose my blade in some mighty battle against overwhelming odds. A mere child got the better of me. And even if Lady Kerris decided it was excusable, the road back to the First Setting is a long and dangerous one. If I ever had any bravery in me, it's long spent. Maybe I'll get lucky though. Maybe Kerris will make me a cook, or let me work in the kennels, or even make a librarian out of me. There would be some dignity in that at least."

They were passing the library as Ander said this. Through the double open doors he could see their precious copy of *The Book of Better Creation* on its pedestal. It was huge and ancient. Even from out in the hall Ander could feel the power and inspired authority it radiated.

"I wouldn't mind spending the remainder of my days tending the Great Book," Ander said.

"It's a lot of work," Hywel said. "The book changes so often. So many subjects to keep track of. The hero of yesterday becomes the rogue of today. Max himself used to be well thought of in the old days. We used to hold him up as one of the examples of a boy of unimpeachable good character. We looked forward to the day when we could welcome him into some part of the Settings, not to cut him but so we could celebrate him. And now he's considered a dire villain that needs to be cut or killed. The winds constantly change and any breeze disturbs the leaves. Especially those in the Great Book. Keeping up with all of that would be a harder job than being a Cutter in the fields."

Once he was back in his own rooms, and his warm bed, Ander thought about Hywel's words long into the night. Was Lord Hywel actually being critical of the Cutters and their Great Book? If he denounced Hywel to

Kerris might she look with favor upon him? Was it possible Ander could still redeem himself in some small way?

I n the woods below Cutters Keep, the man in green watched as the two groups of Blue Cutters emerged from the fortress and sped off in different directions. Something big and important is afoot, he thought, but which group should I follow?

After a short time he determined that it was best to follow the riders. The hounds in the one group might detect even a woodsman as stealthy as he, and besides, the riders would get to wherever they were going first, meaning that's where the man in green needed to be.

It would be difficult keeping up with the horses, but he was nearly tireless, swift of foot, and wouldn't be confined to the narrow mountain road and its many switchbacks that would force the riders to slow down often.

He took up his bow and followed, running almost silently through the forest.

Cliffhangers and What to Do About Them

6 "This is not a good time to find ourselves trapped with our backs to a cliff," McTavish said. The baying of the dogs seemed louder, but it may have been only because they'd all started paying close attention to the sounds. The sun was still high in the sky, but already clearly on the downward part of its arc.

"We should probably consider our options now, while they're still far away," Banderbrock said.

"That's a good idea," Max said. He was next to a big curl-leaf mountain mahogany tree that grew so close to the cliff's edge that one of its larger roots hung out over the precipice. He'd been lying on his stomach, holding on to the tree root to support hanging his head and upper torso out over the cliff. He scooted back a bit to look back over his shoulder at Banderbrock and McTavish. "First of all, let's consider what we know. We know that the hunting dogs are out again and on someone's trail, but we don't know that it's our trail."

"But . . ." Banderbrock began.

"Yes, I was getting to that," Max said. "But, as the wise Banderbrock taught me last night, we don't prepare for what we'd prefer to happen; we prepare for what could happen. So, let's assume that the hounds are indeed after us again. We can't go uphill, because that's where our enemy is. We can't go west along the cliff top, because we've just come from that direction, and we know there is no path down for at least a mile or so. We can keep going east along the top of the cliff, but there is no guarantee we'll find a way down before the dogs arrive."

"Then we're out of options," McTavish said. "We could scatter, so at least there might be a good chance that two out of three of us get away."

"Or we could go down the cliff," Max said.

"There's no path," Banderbrock said.

"I think there is," Max said. "If you look down here,

where I'm looking, there's a ledge about seven or eight feet down. And look how it descends back along that way. I think it's a path down the cliff."

"Even if it is," Banderbrock said, "it's no use to us. You're the tallest of us, and you're well short of seven or eight feet. There's no way to reach the ledge, so it might as well be thirty feet down, or not exist at all."

"Not if I use the Blue Cutter's cloak," Max said. "See? I can loop it over this thick root and hang down from it. The combination of the length of the cloak and my arms should be enough to be able to touch the ledge. Then I let go of one end of the cloak, pull the other end off from around the root, and I'm safely down."

"And how do we get down there with you?" McTavish asked. "Or is this just how you plan to escape, leaving us to fend for ourselves?"

"I'll ignore the implied insult for a moment," Max said, "because I'm sure we're the very first friends you've ever had, and you don't know how it's supposed to work yet. You two can get down because I will already be there to catch you."

"That's your plan?" Banderbrock asked.

"Not a chance," McTavish said. "You'd miss, or drop me."

"No, I wouldn't," Max said.

"How can I be sure?" McTavish said.

"Because in this time, in this place, all we have is each

other," Max said. "I'd never let you down, which is a statement with literal implications in this case."

"That's good enough for me," Banderbrock said. "It has the added advantage of desperation. I can't imagine many hunting dogs would be willing to take the same chance to get down the cliff. If we make it, we should achieve quite an increase in our lead."

A few minutes later, Max was dangling from both ends of Lord Ander's gray wool cloak, which was looped over the tree root that hung over the cliff. Banderbrock and McTavish crouched as close to the cliff edge as they dared.

"Are you down on the ledge yet?" Banderbrock called.

"Not quite," Max called back. "My feet still don't quite reach, and I'm just not really in a position to see for myself. But I'm sure I'm close."

"That's not good enough," Banderbrock said. "Don't let go yet."

"I won't," Max said. "But I'll have to sooner or later."

"McTavish, crawl out on the root and look down to see how close his feet are to the rock shelf," Banderbrock said.

"Me?" McTavish said. "Why should I have to do it?"

"Because one of us has to do it, and cats are better at climbing about on roots and branches than badgers are," Banderbrock said. "We each have our areas of expertise, and I assure you that the first time a digging job comes up, I'll be the one to step forward."

"Hardly a fair distribution of risk," McTavish said. "No one ever fell to his death down a rabbit hole."

"The longer you delay, the more tired Max gets," Banderbrock said.

"Okay, fine! I'm going," McTavish said in the sulkiest of all possible voices. "But if I die I'm coming back to haunt you."

The cat slowly crawled out on the root, which was easily thick enough to support him, but McTavish knew even the slightest whisper of breeze was directed specifically to throw him to his doom. He had to get beyond the part that had the cloak draped over it, or it might pull McTavish off with it, when Max let go of one end.

Once he was out far enough, McTavish risked his first glance down. At first all he could see was how far down it was to the bottom of the cliff. His claws dug so far into the trunk that few powers on earth could have dislodged him.

"This isn't fun!" McTavish cried.

"What can you see?" Max called, dangling below him.

"It's a very long way down and we're going to die horribly," McTavish said.

"A long way to the ledge?" Max asked.

"What?" McTavish said. "Oh, no, not to the ledge. It's a long way to the very bottom of the cliff."

"I'm really more concerned about the ledge at this point," Max said. "I don't want to complain, but my hands are beginning to get tired."

"Oh, sorry," McTavish said. "One second." With an effort of will, McTavish pulled his eye—just one, because the other had been gouged out years ago—away from the dizzying sight of the cliff bottom, to the ledge under Max's dangling feet. "Hold on, my eye is watering."

"Take your time," Max said, as casually as he could. He didn't want to further panic the already frightened cat.

"Don't listen to him," Banderbrock called from the safety of the cliff top. "He needs that information now, rather than later."

McTavish shook his head back and forth as vigorously as he dared, to shake the tears from his eye. When he did, he saw something to one side that wasn't visible from anywhere but far out on the limb where he was. Forgetting his fear, he looked down at Max again. "Can you hold on for just a minute longer?"

"I suppose so," Max said.

"I'll be right back," McTavish said, and then backed rather rapidly along the root, until he'd reached solid ground again.

"McTavish, what are you doing?" Banderbrock cried in alarm, when he saw the cat abandoning his duties to Max, leaving him hanging out over the cliff. McTavish didn't answer right away. Instead he dashed into the tree line bordering the cliff edge, in the direction they had originally been heading.

"Banderbrock, follow me," McTavish cried, as he dashed away.

Below the cliff ledge, Max hung on to the cloak and gently swung back and forth. McTavish had been gone much more than the minute he promised and, from the sound of things, Banderbrock had gone off somewhere with him. He tried hard not to feel abandoned. He trusted his new friends and was confident they were up to something that would be helpful to him, but his fingers were cramping against the rough fiber of the woolen cloak, and he knew he'd have to let go soon. Whatever they were up to, Max worried that they wouldn't make it back in time to help him.

"How long do you think he's going to dangle like that?" McTavish's raspy voice said from somewhere below Max.

"I'm not sure, but it looks uncomfortable," Banderbrock's voice said from the same general location.

"How did you guys get down there?" Max said.

"We had a leisurely stroll down the path," McTavish said.

"How did you . . ." Max began. Then, "No, never mind that for right now. I can't hang on much longer. How far above the ledge am I?"

"I'd say about half an inch," Banderbrock said.

"Less than that, I'd say," McTavish said.

"I can drop safely?" Max said.

"Unless you have a reason to want to continue hanging like that," Banderbrock said.

Max didn't quite know what was going on, but he was out of time anyway. His fingers had no more strength in them. Whispering a quiet prayer, he let go with his right hand and found himself standing on solid rock, after no perceptible drop. Now that he was able to look at more than the rock face in front of him, he looked down to see the reasonably wide rock shelf he was standing on, and his two friends standing next to him.

"Okay, how did you get here?" Max asked sharply. He didn't think the situation was nearly as amusing as the others did. He yanked the cloak down from the root over his head.

"Just around that bulge of rock, the path slopes right up to the top of the cliff," McTavish said. "But you can't see it from the land side, because someone piled a lot of brush where the path meets the cliff top, to hide the start of the path. You'd have to be suicidal enough to crawl out on some branch hanging over the cliff to see it."

"Don't start crying about that again," Banderbrock said. "If you hadn't had to crawl out there, you would have ended up having to throw yourself off the cliff, hoping that Max would catch you."

"I would have caught him," Max complained.

"I share your confidence," Banderbrock said. "And I would have risked everything on your ability to prove it, but I confess I'm pleased we didn't have to find out."

"Me too," Max admitted. "Now, we'd best be on our way. I don't want to be caught still clinging to the side of this cliff when the sun goes down. But first, if it's not too far away, I'd like to go up and get a look at the trailhead and the brush hiding it."

"Why bother?" McTavish said. "It's just a bunch of bushes."

"Indulge me," Max said. "I can't very well call myself a boy detective if I don't do a little detecting every day."

The cat and the badger followed Max back up the trail, clinging close to the rock wall. The ledge they walked on was alternately wide—like the place where Max had hung and eventually dropped onto—and narrow, but the footing was sound and, as long as they walked carefully and in single file, there was no great danger of falling. The small company quickly reached the summit and the end—or the beginning if you like—of the trail there. As his companions claimed, Max found the place covered in concealing leaf-covered branches, separated a bit where the two animals had recently pushed their way through it.

Max carefully looked at a few of the leaves attached to the piled branches. Then he looked at the ends of the branches where they'd once been attached to some tree or bush. He didn't comment while doing this and, for once, the two animals didn't either.

"Hmmmm," Max finally said.

"What?" McTavish said. "What did you find out?"

"Stay here," Max said. "I'll be right back."

Max pushed his way through the break in the pile, disappearing into the brush. After a few minutes he reappeared, pushing back through the leafy branches. Then he carefully rearranged the brush to mask the hole he and the other two had made, once more completely hiding the beginning of the trail.

"Okay," Max said, "I'm done, and I apologize for making you wait on me. Banderbrock, if you will lead the way, we can go now."

They set off back down the rocky trail down the cliff, Banderbrock in the lead, followed by Max, with McTavish bringing up the end. In little time at all they'd passed the spot where Max had dropped down. The trail continued to wind down the rock face, always wide enough for a single person—or cat, or badger—to negotiate, but sometimes just barely. When they were at least halfway down the cliff, making good time, and the path became steeper than usual, they discovered that a set of steps had been carved into the rock.

"I expected to find something like this," Max said, when they encountered the steps. "This isn't a natural trail. It's manmade. Or if natural, it was at least greatly improved by someone. We should consider that the Blue Cutters may know about this path, so our lead on them may not be as great as we might have wished."

"Is that what you found out by your detecting up there?" McTavish said. "Were the Cutters the ones who hid the trail?"

"I doubt it," Max said. "The leaves on the branches were still green and hadn't begun to dry out. That tells us the work was recently done, probably within the last hour. My guess is someone preceded us down this trail, and covered its beginnings to prevent or delay anyone following."

"I understand now," Banderbrock said. "You asked me to take the lead because we couldn't count on this trail being wide enough to switch places, and you wanted our best warrior out front, in case we ran into whoever it is ahead of us. Smart thinking."

"If that were true, he would have put me in front," McTavish said.

"Oh, be serious for once," Banderbrock said.

"I am serious. On my worst day, I could beat a sackful of badgers. I could beat you if I was two days dead, rotting, and partially eaten."

"What do you mean if you were dead and rotting?" Banderbrock said. "The way you smell, you already are."

"As amusing as this is," Max said, "I do wish you would both quiet down. We're following behind an unknown party, and we have no idea if he—or they—are allied with our adversaries."

"Is it one of the Cutters, do you think?" McTavish said.

"I doubt it," Max said. "I saw firsthand what one of their swords could do to a grown tree with one chop. But I examined the ends of those branches, and then took a look at the Bebb willow bush they came from. The branches were clearly ripped from the bush, not cut. Whoever it is in front of us, I don't think it's a Cutter. But whoever it is will certainly know we're behind them, if we don't quiet down now."

"Fine," McTavish said.

"Shhhh," Banderbrock said.

They proceeded around a corner of the rock face and saw the rather large black bear sitting in the trail, munching the berries off a stunted squawbush that grew out of a crack in the rock and hung out over the edge of the ledge.

"It doesn't really matter," the bear said, looking back at them. "I heard you all the way, since you first arrived at the top of the cliff."

The Fair Distribution of Honey and Borrowed Coats

7 Walden the Bear was a black bear, even though, except for his nose, and possibly his eyes, he wasn't black. If one looked carefully, one would see that his fur was actually a very dark reddish brown in color. He weighed a little more than four hundred pounds, which is big for a black bear, but wouldn't be at all impressive for a grizzly. However, since no grizzly bear had ever been known to visit the gently rolling woods known as the Grand Green, Walden was generally considered by one and all to be mightily impressive indeed. On all fours he stood thirty-two inches at the shoulder. Standing on his hind legs he was just an inch or two shy of six feet tall.

For the last six years of his life Walden had been sheriff of the Grand Green. He'd taken over from Rambler the Bighorn Sheep, who'd retired to move back to the beloved mountains of his childhood.

It wasn't all that hard being sheriff of the Grand Green. With his deputy, Dudley the Raccoon—who only got the job because he ran against Walden every year for sheriff, but always lost, which made Dudley feel sad, which in turn made Walden feel sorry for him—he patrolled the woods tirelessly.

Of course if he found a good place to fish, or an old rotted log with some tasty grubs, or a nice tree to nap under, some of the patrolling didn't always get done. And since the Grand Green had a bunch of good fishing spots, and lots of old logs, and an endless number of nice trees to nap under, one might say nearly all of the patrolling never got done. But that was okay, because there wasn't an awful lot of crime in the forest.

Walden was mostly on the constant lookout for Rake the Cougar, who could certainly get up to some mischief at times. Since Rake never seemed to be in any of the places Walden looked for him, which was usually at a fishing hole, or near an old grub-filled log, or under a really excellent napping tree, he never got caught. But Walden would tell anyone who'd listen that he was bound to catch Rake someday.

Every election Walden ran on the platform of, "This year I'm confident I'm finally going to catch Rake." And since everyone but Rake thought that was a good idea, they always reelected him. Every year Dudley ran on the platform of, "Since no one can ever catch Rake anyway, a raccoon would be just as good at not catching him as a bear would be." But everyone thought Walden was much better at not catching Rake than Dudley was—after all, he had proven time and again he could do the job—so no one ever voted for poor Dudley, except Dudley himself, and sometimes Rake, by absentee ballot.

One day Walden the Bear went to sleep nestled under a comfortable old sycamore tree, in the heart of the Grand Green. When he woke up, he found himself nestled in a less than comfortable thorn bush, in a strange high hilly forest, under a range of white mountains, far away from the familiar woods of the Grand Green. At first he thought this was another trick Rake the Cougar had played on him. Rake played an awful lot of tricks, and usually Walden was the victim of them. But Rake liked to enjoy his handiwork firsthand, and in several days of wandering around this big new place, Walden hadn't seen his old adversary once. But he'd been chased a couple of times by two very rude men with blue swords, which he didn't like at all.

On his third day in the new land, he met Jackpaw, a

well-spoken yellow-bellied marmot. In exchange for help getting honey from a tree, he told Walden about an oracle called Prince Aspen, who might be able to answer all of his questions, number one of which was, "How do I get back to my own forest?" but was closely followed by, "Who are those rude men and why do they keep chasing me?" Walden thanked Jackpaw, and didn't bother to mention that he'd eaten most of the honey while he was up in the tree, saving only a small bit to carry down to his new friend. He correctly reasoned that the news about the missing honey might make Jackpaw sad, and Walden was too nice a fellow to say anything that would make even a new friend sad.

He followed Jackpaw's directions faithfully. Whenever he began to forget the way, he'd just imagine Jackpaw actually gave him directions to a fallen log packed full of grubs and ants and black beetles. Then he'd remember every detail of the marmot's directions again, but he'd also feel very hungry. He found the path down the cliff right where Jackpaw said it would be, and even thought to conceal it from the rude men with the blue swords, if they chanced to come by. Piling bushes up to hide something was just the kind of thing old Rake would do, and a bear of law can't spend half his life chasing a wily trickster without learning a few of his tricks.

Halfway down the cliff he paused to munch some berries off a scraggly shrub when he heard someone coming down the path behind him. He decided if it were the rude men, he'd just wait in the trail and swat them off the cliff when they came close to him. They turned out not to be the rude men at all, but a badger and a boy and a thing that was possibly a cat, but he couldn't be sure.

"It's a bear," the badger said.

"A big black bear," the boy said, even though Walden was clearly dark brown.

"Kill it, Banderbrock," the possibly-a-cat said. "You wanted to be out front, so show us all what you can do."

"Now wait a minute," the boy said. "We're not going to kill anything that doesn't deserve it. We don't even know whose side he's on."

"As a law enforcement officer, I'm naturally on the side of law and order," Walden said. "Folks who go around killing anyone they want are the kind of folks who would end up in my jail, if I ever had a jail."

Every so often, back in the Grand Green, Walden would tell Mayor Landhart the Mule Deer that a sheriff really ought to have a jail to put criminals in. Landhart always answered that, since Rake was the only criminal in the Grand Green, and since Walden would never catch Rake, there wasn't much point in building a jail. Walden couldn't argue with reasoning like that and would usually end the conversation by taking a nap under the big old oak tree that was the City Hall.

"Are you going to let us get down the cliff?" the badger asked.

"One way or another," Walden said.

"What's that supposed to mean?" the badger said.

"It means I'm going down the cliff myself," Walden said, "and I don't want to have my unprotected butt facing a band of homicidal creatures the whole way. So I might just send you three down the cliff ahead of me."

"I don't think there's room on the trail for us to squeeze past you," the boy said.

"Who said anything about letting you past me?" Walden said.

That's when the badger started to make a very unpleasant growling-hissing sound.

"Does everything in these woods want to fight every other thing?" the boy said. "No wonder the Blue Cutters want to chop all of us up."

Max was getting cranky, because he hadn't gotten any sleep since he'd been woken up in the middle of the night to fight for his life. Suddenly all the tension of the past two days burst out of him and he began to describe the faults of his two companions in some detail, scolding them harshly for their readiness to cause trouble when there was no need. In the process he described their troubles with the Blue Cutters well enough that Walden began to wonder if the Blue Cutters were the rude men with the blue swords who'd been so bothersome to him.

"If you're enemies of the Blue Cutters, we may be friends after all," Walden said, after it looked as if the boy had run out of things to scold the badger and the possibly-a-cat about. "I hate those guys."

"We do too!" the boy said. Then he introduced himself as Max the Wolf, being very careful to explain that he wasn't trying to pass himself off as a real wolf, which was good, since Walden was pretty sure impersonating a wolf was at least a misdemeanor offense. He learned that the badger was named Banderbrock and the possibly-a-cat, which remarkably turned out to be an actual cat, was called McTavish.

Walden introduced himself and told them all about the Grand Green and how he was trying to find his way back there. In return, Max and McTavish and Banderbrock told about all of their adventures, and what had brought them to the middle of a cliff in this strange wood.

"You should come with me to the oracle and see if he can answer your questions too," Walden said.

"I don't need a strange bear telling me what to do," McTavish said. "These two already think they know everything I should do, and everything I shouldn't do, and that's already too many folks with too many unwelcome nopinions."

"Nopinions?" Walden said.

"McTavish is proud of his elocution," Banderbrock said, with a wry smile.

"What's that supposed to mean?" McTavish said.

"Now hold on," Max said. "Let's not get off track. We

all want to know how we ended up here and why. It would be foolish to dismiss out of hand the idea of talking to someone who might have the answers we need."

"I agree," Banderbrock said.

"You agree with Max every time the choice is against me," McTavish said.

"Can we at least discuss it?" Max said.

And they did. McTavish was eventually reluctantly persuaded, but only since the oracle seemed to be on their way. Max was a little concerned because sometimes Walden called the oracle Prince Aspen, and at other times called it a fallen log full of grubs and ants and black beetles. But he decided the bear might be speaking metaphorically, or maybe in this odd place, fallen logs were given names and royal titles.

As they walked single file down the cliff, the sound of the hunting dogs could be heard again. "They're definitely getting closer," Banderbrock said.

Walden, who'd had more than one run-in with hunting dogs back in the Grand Green, wasn't surprised that the Blue Cutters would employ such ill-mannered creatures. The discovery simply cemented his dislike of the whole bunch of them.

"How far away is this Prince Aspen?" Max asked Walden's broad hind end, as they walked along the narrow ledge.

"A day or two, I think," Walden answered. "My friend

Jackpaw said it was almost midway between the bottom of this cliff and the nearest part of the road that leads down to the big river."

"The Mysterly River," McTavish said proudly. "I named it!"

"Then I suggest we make camp once we get to the bottom," Max said. "It's getting late and the three of us have gone a long time without sleep. The cliff path might be a good avenue of retreat in case they catch up to us down there. On this trail they could only come up at us one at a time."

They made camp as soon as they found another stream to drink from. Max didn't light a fire this time, not wanting to risk giving their position away to the Cutters. Now he had Lord Ander's heavy cloak to keep him warm in the chilly night air. Walden had eaten all throughout the day, and the other three were too tired to hunt and gather, so they all went straight to sleep. Despite the warmth of the cloak the night continued to get colder. The next morning Max was surprised, and a bit alarmed, to discover that, sometime in the night, he'd snuggled up to Walden's large furry body.

"That's perfectly okay," Walden said. "I don't mind sharing. It's only those who prefer to wrap up in a warm bear pelt without the bear attached that I find fault with."

"No dogs barking this morning," Max said. "And I don't recall hearing them last night. Did you?"

"No, but we still should have taken turns standing watch," Banderbrock said in his grumpy morning voice.

"I know," Max said, "but I was too tired to think of it."

"Me too," Banderbrock said.

"We'll be more careful from now on," Max promised.

"I'm hungry," McTavish said, after returning from a visit to nature's privy.

They decided to forage for breakfast along the trail. As they walked, Max and Walden compared methods of investigation. Max told about the various mysteries and adventures he'd been involved in during his Boy Scout career. Walden was impressed that Max had named each one of his cases, and decided to do the same thing. By midday Walden had thought of many names for his cases, but none that were as good as Max's. Each of Walden's titles seemed too similar in tone, and always began with "The Time Rake Got Away With . . ." or "The Time Rake Tricked Me Into . . ." and so on.

Eventually Max got around to listing his various rules of detection, which Walden loved, wondering if some of that detection stuff wouldn't have helped him keep Rake the Cougar from getting away with so many things.

"The main thing to keep in mind," Max said, as they walked along, "is that most detection is simply a process of elimination."

"You think better after you poop?" McTavish said. "Me too! Maybe I could be a detective."

For most of the morning the company walked along a forest trail that was mostly so overgrown it wasn't much there at all. Gradually though, the brush thinned out as the woods changed into old-growth forest with its high tree canopy and very little undergrowth. This made walking much easier, but also drastically reduced the number of wild blueberry and blackberry bushes they found along the way. As they walked McTavish would constantly dash off like a rocket, rejoining them later with a fat mouse or bird in his jaws. It appeared even talking cats were ultimately cat-like, and McTavish seemed incapable of eating anything without first dragging it back to show the group. On one of his side trips he came back with news of a discovery. He'd found the overgrown ruins of an old stone house. The ruins turned out to be little more than a few foundation stones, but next to the house's meager bones was a small stand of peach trees that must have been a planted orchard long ago.

They took a long break for lunch among the peach trees. Max and Banderbrock and Walden gorged them-selves. When Max was so full he couldn't eat another bite, he picked as many peaches as he could carry wrapped up in his borrowed cloak. Not borrowed, he reminded himself. Spoils of war. After lunch, Banderbrock and Walden, as true to their animal nature as McTavish was to his, insisted on taking a short nap before they continued.

Max used the time to search out a straight young ash tree whose trunk was approximately two inches thick. Us-ing the very small saw blade in his knife, he sawed it down and then cut and trimmed a five-foot length from the ash sapling. It took a long time for the tiny saw blade to cut through the sapling, but by the time his companions woke up, he had himself a stout walking stick. Or a weapon, should the hunters find them again.

Back on the trail, Walden entertained them with more stories of Rake's exploits.

"He sounds like a crafty one," Banderbrock said. "But no creature is as cunning as the badger."

"Not likely," McTavish said. "I'll give you that badgers can be mean, almost as mean as a barn cat, but your kind has never impressed me as the clever type."

"We've been so clever that we've avoided getting the reputation," Banderbrock said. "Brock, the first badger, was the original trickster. Once, back in the First Garden where all the first creatures lived, Brock even pulled one over on the Creator himself."

"How so?" Walden asked.

"I detect a story coming up," Max said.

In the beginning of time," Banderbrock said, "when all first things lived in the Garden, Brock, the first badger, didn't have any fur; not one hair to cover his grand warrior's body. You see, the Creator distributed gifts equally among his creations. So, because the badger already got the teeth and claws and ferocity to be a great warrior, and the wisdom that made him the most clever of all the creatures, he wasn't given a pretty fur coat like the one Gromp, the first toad, was blessed with.

"Now the Creator was accustomed to taking a walk through the Garden in the cool of the evening, and one such evening Brock the Badger came up to Gromp the Toad at the side of a pool near where the Creator would soon pass by. The toad looked nervous and uncomfortable, so Brock asked him why he was in such a state. 'I am waiting here to wish the Creator a good evening when he comes by,' Gromp said. 'But I am worried that I won't remember what to say, and he will think me a dullard.'

"Seeing an opportunity, Brock said to the toad, 'If he sees you sweating and fidgety like that he will think you're not happy with him and all the wondrous gifts he's given to you. You should take a dip in this cool water so that you'll be refreshed and relaxed when he comes by.'

"But the toad looked forlorn and said, 'I'd love to do that, but I can't because he will be by here soon and there wouldn't be enough time for my lovely coat to dry before he comes.'

"Clever Brock answered him saying, 'I see your dilemma. It would not be fit to greet the Creator in a wet coat. But you are my friend, so I will help you by holding your coat so that it doesn't get wet while you take a swim in the cool water. Give over your coat to me.'

"Gromp was suspicious because no creature in the Garden was more cunning than the badger. 'How can I be sure you will return my coat after I swim?' Gromp said. And Brock answered him saying, 'If you ask for your coat back before the Creator comes by, and I don't give it over to you, then I promise by the teeth of the Creator himself that I will forfeit my cunning and my claws and my own fine teeth.'

"Now the toad envied the badger all those gifts, and knew that no promise made on the teeth of the Creator could be broken, so he gave his coat over to Brock and took a swim in the cool waters of the pool.

"This was the first time the toad had ever swum without his heavy fur coat, and the feeling of the cool water against his naked skin was glorious. As Brock knew he would, Gromp kept swimming too long so that he was still frolicking in the pool when the Creator came by to take his accustomed walk through the Garden in the cool of the evening.

"The Creator saw Brock wearing the fine coat with all of its lovely stripes of black and white, and its back of long gray and brown fur, and said to him, 'How is it that you have the fine coat I gave unto the toad?' And Brock said to him, 'The toad gave it over to me to hold while he swam in the cool waters of this pool. We agreed that if he wanted it back he would ask for it before you came by, so he could wear it to wish you a good evening. But he loved his swim more than he wanted to have his coat back, or to wish you a good evening, so the coat is now mine to keep.'

"Now this news made the Creator very angry and he said unto the toad who was swimming in the cool waters of the pool, 'If you prefer to swim more than you desire to wish me a good evening, and you value my gifts to you so little that you'd give them over unto the badger, then I will give you sick green skin and warts, and I will turn your sweetest sounding of all voices into a wretched croaking!' And all these things came to pass.

"And that is why," Banderbrock finished, "to this very day, badgers have the most lovely fur coats in the animal kingdom, in addition to all the other great gifts, while toads are fine swimmers but have very few other gifts at all."

"That's a wonderful story," Max said, when the badger had finished.

"It makes me want to go for a swim," Walden said.

"It's a load of poo," McTavish said.

Later that night they camped again without a fire, and ate more of the wonderful peaches Max had carried throughout the afternoon. Banderbrock told more stories about cunning Brock when he was in the Garden, and later, after all creatures had to leave the Garden, and how Brock's new fur coat came in handy once the first of many winters started. Max took the first watch and then woke Walden to take the watch when it was his turn. Minutes after Max fell asleep it began to rain, waking him up again. It rained all night and the company was cold, wet, and miserable and got little sleep.

What Cutters Cut

By midday the eight riders in Lord Robert's group had finished the treacherous overland race east, from Cutters Keep to the high mountain road. Above them the dirt road picked its careful way up to the pass at the saddle between Sentinel and Barrier mountains. The pass would be closed in another two weeks with the snow that would stay until the late spring of the new year. Below them the road zigzagged down the mountainside, up and down, over a series of false summits, only to turn down again, winding back and forth into the green foothills, ever farther down to the river valley.

On reaching the road they dismounted to rest the nearly blown horses. They brushed them and then walked them down the road for a few hours before mounting again. Though Lord Robert was in charge of this expedition, Lord Stephen was the master of horses for the chapter, and Robert willingly deferred to him in all matters regarding their care. They'd never be able to complete their mission on ruined mounts.

By nightfall, alternating between two hours of riding and two hours of walking, the party had descended well into the wooded foothills. They camped early to give the mounts as much rest as possible before the next day's ride. Lord Michael brought down a whitetail buck with a well-placed arrow and they feasted. Unlike the company of fugitives far below them, they had no fear of lighting open fires. They were the Blue Cutters and, in these numbers, nothing in this land was a danger to them.

From a short distance away, the man in green crouched in the deep shadows of the trees, watching the Cutters in their camp. No one saw him. No one heard him. He ate a dinner of green thistles and the uncooked meat of a rabbit he'd shot earlier in the day, with a single well-placed arrow. When the Cutters slept he slept, and when they woke he woke.

The next morning—at the same time Max was telling

Walden about the Mystery of the Missing Star and other past adventures—Robert's team was already mounted again and pushing hard down the road, changing directions with each turn of the countless switchbacks that stepped down the steep hills in more reasonable grades than the actual slope would otherwise allow. By the time the fugitive company was gorging on a lost orchard's peaches, Robert's riders had crested the last hill that hid the river valley from view. They looked at the mighty river so far below them, snaking its way to a far, unseen ocean.

The river had a thousand names. Each new arrival in the land called it something different and, until such time as the Blue Cutters found and redeemed them, each new arrival's pronouncements carried authority. So the names piled up. The river was called the Silver Veil. The river was called the Snakedance. The river was called the Mysterly. So many names.

By nightfall the last of the switchbacks was far behind them. They camped where the road began its last steady fall in a long gentle slope down into the valley. Sometime in the night the rains came. Huddled under their long warm cloaks, the riders clip-clopped slowly along a dirt road that had become a ribbon of mud. An hour after dawn they spotted a lone horse-drawn caravan wagon ahead of them on the road and traveling in the same direction, but much slower than the mounted riders. It must have come over the high mountain pass days ago, before the latest snowfall closed it off for the winter. Whoever it was, he'd be stuck in this valley until the next spring.

As they began to close with the brightly painted box-covered wagon they recognized it, and most of them lost their bravado of the previous days. It was the Eggman's wagon. As they overtook it, they circled well off the road to give the single caravan, with its solitary driver and white draft horse, a wide berth.

There were powers in the world not even the combined strength of the feared Blue Cutters could overcome, and the Eggman was one of them.

Far on the other side of the slow-moving wagon, they regained the road and spurred their tired mounts to greater speed. Lord Robert ordered that they put three leagues between them and the Eggman before they allowed the horses to walk again.

The man in green followed the riders as best he could, but began falling behind once they'd put the spurs to their mounts. He could catch up by sacrificing on sleep. He'd keep moving, day and night, while they'd have to stop often to rest their mounts.

Diana stood near the edge of the precipice, looking down over the exposed walls of defiant limestone, punctuated here and there on its nearly vertical face by hardy shrubs and grasses that slowly broke their way into the solid stone, colonizing the vertical face with creeping deliberation. Its fateful and inescapable message: "Even this we own."

"This is where the trail ends?" she said to Lord Patrick, the chapter's kennel master. Two dozen excited hounds yipped and barked at their feet, paying no attention to the rain, but generally giving the edge of the cliff good clearance.

"Yes, Lady," Patrick said. The rain had soaked his short reddish hair into a thin cap pasted against his skull. It would be impolite to address Lady Diana with his hood up, so he endured the rain. "There's a trail down that wall you can just see if you scoot far enough over the edge, and have someone you trust holding your feet. You can bet your last silver they went down it."

"Is there a way down to the trail short of lowering ourselves on ropes?" She clutched her cloak tighter around her against the rain. She had her hood up and idly wondered why Patrick chose not to.

"Probably," Patrick said. "We're looking for it now, but it may take some time. This rain has spoiled the scent trail."

"Call me when you've located it," Diana said, and walked back into the tree line where some of the others had erected a shelter by stringing the square of a large oilcloth tarp among four trees, slightly angled to allow the water to run off. Most of the Cutters under her command were gathered under the tarp, surrounding a small, terrified creature.

"Is this the prisoner?" Diana asked, as she slipped under the makeshift awning.

"Yes, Lady," Lord Jeven answered. He was one of the two men not originally assigned to her party, but who'd recently joined up with them. They'd been hunting Walden the Bear for the past few days and had come into her camp with the small captive creature in custody.

Diana looked down at the shivering beast trapped between the Cutters. It was some sort of large member of the rodent family, about a foot and a half long. It had short bristly brown fur that turned mustard yellow on its underside.

"What can you tell me about him?" Diana asked.

"His name's Jackpaw," Jeven said. "He's a minor fugitive that wasn't worth the effort to hunt down, as long as he didn't show any inclination to make a run for one of the sanctuaries. But Walden's trail intersected his a few days ago, so we picked him up."

"What has he told you so far?" Diana said. Even under the trees, rain fell in a hard patter against the top of the stretched oilskin barrier above them.

"Nothing useful," Jeven said. "He's a defiant little rat."

"Marmot," Jackpaw corrected.

"What do you think he has to tell us to help my mission?" Diana said.

"Maybe nothing," Jeven said. "But since the trails of your quarry and ours converge here, maybe they've met up. If this fellow knows something about Walden, it might also apply to your group."

"That sounds reasonable," Diana said, pulling out her short sword. The blue metal glistened in the diffused light under the tent. "Do you mind if I do the cutting?"

"Be our guest," Jeven said.

Diana took her time cutting into the creature. She made no broad slashes but made instead a hundred tiny and particular cuts, bit by bit discarding details of the thing's past life. She didn't stop when she'd learned everything about his encounter with Walden the Bear, and the directions he'd provided to Prince Aspen's grove. She continued cutting for more than two hours, until the creature that remained resembled the former Jackpaw in name and appearance only. When she finally turned it loose, it thanked her profusely and scampered off to enjoy its new and approved life.

"I've never seen more precise and delicate work, under more difficult conditions, cutting in the field, in the mud and rain," Jeven said, when she'd finished with the yellow-bellied marmot. "I've ever only worked in the warmth and comfort of one of the keep's cutting rooms. You make me ashamed of my own poor skills."

"I've been at this awhile," was all Diana said.

She was excited about learning the directions to

Prince Aspen's secret grove. If they proved out, this was already the most successful single mission she'd ever undertaken. They'd been hunting for Prince Aspen for a decade in every corner of the Heroes Wood. Who ever suspected he was rooted in the heart of the beast section?

If Diana located Prince Aspen she'd almost certainly be offered Lady Kerris's place as head of this chapter. Diana had an odd, wavelike track of ambition. She'd risen to chapter command half a dozen times, only to eventually get bored with the pressures and tedium of administrative duties, and beg a return to field assignment. Then, in a year or two, her ambition would reassert itself and she'd claw her way to the head of another chapterhouse.

Maybe it was a strange form of wanderlust. She was always reassigned to a new chapter at each return to field duty. It wouldn't do to have her serve in a subordinate position in the same chapter she'd once commanded. It might cause a dangerous rift in loyalties. In any case, she'd never been the leader of this particular chapter yet, so she intended to win the seat away from Kerris or anyone else who might stand in her way.

"We've located the top of the trail down the cliff," Patrick said, stepping under the protection of the tarp. He was followed, as always, by a number of his more boisterous hounds.

"Show me," Diana said. She preceded him back out into the cold hard rain.

Patrick and his canine retinue caught up to Diana and he led her along the cliff edge to a place where a number of severed branches had been cleared away from the head of the trail. Diana stepped out on it a little ways to get a better look at its path as it wound down the rough face of the granite wall.

"Can the dogs get down this?" she asked.

"Not in the rain, and I'd call it at no better than possibly if it were dry," Patrick said. "I'd never give such an order myself."

"Then I'm placing you in temporary command of the company," Diana said. "I'm going down this way immediately on my own. You take the rest of the company and find a better way down and meet up with me when you can. I'll leave plenty of trail-sign for you to find me again. In any case, you know our new objective."

Diana returned to the rough encampment long enough to repeat her instructions to the others, and gather a few light provisions. Then she set off down the rain-slicked rock of the narrow ledge, where Max and his company of fugitives had descended two days earlier. She was quick and sure on her feet, and never made a misstep.

Quaking Aspens, Good Manners, and Stories Told

 Diana reached the bottom of the escarpment without mishap, though the rain made the rounded stone surface of the narrow ledge slick and deadly. At the bottom of the cliff she began to run, springing light and agile over boulders and fallen logs, splashing through the mud and pooled water, enjoying herself despite the miserable weather. Deep into the woods she ran, trailing the fugitive company, no longer needing to constantly pause and search out their sign. She knew where they were going

because now she followed the same directions they did. They'd be limited by the speed of their slowest member, and badgers, for all of their other qualities, weren't built for long, hard travel. If she hurried, she could overtake them in little more than a day.

When the rain finally let up, she shook the water out of her cloak, then rolled it up and tucked it under one arm. In the other hand she carried her sheathed sword, unhooked from her belt, to balance the weight of the cloak on the other side, and to keep it from slapping against her leg as she ran. At every small stream she stopped briefly to drink and rest, before running on again, lithe and beautiful through the rain-sparkled greenwood. When darkness closed in she had to slow to a brisk walk. After a while she slept, but only for a few hours—she didn't need more—before setting out again. She ate up miles quickly.

By the time the small company met Prince Aspen, Max had abandoned all hope of finding some reasonable explanation for the bizarre turn his life had taken. He resigned himself—reluctantly—to talking cats and badgers and every other impossible thing. On the trail earlier that v, he'd refused to let Banderbrock kill another rabbit for

't eat anything that I might have a conversation

with under different circumstances," he'd said. His friends found such an idea amusing.

Walden patiently explained to him that one thing had nothing to do with the other. "One kills what he needs to eat, according to his nature," he'd said. "As a law enforcement officer I had to learn long ago that killing and murder are two different things. Back in the Grand Green I never arrested anyone for simply getting his dinner, even if the dinner used to be someone I knew."

Max admitted that he understood the bear's reasoning, but he couldn't personally subscribe to the grim philosophy behind it. "I'll limit myself to eating fruits and vegetables from now on," he'd said. "At least plants don't talk." This seemed to amuse his friends even more, which confused him, until he met Prince Aspen.

After a long morning's walk in the pouring rain—McTavish had been even more annoying than usual, constantly wailing dire curses against the sadistic sky—they came to a bluff overlooking a stand of aspen trees, surrounded by a wide protective circle of lodgepole pines, forming a secluded grove, almost like a living woodland temple. The rain let up and their spirits rose as they worked their way down to the aspen grove. They had to squeeze their way past the close-standing trunks of the lodgepole pines to get in amongst the aspens. Walden had the most trouble, and for a while it looked like he was going to get stuck between two tree trunks, until a well-placed claw from Banderbrock, enthusiastically applied to Walden's rear end, helped him get past the pine trees just fine. The largest tree was the one in the center of the grove. Max recognized it as the variety known as quaking aspen, so named because of the way its leaves tremble in the slightest breeze.

This particular tree was huge, about seventy to eighty feet tall, with a trunk at least six feet thick. Its relatively thin branches started high up on the trunk, and were covered with small green heart-shaped leaves that were just beginning to take on the golden yellow color that would see them through to the fall. Its bark was thin and white and unblemished by the cuts and scratches of bear, moose, and elk that are common to most aspen trees.

There was a breeze that afternoon, and it caused all the millions of leaves in the private grove to quietly tremble and rustle, like the excited whispering of a concert audience before a grand performance is about to begin.

"So, we're really going to talk to a tree?" Max said, standing with his friends at the base of the giant. He felt just a touch of guilt to be holding his recently made staff, which made him feel silly that he actually took this seriously. Would the tree blame him for murdering an innocent ash sapling, just to get a walking stick? "How do we start? Is there some sort of druidic ritual we have to go through first?"

"Not that I know of." A voice came from far above them. "Most visitors begin with the usual 'hello' and 'nice to meet you' common to anyone with reasonably good manners."

"Oh my," Max said.

"This is spooky," Walden said.

"If he insists on good manners, then I probably shouldn't be chosen as our spokesman," McTavish said.

"Hello, sir," Banderbrock said, after it began to look as if none of his companions were going to continue. "My name is Banderbrock the Badger. These are my friends, Max the Wolf—which is strictly a metaphor—Walden the Bear, and McTavish the Monster, which isn't entirely metaphorical, though it's obvious he's also a cat."

"I'm pleased to meet each of you," the voice said. "My name is Prince Aspen, neither word of which is intended to be taken in any but the most literal way, though I have to confess, my principality was in a land far removed from this one, and is no longer mine to claim."

Prince Aspen's voice wasn't booming or overpowering in any way, though it was omnipresent. It seemed to be formed from the combined rustling movement of all his high leaves and branches. In tone, it was both light and resonant, as if a young man, in a good mood, were talking against a tightly stretched drumhead.

Each time Prince Aspen spoke, a light spray of the water that had accumulated on his leaves during the recent rain shook loose and sprinkled down on the company below him. McTavish moved far enough away to avoid getting further soaked by Prince Aspen's secondary rainfall, mumbling something along the lines of, "Say it, don't spray it," as he went.

"Sir," Max said, "we've come to see you because we were told you're an oracle who can answer our questions, and solve the mystery of how each of us got to this land. We'd also like to know how we can find our way home. Or, if that's not possible, we'd at least like to know why we're here, and what we're supposed to do."

"That's quite a list, young wolfling," Prince Aspen said. "And I may be able to answer some of those questions, but I'm sorry to have to tell you that I'm not a real oracle. I can't see the future. I don't have special insight into the minds of whatever great powers rule the universe. Nor do I have knowledge of events I didn't witness, unless someone comes here and tells me about it.

"I'm only helpful, if at all, because I've got a good memory, and I've been here long enough to hear the stories and adventures of many a passerby. It's an unfortunate truth that tales tend to grow in the telling. Through rumor and wishful thinking, the news of my store of useful information has grown into a belief that I possess extraordinary wisdom or supernatural powers. I regret that you may have come here thinking I could provide easy solutions to all of your problems, which isn't so. That said, I'll gladly answer what questions I can."

"Is there a price for such information?" Banderbrock said, knowing that such things are best worked out in advance, to avoid unhappy surprises later.

"Of course there's a price," Prince Aspen said. "First, I require a binding oath from each of you never to reveal my location to those who call themselves the Fellowship of Justice, and sometimes the Ring of Truth, and whom most others refer to as the Blue Cutters. Then, equally as important, I want gossip. Lots and lots of gossip.

"Long ago, in my youth, I was as mobile as any of you. As a dryad prince of the royal sapline, I went everywhere and had many wonderful adventures. But, in the folly of my youth, I made a serious political error and was forced, as a penance, to take early root here, long before one of my kind usually does. As a result, I'm bored unto tears. So I want your stories. I want to hear all about everything that's happened in this land and in whatever lands you originally came from."

Many oaths were then sworn. Banderbrock swore in the name of the first badger, and Walden swore as an officer of the law. Max swore on the *Boy Scout Handbook*, which was—he assured everyone—still binding on him, even though he didn't have his copy of the book with him.

McTavish couldn't decide what or who to swear on, because—as he explained—he'd never encountered nor acknowledged an authority greater than himself. After all, he was a mighty king in his old home, compared to poor

Aspen, who only made it as far as prince. He'd been undisputed king of the McDonald's farm barn cats, which had to make him king of the whole farm as far as any reasonable person could be concerned. And the McDonald's farm was obviously the most important farm in all the land; otherwise McTavish wouldn't have been king of it. His logic was odd but unimpeachable.

After some discussion on the matter, Prince Aspen eventually agreed that the cat should swear on himself, since he was clearly the greatest of all things in the official McTavish cosmology.

Once the oaths were sworn, following a short break for the company to find lunch—which went quickly after Prince Aspen directed them to all the best sources of fruits and nuts in the area—the stories began, and continued long into that night and the day following. Each member of the small company took their turn, while the others listened along, or slept, or gathered more food, of which there was an abundance in the area surrounding the hidden grove.

Walden told every story about life in the Grand Green that he could remember. Not surprisingly, every tale that didn't directly involve some clever trick played on the sheriff by Rake the Cougar concerned a beloved memory of where a particularly fat and tasty trout was caught, or where a particularly fine bunch of grubs, or ants, or black beetles had been located, or a long and detailed list of some of the very best naps the bear had taken. He also told of his few adventures in this land, his encounters with the Blue Cutters, and of meeting the prince's old friend Jackpaw.

When it was Banderbrock's turn, he told of his own warrior's adventures on the wooded slope of his home sett, and all of the instructional tales of Brock, the first badger. Prince Aspen particularly liked the legend of how Brock convinced Weylin, the first skunk, to take Brock's horrible scent, if he also gave the skunk the best white stripe off his new fur coat. Banderbrock taught Prince Aspen many of the military songs he'd learned in the two great wars, and many isolated battles he'd fought in during his years in the Army of the Misty Hills. The badger sang in a low, nearly monotone voice, complemented nicely—when he'd learned enough to join in—by the prince's impressive vocal range.

Max told the prince each and every one of his adventures, from the fairly innocent Mystery of the Tardy Tenderfoot, to the horrifying Mystery of the Fallen Eagle, and everything in between. Prince Aspen had many questions about the nature of Max's homeland in general, and the origin and history of the Boy Scouts in particular.

"My father's name is James," Max said. "He's a precision steel cutter for airplane construction in Seattle, a really big city near where we live—where I used to live," he corrected himself. "My mother's name is Hazel and she mostly stays home with my baby sister Lilly, but she also does small business accounting from her home office downstairs."

"And what do you do?" Prince Aspen asked.

"What do you mean?" Max said. "I already told you, I go to Scout meetings and do Scout projects, and go on campouts and Jamborees, and also solve the many mysteries that come up surprisingly often."

"And is that all? Don't you go to school, or play, or have hobbies outside of this scouting organization?"

"Of course I do," Max said, "only—"

"Yes?"

"I can't seem to think of what my hobbies are right now. I can't even remember what grade I am in school."

"That seems odd," the prince said.

"It sure is," Max said. Shortly after that he went off to be on his own for a time. A troubled look cast a shadow on his face.

McTavish stepped in then, telling about life on the McDonald's farm and its surrounding territories, from the time he was a tiny but feisty kitten, to the height of his reign as king of the barn cats, uncontested monarch of all the land. The prince didn't seem to mind when the cat's tales devolved into nothing more than a seemingly endless list of all the creatures he'd killed, with particular emphasis on any especially brutal or gory injury he'd inflicted on his opponents during such battles.

Finally, in the waning hours of their second day in the secret grove, the time came to question the prince. The company decided that Max would speak for them, with help from the others as it was needed.

Questions Answered, and
Sometimes Not

"First," Max said, when it was time to begin, "is this land the afterlife, as Banderbrock believes? Did we come here because we're dead?"

"I don't know if this is the afterlife," the prince answered, after considering the boy's question for a long moment. "Not everyone arrives in this land, like each of you did, from some other far territory. Most creatures are born, live their lives, and die here in nature's normal cycle. But some of the ones who come here like you did remember dying first in their previous land. Some don't. Whatever the truth of the matter, you're certainly not dead here. You're as alive as anything else in this land, and can be killed like everything else as well."

"Are the Cutters native to this land?" Max said.

"Some are," Aspen said. "Or so I'm told. Then again I also hear that they come from other lands, far beyond the fields that we know. There certainly seem to be a lot of them, so I imagine both answers could be true."

"Do you know any good barns I can conquer?" McTavish broke in, before Max could ask another question.

"There are many farms far down your Mysterly River," Prince Aspen said. The amused tone in his voice did not prevent him from giving the serious question a serious answer. "You'll begin to find them where this great forest begins to thin out. I hope you'll be less brutal in your new quest for a kingdom than you were in your last. There are good and noble creatures on those farms, many of whom have been good friends to me in the past."

"I won't kill anything smart enough to roll over and show throat when I move in," McTavish said. "That's as much mercy as any king can be expected to show."

"Why are we here?" Max continued quickly, before the feral cat could think of another question. "Were we brought here by someone, and if so, to do what?"

"I don't know," Prince Aspen said. "This land, in every direction, from north to south or east to west, is called the Heroes Wood, even in those places where the woods have been stripped away. I believe it is so called because each one like the four of you, who've come here from other places, has in some way been a hero in their homeland."

"That's not true of us," Walden interrupted. "Or not me at least. I'm no hero. In fact, for all my bragging about being an important bear of law, I pretty much played the fool. My only job as sheriff of the Grand Green was to catch Rake the Cougar, or at least stop him from playing so many cruel tricks on everyone. But I never caught him once, and as far as I could tell, all of his schemes and tricks worked out exactly as he planned."

"I think you should have paid closer attention to the same stories you told me," Prince Aspen responded. "Didn't Rake get away with spoiling Mayor Landhart's birthday party only because you were busy pulling Mrs. Otter's cubs out from Conrood Beaver's dam, where they'd become entangled under the water line and were in danger of drowning?"

"Well . . ." Walden said.

"And didn't Rake get away with stealing all of Miss Fisher Martin's Christmas pies precisely because you stayed to evacuate everyone out of the path of the fire Rake set to divert you?"

"True, but . . ." Walden tried again.

"I could go on, but I suspect my point is made," Prince Aspen said.

"That may explain Walden," Banderbrock said. "And Max the Wolf obviously qualifies, and even me, if I can risk being thought of as less than humble. But it doesn't explain why McTavish is here."

"What could possibly be a mysterly about me?" McTavish said. "As beloved king of the McDonald's farm, I was a hero to all my subjects. If you asked any one of them they'd tell you the same, or answer to me later."

"See?" Banderbrock said. "If he's a hero, then I'm the long-lost son of an improbable union between a flounder and a mountain goat."

"No less than I suspected," McTavish said.

"My guess is that all of McTavish's colorful history has yet to be revealed," Prince Aspen said. "Whatever other purposes this land has, and no great land ever has only one purpose, it appears to be a gathering place of heroes from other lands. Were it not for the Blue Cutters, I'd believe that this land was intended to be a place of rest and reward for heroes."

"Then tell us about them," Max said. "Who are the Blue Cutters and what do they want? Why are they hunting us?"

"I don't know much about those mysterious people," Prince Aspen said. "They live in the high places, behind impenetrable stone walls, venturing out only to hunt down any like you who're new to this land. No one knows their purpose for doing so. I've never seen one, and never want to, because I hear that they hunt me as well. They're each said to be great lords and ladies, and each one carries the blue sword, a weapon of such power that it can cut through and destroy anything it touches. They never give up, except when their prey makes it to the safety of one of the sanctuaries."

"They kill every one of us they catch?" Max said.

"Worse than that," Prince Aspen said. "They cut out and kill what was true and original in their captives, leaving a new and alien thing of their own design in its place. The creature they eventually release is no more than a foul distortion of the one they caught, a strange new creature masquerading in a familiar body."

"Like demonic possession?" Max asked. "They kill our mind and soul, so that something else can move in and take over our old bodies?"

"Perhaps," Prince Aspen said. "Though I caution you, all my wisdom on those people comes secondhand. Who's to say how much those tales grew in the telling? And I've only heard one side of the story, from those who stand against the Blue Cutters."

"Well, one of them sure tried to get me," Max said. "And he knew who I was too, so there was no mistaking that he wanted to chop me, specifically."

"Me too," McTavish said.

"What about these sanctuaries you mentioned?" Max said.

"There are a few places of safe refuge from the Blue Cutters, dotted throughout the Heroes Wood," Prince Aspen said. "The closest is over the high pass between Sentinel and Barrier mountains. But the Cutters stronghold stands between here and there, and the pass will soon be blocked by the winter snows, if it isn't already."

"And the next closest?" Banderbrock said.

"That would be the castle of the Wizard Swift, far to the south on the banks of the Mysterly River."

"A real wizard," Max said, "who can do real magic?"

"Of course," Prince Aspen said. "All the sanctuaries are held by great and powerful wizards. How else could they stand against the might of the Blue Cutters? Come to think of it, I have little doubt the Wizard Swift can give you the answers I've failed to provide."

"Then I vote that's where we go," Walden said. "We'll go to the Wizard Swift's castle and be safe from the Cutters, and get all our questions answered."

"I'll go, unless we find the Great Sett on the way," Banderbrock said.

"Or a good barn to rule," McTavish said.

"One last question," Max said. "Can we get back to our own homes? Or are we stuck here for the rest of our lives?"

"I never heard of anyone finding their way back to their old lands," Prince Aspen said. "But maybe that's because they did reach home and so weren't able to come back and tell me."

"Then, if we're all agreed, we'll continue on to the castle of the Wizard Swift," Max said. "Can you tell us the way?" he asked the prince.

Directions were given, and after profusely thanking the noble prince of the secret grove, the company of fugitives set off southward, for the road to the Mysterly River and farther on to sanctuary.

Revolutions Lost and Forgotten

11 From the bluff overlooking the secret grove, Diana looked through a small spyglass down on the company of fugitives talking—she supposed, since she couldn't hear them from so far away—to a particularly large aspen tree in the center of the grove. The boy, wearing some sort of military uniform, had Ander's stolen cloak with him, but she couldn't see if he also had the blue sword.

Lord Ander had suffered disgrace in the eyes of his fellow Cutters by losing his sword. No matter what the reasons he gave, no matter what string of events led to it, no excuse was ever really good enough for a Cutter to lose his sword. If Lady Diana were able to recover Ander's sword, it probably wouldn't help him—Ander's work had already been slipping and was probably beyond saving by this time—but it would help Diana's reinvigorated ambitions. It's too bad the boy didn't seem to still have it, because Diana would enjoy taking the nearly sacred weapon away from him.

In any case, the boy looked to be packing up his few belongings and his animal companions acted as if the company was about to leave. Diana's exhausting two-day marathon run through the forest had paid off. The company of fugitives couldn't escape her now, not even after she spent a few hours with Prince Aspen while they continued on their way. At the slow pace they traveled, she'd easily be able to overtake them again, and she wanted them to be well on their way before she dealt with the prince. She didn't want to be interrupted while she tended to him.

Diana was slim and agile. She had long hair that she kept tied back in a ponytail with a leather thong. It was a blond color so pale as to be nearly white. She had pleasant, youthful features that disguised her actual years, and would break into a large bright smile at almost any provocation. In every visible way she seemed affable and sweet, which caused more than one adversary to underestimate her. No matter how nice she looked, she had an inner resolve of cold, hard iron. She could be surprisingly ruthless when ruthlessness was called for.

She crouched on the velvet crown of a moss-covered boulder, wearing her warm cloak in the coolness of the autumn afternoon. She waited until the company below had moved out of Prince Aspen's grove and disappeared along the forest trail before she stirred from her place on the overlook and strolled down to confront the prince. When she reached the ring of guardian lodgepole pines, she couldn't find any space large enough between them to slip through to the stand of aspen trees inside. That was strange, since she'd just watched a fat black bear pass through the same ring of trees moments ago.

Diana didn't waste time trying to work out the cause of the interesting puzzle, but simply drew out her blue sword and began to cut her way through. With easy slashes of her amazing weapon, she chopped one of the pine trees down— making sure it fell outward, away from the aspens—and stepped through the breach, into the protected grove.

"We had the devil's own time finding you, Prince Aspen," Diana said, stepping boldly up to the largest tree in the center of the grove. "But it was always just a matter of time. It's not as if you were able to run from us. If you had to take root somewhere, you should have done it in the garden of one of the sanctuaries."

"I didn't have much choice in the matter, and besides,

it didn't seem necessary at the time," Prince Aspen said in a tired voice of deep resignation. "This place seemed safe enough because of its seclusion. Who would ever look for me here?"

"I doubt we ever would have," Diana said, "if we hadn't run across one of your friends. If you wanted to remain hidden, you shouldn't have let so many creatures come visit you. A secret shared by so many was bound to come out eventually."

"I guess I knew that, but I couldn't help it," Prince Aspen said. "I'm a social creature at heart, and I couldn't survive without interesting conversation. I take it then that you're one of the Blue Cutters?"

"Yes," Diana answered.

"And you're going to cut me now?"

"Yes," she answered again.

"I'm afraid."

"You don't seem so."

"Only because the passions of treekind are slow to reveal themselves. Will it hurt?"

"It will at first," Diana said. "But it will get easier as I go along. Soon enough you'll get to like it."

"I doubt that," Prince Aspen said.

"Nevertheless . . ."

Diana drew her sword out and buried its blade deep into Prince Aspen's thick trunk, like a re-creation of ancient Branstock. The wounded tree's scream of agony reverberated throughout the small valley, nestled between two of the wooded hills that stepped their way down to the larger river valley below.

In his youth, living in a great forest, worlds away from the Heroes Wood, Prince Aspen had been a dryad, a forest spirit in a borrowed human shape. For the most part he lived a happy-go-lucky existence, with no cares for anything other than tending to his own constant needs for entertainment and pleasure. He planned to live that way for centuries at least, before finally taking root and taking up his duties as one of the noble elders who'd serve in the court of Old Grandfather Oak, the dreaded Wood King of all the forest.

But his plans changed when it became clear that Grandfather Oak had turned black and evil over the countless centuries of his rule. The young and often impetuous dryad prince allowed himself to be caught up in romantic talk about revolution against the dark king. He met in secret with noble Annoras, the great lord of the centaurs, and many other leaders of men and beasts, to plot the overthrow of the corrupted Wood King. But, along with the loss of his benevolence, Grandfather Oak had lost none of his cunning over the years, and his spies among the would-be revolutionaries betrayed them into his clutches.

Most of the conspirators were killed outright, but the foolhardy young dryad was spared. Grandfather Oak was reluctant to kill one of his own nobles, a prince of the royal sapline, no matter what his crimes. Instead the old king banished the prince from his kingdom, and laid upon him a compulsion to take early root as punishment. Never again would Prince Aspen be free to run and dance and play amongst the woods and creatures of his beloved childhood homeland.

As Lady Diana continued to cut, time and again, into the tree, his story, the entire history of his life began to change. It was no longer true that he'd taken part in a doomed revolution against his own king. In fact Diana's power was such that that story had never been true. Now the truth was this: Prince Aspen had fought beside his beloved king in a brave and valiant war against evil men, who invaded the wood, seeking to cut down all the trees in the realm. The men were filthy loggers who wanted to clear-cut all the land for their farms, and steal all the wood to build their ever-expanding cities.

Though the dryad prince fought well and bravely against the men and their evil plans, their cause was doomed. The men won, killing Old Grandfather Oak and forcing Prince Aspen to flee to a far land and take root there, trembling against the day they would come to pillage this forest as well. That was Prince Aspen's new history, and because of the way the Blue Cutters' powers worked, that had always been his history. There never was a Prince Aspen who joined a doomed revolution against the dreaded Wood King.

It took Diana more than four hours to finish her work. In the process of cutting the prince into his new and better version, she'd learned from him everything he'd told the fugitives and everything he'd learned from them. Now she knew enough about each of them to cut them into better creatures, without the need to first study their records back at Cutters Keep, where she would possibly have to surrender them to one of the other Cutters, to do the hard work of redeeming them, and get all the credit for doing it. As with Prince Aspen, she planned to do the cutting in the field, as she found them. She also learned of the fugitive company's immediate plans and where they were going. She set out to follow them, leaving Prince Aspen to sulk alone and bitter over all of the evils mankind had visited upon him and his kind.

Cold Camp Memories, and the Lack of Good Conversation from Fresh Fish

12 According to Prince Aspen, it wasn't more than an easy two-day hike through gently rolling woodlands from the location of his hidden grove to the road that led down into the Mysterly River valley. But the small company took three full days to travel that distance, which made Max nervous. He had to keep reminding his companions that they were fugitives, on the run from a deadly enemy. They had to assume the Blue Cutters were still after them, even though they hadn't heard their hunting dogs for a considerable time. Unfortunately it was hard to keep one's mind on a danger that hadn't appeared lately, especially while walking through a lovely and seemingly peaceful forest that was ripe with every kind of fruit and nut, free for the taking, and crisscrossed with streams of cold, pure water to drink.

Max had to admit to himself that he was also having a tough time keeping his mind focused on the danger they were in. Though it still rained off and on, which made McTavish whine and cry as if he were being tortured, the showers were light and infrequent. Most of the time the sun was out, painting the woods in a thousand shades of sparkling green. Every possible variety of bird gossiped and scolded each other among the overhead branches, occasionally taking flight in wonderful bursts of bright colors. It was when Max suddenly realized he couldn't understand anything the birds said that he began to form his theory on how some things worked in this enchanted land.

"Walden," Max said, as they walked along, single file through the underbrush, "can you tell me what those birds are saying?"

"No," Walden said. He was walking just in front of Max and paused to look back at him as he answered. Walden was an undisciplined hiker and took every opportunity to pause and rest. Usually it coincided with the discovery of some inviting morsel of food along their path.

"You can't understand a thing they say?" Max said.

"No, I can't," Walden answered.

"Doesn't that strike you as unusual?" Max said.

"Yes it does, now that I think about it," Walden said. "Back in the Grand Green I could understand every kind of talk there was, from the Widow Robin's constant chattering about how successful each of her chicks were, to every horrible thing Rake used to call me. In fact, the only folk no one in the Grand Green could understand were you men people, and now here I am talking to one of you with ease. You don't even have much of an accent."

"What about you, Banderbrock?" Max called to the badger, who was ahead of Walden. "Could you understand every creature's language back where you came from?"

"No," Banderbrock answered, in a muffled voice, around a mouthful of food. Taking advantage of the current pause in hiking, he was digging under a dark green bog birch bush for a quick snack of juicy earthworms. After he swallowed his treat, he continued more clearly, "I could speak to most of our neighbors well enough, but there were all sorts of odd creatures back where I come from, and they all had their own strange ways of talking. As I said when we first met, you're the first among the fire callers I ever understood."

"What about you, McTavish?" Max said to the cat, who walked behind him on those rare occasions when he wasn't off hunting something.

"Back on the McDonald's farm, I could understand everything and everything could understand me, except Old Farmer McDonald himself. We could all understand him well enough, but he didn't know my language. At least he never followed a single order I gave him, and most of the time even talked like he was the boss around there. Of course that proves that the old man had gone senile, which might explain why he couldn't understand me."

"Where I come from," Max said, "only men, people like me, could talk and be understood by each other. We couldn't understand the talk of other animals. In fact, we believed all of the other animals were incapable of using language."

"Meaning no offense, but it sounds to me like your kind is maybe just too dumb to understand other folks," McTavish said, "just like Old Farmer McDonald."

"That could well be," Max said, taking no offense whatsoever. "In my world, even among mankind, there were so many thousands of languages, chances were that any two randomly chosen people wouldn't be able to understand each other."

"That's no way to run a species," Banderbrock said.

"I agree," Max said. "But I find it interesting that a different set of rules seemed to apply in each different place the four of us came from. Some of those differences were subtle, I admit, but substantial all the same."

"Are you about to solve another mystery?" Walden

said. He'd very much like to see a mystery getting solved, because he wanted to learn how it was done.

"Possibly," Max said. "Not the entire mystery, but maybe one piece of the overall puzzle. My guess is that this land is most like the world I come from, in that members of the various native animal species aren't able to communicate with each other. Remember the fight with Lord Ander and his dogs on the first night, Banderbrock?"

"I've got enough new scars from that encounter that I'm not likely to forget," Banderbrock said.

"Could you understand anything the dogs said?" Max asked.

"Not any words, if that's what you mean," the badger said. "I could sure understand the intent of all their growling and barking."

"Me too," Max said. "So why is it I can talk to a badger, a bear, a cat, and even a tree in this world, but not to a dog?"

"I don't know," Walden said, looking a little embarrassed, because he never was very good at quizzes.

"I think it was a rhetorical question," Banderbrock said. "I think Max is about to tell us why."

"My guess is because those particular dogs were native to this land and therefore subject to the rules which pertain here," Max said. "In this land, like where I come from, dogs and birds and men and every other kind of creature can't talk to each other. But those of us who come from other places, like each of us, operate under some different set of rules. Each of us has the advantage of being able to understand each other."

"Why is that?" Walden said.

"I have no idea," Max said.

"Then you were right to warn us that you weren't really about to solve an important mystery," McTavish said, in a most exaggerated voice of disappointment. "You didn't accomplish much at all."

"On the contrary," Max said, "I've solved two of our most immediate dilemmas. First, I can go back to eating meat again, now that I'm not likely to eat anything that could talk back to me. I have to confess that I'm getting a bit tired of nuts and berries."

"Who was stopping you from eating meat in the first place?" Walden asked. "I still don't understand why you wouldn't eat something just because it could talk to you. Back in the Grand Green, half of the population would starve if they believed such a silly thing."

"There's no sin in being true to your nature," Banderbrock said.

"Yeah," McTavish said. "As a matter of fact, for me, the best part of eating a mouse was when I had him bloodied but still alive in my claws and he would plead and cry in his tiny little mousy voice, 'Please, Mister Big Bad Cat, don't eat me. I have a wife and thirty-seven children at home, so please have mercy on poor little me.' It's too bad the mice here don't do the same. Instead they just chirp away in frightened, squeaky gibberish. It makes dinner taste bland not to have it beg for its life first."

McTavish's admission briefly brought the conversation to a halt, as Max, Walden, and Banderbrock each stared at the feral cat with varying expressions of disturbance on their faces.

"What did I say that was so bad?" McTavish asked. "I'm just trying to contribute to the discussion. You all said something, so I thought it was my turn to speak. This business of having friends is still new to me, but isn't that what friends do in a friendly conversation? We each take turns saying stuff, right? So I said stuff.

"Quit looking at me like that! Honestly, sometimes you guys make it hard for me to treat you nice. I'm not sure that having friends isn't overrated. Things went better back in the barn days when I gave orders and everyone else obeyed."

"Perhaps we should return to the subject," Banderbrock said. "Max, I believe you said that there were two problems solved for us by your discovery. What's the second one?"

"I think we should be wary of any other creature we can talk to," Max said, "unless they are new arrivals to this land like we are."

"Why is that?" Walden asked, still looking suspiciously at McTavish.

"If the Blue Cutters hunt each new creature that arrives, most of the ones still at large will be those the Cutters have already caught and altered with their magic swords. They may now be allies of the Cutters and give us away to them, if they have a chance."

"That's true," McTavish said. "Maybe we should kill anyone we meet from now on."

"I don't think we have to go that far," Max said. "But we should be wary."

After Max got their minds back on their fearsome enemy, the hiking pace picked up a bit and they made good time for several miles. But soon enough the distractions began to occur again, as such things will. When the company crossed a stream big enough to be called a river in its own right—McTavish made the crossing fearfully clinging to the middle of Walden's furry back—they decided to stop long enough to fish out some of the trout they could see swimming and darting in the swift water.

By the time Max got his hook and fishing line out of his Lost Kit, and had dug up a few worms to use as bait, Walden had already splashed back out to the center of the small river and caught a dozen fat trout. He would simply crouch on the big boulder he had chosen in midstream and watch for the silvery flash of a fish trying to swim by. Then he'd quickly splash his toothy muzzle into the cold water and come up—most times—with a fish in his jaws. With one flip of his head, Walden would toss his catch onto the shore, where it would flip and flop on the rocks while the bear went back to work. Since Walden announced he'd be glad to share his catch with the rest of them, Max rolled his fishing line back up and put it away, but dug out the candle and one of his matches to light a fire.

"If I use only dry wood that won't give off smoke, and shelter the fire under these big boulders, there shouldn't be much danger of giving our position away," Max said. "Although I learned to eat raw fish during the Mystery of the Minor Samurai, I prefer it cooked whenever possible."

Even though the four of them had become reliable friends on their journey together, Walden, Banderbrock, and even McTavish shied away from the fire, and looked with superstitious wonder at Max, who had such amazing powers at his command. Then the spell was broken when Max carefully questioned each of the two wiggling fish Walden gave him.

"Hello? Can you hear me? Can you understand what I'm saying?" Max said to each gaping fishy mouth, much to the amusement of his companions. When he was sure there would be no reply, only then did he use his Scout knife to cut and clean his lunch, which he then speared on a stick and roasted over the fire. McTavish ate a single trout, plus the two heads from Max's fish, which the cat couldn't believe anyone would willingly throw away.

"You're giving up the best part," McTavish said between hungry gulps.

Banderbrock declined any of the catch, sticking to his usual diet of worms and nuts and berries. That left Walden with nine tasty trout all to himself, which he gulped down in just a few minutes. Then he waded back in the river to catch himself a dozen more, while Max cooked the two he had.

After such a big meal, the customary afternoon nap was called for, and the sun was low in the sky before the company set out again. At the next open space they passed, they could see where the river they'd recently crossed and fished from wound its way down into the great valley below, and toward the much larger Mysterly River, still many days' journey ahead of them.

That night—the third night out from Prince Aspen's grove—they camped on the top of the last hill separating them from the road they originally expected to reach a day earlier. As usual, Max didn't build a fire, because a flame at night was too easy to spot from many miles away. Instead Max wrapped himself again in the warm gray cloak, and snuggled into Walden's even warmer fur.

"I miss my folks," Max said, while they were waiting for sleep to come. "And my little sister, even though she keeps getting out of the playpen and chewing up my books. And I miss cheeseburgers and pizza, and my friend Joe King, who'd come over to my house and play the piano. Joe and I were in charge of entertaining the parents and other guests at our Court of Honor."

"What's that?" Walden said.

"It's the ceremony every Scout troop has once every two months to award the badges and achievements the Scouts have earned. Joe and I would rewrite popular songs with new funny lyrics, and write skits we'd perform. Except for the actual camps and hikes, it was the best time ever."

"I wish I could miss my parents too," Walden said.

"Why don't you?"

"Because they probably died a long time ago," McTavish said, "shot dead by hunters and skinned. They're probably fur rugs in some rich man's cabin now. Didn't you never think of that, Max? Huh? Didn't you? Some friend you are, bringing up all those sad memories and throwing them in Walden's face, like he never had no feelings to get hurt or nothing!"

"But I'm not the one who—," Max began, and then said, "You were the one who brought it up, McTavish!"

"I did not!"

"It doesn't matter," Walden interrupted. "I don't think I ever had any parents to miss. At least I can't remember them. I can't remember anything at all before the year they first elected me sheriff of the Grand Green."

"That's odd," Max said.

"Is it a mystery?" Walden said. The possibility of being so directly involved in one of Max's mysteries excited him.

"It might be. McTavish, what's your very first memory?"

"When I was just a wee kitten," McTavish said, "the first time I dreamed of someday becoming the king of the barn cats."

"Do you recall your parents, or at least your mother? Did you have any littermates? Brothers or sisters?"

"I have no idea," the cat said. "That's a puzzler, isn't it?"

"And, Banderbrock," Max said. "What's your very first memory?"

"The morning of my first battle, when I was just a new recruit in the Army of the Misty Hills."

"Hmmmmm," Max said. There was a deep frown on his face.

"What's the matter now?" McTavish said. "What have you figured out?"

"I'm not sure," Max said. "I need to think about this some more. In the meantime we'd better try to sleep."

And in time they did. They slept under the twinkling stars and a full moon that, like a giant Philosopher's Stone, had transformed each branch and leaf above them into glistening silver.

From less than a hundred feet away, as she'd done for the past two nights, Lady Diana watched them in their peaceful slumber. She'd easily been able to catch up to the slow-moving fugitives, as she knew she could, and trail them for the past three days, without being spotted in turn. She made no attempt to attack them on her own, because any two of them would combine into more of a challenge than she could expect to be able to handle by herself. Instead she continued to blaze markings along her trail so that Lord Patrick and the rest of her excursion force could catch up to her. Once they were reunited in full and overwhelming strength, she intended to lead her troop in capturing the four creatures alive and unharmed.

When that was accomplished, she'd personally handle all of the cutting.

Blood and Battle

13 By the time the company had wakened to continue on their way, winding down the rudimentary forest trail to the roadway below them, Diana had already moved well ahead of them on the path. Since she had Prince Aspen's stolen knowledge, and knew in advance where they were going, she reasoned that she could scout the way ahead of them with little fear that they'd divert to ne other path. The only risk was in leaving some sign r passage that the small company of fugitives might detect as they unwittingly followed behind her. But she was such an able woodsman there was little danger of that. She left no footprints, being careful to step only on rocks and hard-packed earth. She was careful not to snap any twigs or disturb even so much as a single leaf as she whispered through the underbrush.

She picked her way down the hillside, until a break in the trees finally let her see the road below. In the diffused morning light, with long shadows still sown deep into the earth, what she saw in the road filled her with momentary panic followed by an immediate sense of urgency.

She turned and started to retrace her way back into the trees, up the hill, climbing as fast as she could without making undue noise. She needed to reunite with her fellow Cutters as quickly as she could now, so that they could capture all of the fugitives before they reached the road and what she'd just seen there. Then, almost as if on cue, she heard the distant howling of Lord Patrick's hunting dogs, who'd finally picked up the trail. If she hurried there was still a chance to avoid disaster!

Farther up the hill the company, still sleepy from only recently waking, walked single file down the narrow path, toward Diana, though none of them knew it.

"Did you figure out any more parts to the mystery since last night?" Walden asked Max. The large black bear was walking just ahead of the boy again. Banderbrock, as the slowest member of the party, walked in front to set the pace. McTavish dragged himself along in the rear. Of any of the company, he seemed to have the toughest time waking up each morning.

"Well," Max said, "I still need to think some things over more, but I've definitely decided that I miss things from my own world more than ever. I'd give just about anything for a bacon, egg, and cheese biscuit right now. And a glass of fresh-squeezed orange juice."

"I ate some oranges once," Walden said. "They tasted wonderful. But the juice was sticky and got all in my fur and attracted bugs. Then again, the bugs tasted good too, so I wouldn't mind finding some oranges again."

The conversation continued as the morning slowly warmed up, drifting along from one unimportant subject to another, until Banderbrock interrupted in a loud and sharp voice, full of badgerly growls. "Shut up!" he said at the top of his gruff voice, finally making himself heard over Walden's story about a bunch of fallen apples that had fermented in the sun, making every beast who ate them drunk and silly.

"What is it, Banderbrock?" Max asked, once the badger got most of the silence he called for.

"Shush! Listen!" Banderbrock said. And after everyone had quieted completely, Walden first, then McTavish, and finally Max heard the baying of hunting dogs, faint at first, but growing louder so steadily that each one of them knew the hounds were once again hot on their trail.

"The dogs have found us again!" Max said, though he could see everyone in his company already realized it.

"Dozens of them, and they're coming fast," Banderbrock said.

"What do we do?" Walden asked.

"Even I can't fight that many of the beasts," Banderbrock said.

"Since the dogs are behind us, we keep going in the direction we're already headed, but now we'd better run!" Max said.

And so they ran. McTavish was the fastest over short distances, and he shot off like a Fourth of July rocket, between Walden's legs, then around Banderbrock, until he was in the lead. Banderbrock ran as best he could on his short legs. Over very small distances he could be fast enough, and the downhill slope helped. Walden lumbered behind him at an easy lope, huffing and chuffing with anxiety. The bear was capable of much faster speeds, but was reluctant to overrun his friend. Max followed at a quick jog, in the rear of the party now, holding his wooden staff in both hands in front of him, to help force branches out of his way.

The company crashed through branch and brush as they bounded down the hillside, kicking up dirt and dust along with loose leaves and small stones. They cared little about the noise they made, since it was obvious the hounds were steadfastly on their trail. Stealth was no longer of any use to them. Only speed would help them now. Max was as careful as he could be, keeping his eyes on every step he took, even while jumping off boulders, or occasionally sliding in a semicontrolled fall down the slope. Most backpacking injuries occur in the downhill part of a hike, he reminded himself. Still, he couldn't reserve all of his attention for the footing immediately ahead of him. No matter how far and fast they ran, the dogs, and the hunters that followed, would be on them sooner or later. He had to keep an eye out for some defensible place where they could turn and make a last stand.

At that point, McTavish, instead of following the curve of the path that zigzagged back and forth down the slope, cut under some bushes, taking the hill's steepest grade head-on. Banderbrock followed the huge old barn cat, and Walden followed the badger. Of course the bear was too big to slip under the bushes like the other two. He crashed through them, his great bulk, and the momentum behind it, shredding the leaves and thorns and branches out of his way like they were hardly there at all. Max had time to decide on his route. Following the curving path was clearly the safest choice, but that might split him up from his friends.

"Oh well," he cried as he chose the same route the others had taken, "for better or worse, we're in this to-gether." The one advantage was that, having a bear break for him, there was very little left of any branches or bushes that might tangle his feet, or conceal the qualities of footing on the steep grade.

A bit farther downhill, Diana could hear the company of fugitives crashing down the trail toward her position. They sounded close enough to her that she decided to step into the bushes, concealing herself just off the path. She formed a quick plan of action. She'd let the first three of the fugitives pass her hiding place, then step out and take whichever one of them was in the rear, making a lot of noise in the process. Her hope was that the others would turn around to help their companion. She could then retreat uphill, attempting to stay just out of reach, while drawing them with her. In this way she hoped to keep them occupied just long enough for reinforcements to arrive. That was as much of a plan as she could formulate in the short seconds available to her.

But it didn't quite work out that way. Diana realized her plan had serious flaws when, instead of coming down the path, the creatures she hunted suddenly came smashing through the same clump of bushes she was hiding in. None of them saw her until they all collided in a chaotic tangle that sent them tumbling together back out into the center of the path.

Diana recovered quickly enough to find herself lying amid the startled young boy and his three equally disoriented animal companions. If she acted instantly she could still salvage her attempted ambush. She grabbed her

sheathed sword, which she'd still been hand-carrying unat-
tached from her belt. It had landed nearby on the hard
rocky trail. While still sitting among the rocks and dirt, she
drew the short blade from its leather scabbard. Then she
threw the sheath aside and, taking her sword firmly in both
hands, aimed a vicious cut at the huge yellow cat, the
closest target to her.

But as fast as Diana was, she was no warrior badger.
With no regard for his own safety, thinking only of the
danger his friend was in, Banderbrock ran right up Diana's
chest, clawing her as he went, until he was close enough
to bite her unprotected throat. The badger's assault caused
Diana's cut to miss McTavish, but not entirely. Instead of
cutting open McTavish's body, the sword blow was de-
flected enough that it cleanly sliced off most of the rest of
the old cat's already chewed and broken tail.

"Yeow!" McTavish screamed, jumping straight up into
the sky.

Banderbrock failed to sink his teeth into the huntress's throat, because she was able to tuck her chin down
to protect it at the last second. Instead the badger bit into
the soft flesh of her cheek, locking his powerful fangs hard
around her lower jawbone. Dropping her sword, Diana
rolled over on top of the badger, attempting to dislodge it,
but Banderbrock hung on. She punched the badger's body
again and again with quick punishing jabs, but Banderbrock hung on. Copious amounts of blood began to flow

from Diana's torn face, coating the badger's head. Blinded by the woman's blood, Banderbrock still kept his muzzle buried in place, while he continuously raked her chest and shoulders with all four sets of his long digger claws. From some far distant place Diana heard the tortured sobs of a woman crying. Slowly she began to realize the crying was coming from her.

She didn't collapse or surrender, no matter how great the pain, because she was no simple frail woman. She was Diana the Huntress, one of the feared Blue Cutters, a noblewoman of the Fellowship of Justice! She rolled over again on the badger, pinning his body under her so that, at least, he couldn't continue to claw at her. Then, without raising her body, she began to pull herself, and Banderbrock under her, across the hard ground, dragging the badger over the sharp stones of the trail. As much as that hurt Banderbrock, it hurt Diana more, because the badger steadfastly refused to let go. Each movement forward resulted in another dizzying wave of pain from her ruined face, as the badger's weight pulled against her jaw. But Diana kept going in wailing agony, until she'd crawled back to the spot where her sword lay.

Once she had her sword in hand again, Diana rolled over until the badger was on top of her. Then, continuing to ignore the sickening pain, she grasped the animal's blood-soaked fur with one hand, and carefully positioned the deadly sword with the other. Sitting up once more, she placed the tip of the blade to thrust crosswise across her chest and slice open the badger in the process. Blinded by the sticky blood that had coated both of his eyes, Banderbrock had no idea how much danger he was in by continuing to hang on to the woman. But Max saw and shouted to save his friend.

"Banderbrock!" he shouted. "Let go! She's about to cut you!"

Max had recovered from the mass collision to see Banderbrock and the Blue Cutter woman already locked in battle. He hadn't attempted to interfere because his friend was clearly winning, until Diana recovered her blade. I should have picked it up when I had the chance, Max silently scolded himself, but instead I froze up like any dumb, scared kid.

Walden had also stayed out of it. He stood near the fighters, blowing and huffing, clacking his jaws and stamping his feet; all clear signs—to anyone who knows them—of a black bear's extreme agitation.

Walden was as upset as he'd ever been. He didn't want to fight, and wasn't even sure he knew how. He was a peaceful bear, from a peaceful land, and had never in his life been involved in a real fight. Back in the Grand Green, his big teeth and claws and overall bulk had always been intimidating enough to avoid such things. Even Rake the Cougar had never risked a direct battle with him.

"Go away, you nasty woman!" Walden shouted. "Go away!"

But the woman did not go away. And when she was about to stab Banderbrock with her sword, and the badger didn't let go of her, even though Max shouted for him to do so, Walden knew it was time for him to overcome his timidity and act. The instant before the woman could cut into his friend, Walden batted at her with one of his huge forepaws. His blow connected with the woman right under her ribs and sent her small body flying several feet into the brush down the hill. Banderbrock also flew off at a different angle, finally losing his tenacious grip on her jaw.

Now that his slumbering rage had been wakened for the first time, Walden was determined to finish the battle quickly. He charged downhill after the Cutter woman, making the rough *Uh-huh-huh* sound of a black bear's strongest threat warning.

Diana had soft-landed among the dense foliage of a blue oak bush, even managing to hang on to her sword this time. When the bear charged up on her, she simply raised the sword and let the beast run itself onto the blade. Walden howled in agony as the blade sank deep into his breast.

At this point Max had to act quickly to save the bear. McTavish was oblivious to anything else around him, caught up in his own pain at losing his tail, and Banderbrock was too far away, trying to scoop and scrape the drying blood out of his eyes. Max was Walden's only chance. Before the Cutter woman could wound him deeper, Max whacked her head with his wooden staff, causing her to turn loose of the blade's grip. Then he threw himself on the woman in a flying tackle, which caused both of them to continue tumbling down the hill, rolling over and over, bouncing hard off rocks and tree trunks all the way. Their mutual fall was only halted when they tumbled among a group of large boulders piled at the bottom of the hill.

All sounds of fighting had died by the time Banderbrock was able to scrape away enough of the woman's blood to restore most of his sight. He saw Walden lying on his side, gravely injured, the wicked blue sword still protruding from his belly. Blood seeped from the wound. A deep and drawn-out, almost musical moan issued from the fallen bear. Not too far away, McTavish was examining the inch-long slightly bleeding stub where his tail had been.

"Look at me!" the cat cried. "I'm ruined!"

"McTavish!" Banderbrock growled at him. "Where's Max?"

"How should I know?" McTavish said. "Are you blind, or has it somehow escaped your notice that I just lost an entire tail?"

"Walden's in trouble!" the badger said. "Go find Max!"

For the first time McTavish looked up to see what had

happened to the bear. "Oh no!" he said then. "He's stabbed. What do we do?"

"I don't know," Banderbrock said. "We can't help him, but maybe Max can. Go find him now!"

Without another comment, McTavish dashed off to find their missing friend. After a false start, he quickly realized where Max and the Cutter woman must have disappeared. A trail of dust and dry leaves, kicked up by their tumble down the rest of the hill, still hung in the air. McTavish dashed down the hillside, dodging ably around the same rocks and tree trunks Max and the Cutter had hit on their way down. Almost immediately McTavish heard a sound below him, which guided the wounded cat to Max's position among the large boulders.

McTavish found his friend kneeling above the broken body of the Cutter woman. She was obviously dead, her bloodied head lying at an unnatural angle against one of the rocks. Max was crying loudly, not like the hero of many adventures, or a detective that had solved countless mysteries, but exactly like a frightened young boy who'd just done something terrible.

"I killed her," Max said through his tears, once he became aware that McTavish had joined him.

"Yeah, and you did a good job," McTavish said, "but now isn't the time for boasting or handing out congratulations. Walden is stabbed deep and may be dying, and me and the badger can't do anything to help him."

"But I killed her," Max said. "I never . . ."

"Didn't you hear me?" McTavish interrupted. "Your friend is hurt and only you can help him. There's plenty of time to fall apart later, but right now you still have work to do. Hello? Pay attention when I'm talking to you!"

McTavish batted Max across his face—claws out—to punctuate his last remark. The swipe of his paw drew four parallel lines of red across the boy's cheek, not deep cuts, but enough to finally snap Max's attention to what the cat had been telling him.

"How hurt?" Max said, absently wiping tears away.

"Get up and move your skinny butt up that hill!" McTavish yowled.

Max climbed back uphill as fast as he could, arriving at Walden's side winded and struggling for every breath. He found the noble beast awake and in terrible pain, still lying prone, with at least ten inches of the sword buried in his gut. Like any good Boy Scout, Max was skilled in first aid, able to render emergency treatment in any number of situations, but a sword wound was beyond his experience and training. However, the baying of the hunting dogs was much closer and Max knew he was the only one of the company with the ability to do anything helpful. He'd just have to do the best he could.

"Can you hear me, Walden?" Max asked.

"Yes," the bear answered weakly.

"I'm going to pull the sword out of you and it's going to hurt a lot."

"It already hurts a lot," Walden said.

"This will be worse," Max said. "And I want you to get yourself ready for it, because you're too big for any of us to hold down, and you can't move while I do this, or it will only injure you more."

"I'll try to be a good little cub," Walden said with a sad, quiet chuckle.

Before he could lose his nerve, Max grabbed the sword's handle with both hands and pulled straight back with all his strength. At first the sword didn't move at all. The heavy flesh of the bear, pressing down on the blade, created a powerful suction force that resisted any attempt to budge it. Then all at once the blade slid free with a sickening wet sound, accompanied by another moan of pain from Walden. But the bear never moved, and as far as Max could tell, no further damage had been done. Above them they could all hear the sound of the dogs coming over the top of the hill.

"They're on us," Banderbrock said. "If we don't move now, we never will."

"You're still bleeding, but not very much," Max said after watching the bear's wound for a time. "Do you think you can get up and walk?"

"Let's see," Walden said, struggling to his feet. After some effort he stood on unsteady legs.

"Go slowly and stay on the path," Max said. "At the bottom of the hill there's some boulders where we may be able to make a stand. McTavish and Banderbrock will stay with you and I'll bring up the rear."

The company set out again, this time with Walden setting the pace. As the bear walked, softly moaning with each step, a steady drip drip drip of blood seeped down from his furry stomach. Max stayed behind long enough to pick up the sword and wipe the dark blood off its blade in a clump of grass. Then he picked up the fallen scabbard and sheathed the sword in it. Carrying the sheathed sword in one hand, he gathered up his cloak and staff in the other, and hurried after his companions.

By the time Max caught up with them, the trees had opened up enough for the group to look down on the road below them for the first time. The first thing Max noticed on the road was a brightly painted caravan-style wagon. It was parked, having pulled over to their side of the road, and a small campsite was set up near it. A large white horse, unhooked from the wagon, was grazing on roadside clumps of grass. There was no driver in sight.

After looking at the wagon, which was interesting but of no immediate help to them, Max saw the details of the other side of the road and his spirits rose slightly. The road had been partly cut into the next hill, creating a solid stone wall that rose straight up for fifteen or twenty feet before the normal grade of the hill continued. The wall was rough and uneven, creating a number of clefts and depressions in its face. The largest such depression—almost a shallow cave—was directly across from them. It was a place where they had at least a reasonable chance to turn and make a stand.

"Never mind the boulders," Max shouted to his companions. "Cross the road instead!" Walden continued to lope along. He was nearly at the bottom of the hill, only about a dozen yards from the road, but his pace was slowing steadily, and judging by the size of the spatters along the trail, his wound was bleeding more profusely. Banderbrock had no trouble keeping pace with the bear. Even though McTavish was the fastest, and had the best chance of getting away, he too stayed close by Walden.

A quick glance behind him showed Max that the lead dog, howling with a hunter's fury, was at least as close to them as they were to the cleft in the rock face. The sounds of the dogs filled the air now. Some of the faster dogs would be on them before they reached their makeshift fortress, but they had no other choice but to try.

The company reached the road, passing close to the seemingly abandoned wagon, but Walden could barely go on. Each step forward had become a drunkard's stagger. Finally he simply stopped in the middle of the road, bracing himself upright on four shaky limbs, bleeding onto the hard-packed earth of the road's surface. The others stopped with him, not willing to go on by themselves.

Book Two

ROAD AND RIVER

Strange Eggs and the Stranger Man Who Delivers Them

14 As much as a young boy is able to, Max prepared to meet his death as the hunting dogs hurled themselves down at them. There were at least two dozen hounds in the pack that poured out of the woods and scrambled up the small embankment to the roadway.

"If Walden weren't injured, we'd have a fighting chance," Banderbrock said, "but no matter what, I'll be taking some of these howlers with me into whatever afterlife is next."

"I bet you a fat juicy mouse in the next life that I kill more of them than you do," McTavish said.

Fearing his voice would crack, Max didn't try to say anything, even though he recognized that this was a moment when some final bold words among fellow doomed warriors were called for. Instead, he silently took his place beside McTavish and Banderbrock, forming a small protective barrier between the oncoming dogs and Walden, who could stand no longer, and had crumpled down in the middle of the road, with a single long sigh, like air escaping from a party balloon.

Dropping his wooden staff, Max wrapped his thick woolen cloak several times around his left arm. His plan was to shove that into the jaws of whichever dog reached him first, and then hack at it with the dead Cutter woman's sword. With his free right hand he shook the leather scabbard off the short blue blade. Just as he did so, the first few dogs, which had reached the surface of the roadway, skidded to a sudden halt, less than a dozen feet from Max and his companions. The dogs immediately behind them piled into the ones in front, until the entire pack was locked in a churning mass of tangled feet and tails and snouts. Their fierce blood-chilling howling slowly transformed into yips of fear, which rippled back through the piled mass of dogs, until the entire pack was cowering and yipping in confusion and submission.

As each dog was able to untangle itself from the pileup,

it tucked its tail under its hind legs and retreated back off the roadway. Soon the entire pack was whimpering back inside the tree line, as if they'd all been badly whipped.

Max and Banderbrock and McTavish looked at each other with expressions of astonishment, relief, and disbelief fighting for place on their faces. Max felt like a death row prisoner in one of those old black-and-white movie thrillers who'd received a last-second pardon, just as the executioner was about to throw the switch. His knees began to shake and his arms felt suddenly too heavy to lift.

"It's the sword!" Banderbrock cried in a voice of purest exaltation. "They're afraid of the Cutter's sword!"

"You'd think so," a strange voice interrupted. "And the timing was absolutely perfect to support your dramatic theory, but it doesn't happen to be true in this case."

Everyone turned to see who'd spoken. Distracted by the imminent battle, Max had quite forgotten the nearby caravan wagon. An old man stood in the back of the wagon, filling its open doorway. He looked out at them, his frail arms braced on each side of the doorway.

"It's not the sword they fear, it's me," the stranger said. He was short, thin, and stooped, in the way of the very old. His face was deeply creased with countless wrinkles, and loose skin drooped below his jawline, as if his face were slowly melting off his skull. He had large blue eyes that were contained by the biggest and puffiest bags Max had ever seen on anyone's face. Many laugh lines crinkled out from the corner of each eye. His eyebrows were thick tufts of jet-black fur, as if two large crows had perched there, but his wild full head of hair was purest white.

"You're lucky all the noise woke me up in time for the hounds to get a good look at me," the stranger continued. "Otherwise those barkers would've had you for certain."

He gingerly stepped down from the back of the wagon, pausing on each step of the small three-step stairway ladder that was attached on ring hooks below the doorway. He wore a long robe of homespun material that was belted at his waist by a drab green sash. The robe might have been white at one time, but now it was cream-colored at best, and was decorated with an elaborate pattern of brown swirls and loops along the bottom, at the neck, and at the ends of each baggy sleeve. One of the two long ends of his belt sash dragged behind him, on each step down from the wagon, and then along the ground. The trailing end was stained almost black with accumulated dirt.

Max looked back and forth between the old man and the pack of dogs that were still cowering inside the tree line. He was still not quite able to grasp that they'd been saved, and that no further deadly battle seemed to be forthcoming for the moment.

"Who are you?" McTavish asked the old man, who approached the group with short shuffling steps.

"No one of consequence," the stranger answered, in a tone of voice that crackled with such merriment and delight that it was clear his modesty was as false as a law-yer's virtue. "I am Professor Padraic Antipedes Hilde-mark," he continued, "though no one calls me by very much of my full name anymore. My friends call me Paddy, and everyone else simply calls me the Eggman."

"Why do they call you that?" McTavish said.

"No doubt because I deliver eggs," the old man said, "which is both my profession and dearest joy."

"You're a professor of egg delivery?" McTavish said. "I suppose a bit down the road we'll meet a doctor of shoveling manure."

"You're a foul old creature, aren't you?" the old man said to McTavish. His broad smile—full of whitish teeth that were bunched together at every possible angle, as if all of them were crowding toward the front of his mouth to get a better view—took any sting out of his words.

"Perhaps later I'll transform you into a nice green toad, or a small brown titmouse, but first we'd better tend to your fallen friend over here." He walked over to Walden in his small shuffling steps, and bent over to look at the wounded bear, bracing his thin and vastly wrinkled hands one on each knee.

"Hello? Are you still alive?" he said to the bear, in the kind of extra-loud voice one uses when talking over a bad phone connection, or to someone suspected of not speak-ing the same language.

"Barely," Walden whispered back.

"Oh, that's a funny answer," the old man said, straightening up again to look at the others. "Did you hear what he said? He said 'barely' and he's a bear. I do so love a well-crafted pun to start the day off. It's wonderful good luck to meet such a clever and entertaining beast. I suppose we can't risk losing such a treasure, can we?"

"We'll just have to fix you up," he said, turning back to Walden, who was quietly happy to hear that last part, even though he didn't understand most of the rest of what the old man said, and certainly had no idea of what a pun might be.

"Young man, come over here and give me a hand," the old man said to Max, who wasn't sure what to do. He was still looking back and forth between the old man and the hunting dogs, which paced nervously and excited behind the tree line, no more than a hundred feet from their position. He dearly wanted to rush back to Walden's side and give him any help he could, but he didn't quite trust the old man's explanation of what was keeping the dogs at bay. He was reluctant to put away the Cutter's sword, which may be all that saved them from deadly attack.

"Oh, do quit gaping at those dogs," the old man said. "They're harmless, as long as you stay close to me. I need to get a good look at this wound, and my eyesight's not what it used to be. I could ask your comedic friend to raise his wounded belly up to my eye level, but that seems a harsh demand to make of someone in as much pain as he is. It would be a much better idea for me to kneel down to examine him where he's already lying, don't you agree? You'd think a young man in your profession, who's so willing to help any number of old ladies cross a street, wouldn't be so hesitant to help one old man lower his tired old bones down to the ground."

"You know about the Boy Scouts?" Max said.

"Why wouldn't I?" the old man said. "You kids don't exactly go out of your way to escape notice. Now get over here and help me."

Max had a hundred more questions he wanted to ask the man, but the one undeniable truth about all of the bizarre events of that morning was that Walden needed help, and quickly. Instead of sheathing the sword, Max thrust it point down into the hard-packed earth, like Excalibur into the stone, so that it might still stand up as some sort of a barrier between them and the dogs, just in case it was the sword, rather than the old man, keeping them at bay. Then he rushed over to Walden and the old man, after first asking Banderbrock to keep a close watch on the dogs.

Holding him by the elbow and under his arm, Max slowly lowered the old man—who seemed to weigh less than a handful of dry straw—down to his hands and knees, in front of Walden's belly. Then, at a snail's pace, the old man crept forward until his face was not more than an inch or two from the bear's wound, which continued to seep blood into his fur and down to stain the ground. He peered closely at the injury for a long time, never touching it, and said only, "Hmmmmm," and, "Ahhhhhhhhh," as he made his examination. Then he ordered Max to help him back to his feet, which took another long time.

When he was on his feet again he said, "The blood's not too dark, nor watery, and it doesn't smell of bile, so I think we can safely conclude no important guts were punctured. And the flow isn't all that rapid, so I doubt any big veins were nicked. Your friend is lucky to have enough fat and meat on him to take most of what a blade has to offer. I think if we clean the wound good and sew it up, he has a reasonable chance to recover. It will take time, of course, and he'll need a lot of care."

"Why should we wait that long?" McTavish said. "If you can really change me into a toad, why don't you just change him from a wounded bear into a healthy not-wounded bear?"

"Do you think I'm one of those asinine Blue Cutters, that I would treat any creature in such a manner?" the old man snapped at McTavish. "Cutting out anything that doesn't appeal to me, and making him over into whatever sort of thing is fashionable for the moment?

"Despite my joke to the contrary, I've enough respect for original creation that I wouldn't even treat something as grotesque as you in that way."

Then the old man turned to Max. "If you're of a different mind, though, then take up that evil blue device and start chopping away at your friend. Who knows? You might get lucky and accidentally carve him into a pleasing new thing that will amuse and delight you; until he begins to bore you, or fashions change again, and it's time to start cutting him into something else."

"It's the swords that have the power then?" Max said. "The power to change us into different people? Different creatures?"

"That they do," the man said. "It's hardly in the people. Any sort of idiot can become a Cutter, with enough training. Indoctrination might be the better word. You can cut too, if you're that sort of boy. Keep two things in mind though, if you decide to try it:

"Keep a good grip on the weapon, and don't let your concentration slip while you work, or those cuts will turn real. And get ready to fight off a pack of dogs and their masters at the same time, because I won't continue to extend my protection to those who use the blue swords."

During his long speech, every time the old man mentioned the Blue Cutters, he gestured over to where the hunting dogs paced back and forth, growling their embarrassment and frustration at each other. Mixed in among the dogs by that time were several of the Blue Cutters, nine in all, who'd finally caught up to them. Like their hounds, the Cutters made no attempt to approach any closer than the edge of the woods. They were each dressed differently, in traveling clothes of their own choosing, but wore the uniform gray cloak and short sword that identified them as Cutters.

"I was going to announce they'd arrived," Banderbrock said, "but didn't want to interrupt your conversation, as long as they seemed content to stay back there with their dogs."

"And they'll stay at least that far away, as long as I'm here," the old man said. "So we'd best tend to our own business and not give them any more worry."

Under the old man's direction, Max carefully cleaned the bear's wound with a mixture of water and antiseptic that the man brought from his wagon. Then he sewed the wound closed with fourteen individual stitches, using the needle and thread from his own Lost Kit. Through it all Walden remained still, though his frequent moans let Max know how much it hurt. When that was done, Max used his wooden staff, some of the heavy twine from his Lost Kit, and the gray cloak he'd won in his first battle to erect a makeshift lean-to over the bear, to shade him from the worst effects of the afternoon's sun.

"How long will you be here, Professor Hildemark?" Max asked, wondering how long they'd be able to enjoy the old man's protection. He'd put away the dead Cutter woman's sword by that time, finally convinced that it wasn't what was keeping so many enemies away.

"You might as well call me Paddy," he replied. Then,

gesturing over to the Cutters he said, "The fact that you're enemies of that bunch is good enough to start you out as friends by my reckoning. But to answer your question, come the morning, I plan to be moving on from here. My partner should be back from making a delivery by this evening. She's meeting me here, and we'll get another night's sleep, but then we've got other stops to make down the road a ways. We have our schedules to keep."

"Then we'll have to move out sometime tonight, to have a chance of escaping the Cutters," Max said. "We're grateful though for the protection you were able to grant us today."

"It's going to take longer than the rest of today before that bear's able to move," Paddy said.

"I know, but I don't see that we have another choice," Max said.

"My thought is that you'd all come with me for a while," Paddy said. "Unless I miss my guess, you're headed down to the river, isn't that right?"

"Well, yes," Max said, "but I don't think Walden will be able to walk fast enough to keep up with you."

"I was more of the mind that he'd ride in the wagon," Paddy said.

One look at the old man's wagon told Max that no matter how appealing the idea might be, it wasn't practical. Even if they could get Walden back on his feet and up the short stepladder, he'd never be able to fit through the narrow doorway. But when Paddy showed him how the entire back of the wagon could swing open, once a couple of bolts were removed, Max changed his mind, and for the first time in long hours dared hope that they might actually have a chance of making it safely to the Wizard Swift's sanctuary. Thinking of Swift, and then the portable sanctuary Paddy seemed able to provide, Max asked him, "Are you a wizard?"

"As much as anyone is I suppose," Paddy answered, and would speak of such things no more.

The day moved on, as days always will, even in the face of the most interesting events. Paddy introduced them to his draft horse, when he'd returned, whose name was Incitatus. The horse had wandered far afield in his search for sweet grasses to munch, without fear from the Blue Cutters, or their dogs. The respect they had for the Eggman seemed to extend to his well-known horse.

"Incitatus?" Max said, when he was introduced to the large white stallion. "That name sounds familiar."

"It should," Incitatus answered. "I was very famous once in the ever so long ago. I was a senator of ancient Rome. But it was in the darkest times of the empire, and I served an evil man. Now I serve the Eggman, doing humble and honest draftwork as my penance."

"How long will you have to do that?" Banderbrock asked. He knew about animals that served the fire callers, but couldn't understand why. His friendship with Max the Wolf was one thing; they were fellow warriors, and no one served the other. But it seemed to him that an animal that enslaved himself to a fire caller, no matter what the reason, was no different than the dogs that served the vile Cutters. Such an animal was totally alien to the badger's view of nature.

"Incitatus is free to go any time he wishes," Paddy said. "His penance is self-imposed, so only he can decide when he's sufficiently worked out his redemption. I'll be sad to see him go when he does decide to leave me though. He's been a good friend, and a gifted conversationalist on the long road."

"I have some time to serve yet," was all the horse said, putting an end to the subject.

Max built the day's fire for Paddy's lunch and supper, and made several trips to the nearest stream, until the wagon's water barrel was full again. As long as Incitatus accompanied him, which the affable horse was perfectly willing to do, Max was safe from any of the Blue Cutters, who'd all disappeared back into the forest sometime when everyone's attention was directed elsewhere.

"They won't go far as long as you're with me," Paddy said. "But they fear me enough that they'll probably stay out of sight from now on."

McTavish and Banderbrock searched out blackberry and raspberry bushes, and dragged berry-laden branches back to where either Max or Paddy sat next to the wounded bear, taking turns fanning the flies away from his injury. They also hand-fed Walden individual berries and as many spoonfuls of water as he would take. Then, before all the light had gone away, Max unbolted the back of the large wooden box of a wagon, and swung the entire back end of it aside on rusted hinges that complained loudly, not having been put to work in many years.

Under Paddy's direction, Max cleared out enough space in the cluttered compartment for a large black bear to occupy. He moved the old man's chair and writing desk, and packed away his comfortable bed, dismantling the wooden bed frame, which he tied to the luggage rails on the top of the wagon. The mattress went on the floor for Walden to lie upon. As he was moving things around— and there were many odd things indeed—Max noticed that the Eggman's supply of eggs was as small as the individual eggs were odd. Each egg rested inside its own tiny drawer, in a large oaken cabinet that was built along one wall of the wagon. The drawers were labeled with strange words and proper names, and none of it made sense to Max. But, at Paddy's insistence, he made sure that each drawer was closed and securely latched with its small brass hook.

When all was prepared inside the wagon, Max gently woke the drowsy bear and talked him to his feet. With considerable pain, Walden walked over to the wagon and mounted the short stepladder at the end of it. He was too weak to make it up the stairway on his own, and it took some pushing by Max and the helpful Incitatus to get him up and inside. At Paddy's insistence, Walden laboriously turned around in the compartment, so that his head would face the open back end, where he'd enjoy the fresher air and it would be easier for the others to tend to him.

After Walden slumped onto the mattress, quite exhausted by his small effort, Max reexamined his wound to make sure that no stitches had popped. Then, for the next hour or so, Paddy fed him many spoonfuls of poppy oil, mixed with water, until the bear fell into a deep sleep.

While McTavish and Banderbrock hunted food more to their own tastes, Paddy shared a wonderful dinner of goose stew with Max, who marveled at all the rich spices he'd missed over the last few days. During dinner, Paddy's partner returned, fluttering down out of the black, star-filled sky, to perch on one corner of the wagon's roof.

"Max the Wolf, meet Epiphany, my partner," Paddy said, hardly looking up from his soup bowl. Epiphany turned out to be the largest cuckoo bird Max had ever seen. She was closer in size to a falcon or hawk than any normal cuckoo was supposed to get. She had an empty red velvet pouch dangling from her neck on the end of leather thongs.

"Pleased to meet you," Epiphany said. "If you can avoid calling me Piffy, we'll get along just fine."

The Road Down to the River and What Was Learned on the Trip

15 The next day, early in the chilly morning, Max helped Paddy hook Incitatus up to the wagon, and they rolled off at a slow walking pace down the tail end of the mountain road, which meandered into the great Mysterly River valley.

Max rode on the bench seat of the wagon, beside Paddy, who wasn't really driving it, in the sense that there were no reins attached to the horse. Instead the old man just told Incitatus which direction to go, and since there was only one possible direction—unless they were to turn around and head back up to the mountain pass—there wasn't an awful lot of instructions needed or given. This gave Paddy plenty of time to nap in his seat, and he took full advantage of the opportunity, snoring merrily as they rolled along.

The horse seemed to have only one speed, which was so slow that Banderbrock had no trouble walking along on his own, which he preferred to do, rather than ride on the strange vehicle. McTavish slept back in the compartment, where he could keep an eye on Walden. Epiphany, when she wasn't flying off somewhere, liked to perch on the foremost luggage rail on the wagon's slightly curved roof.

From time to time, Max would get down from the wagon, to stretch his legs, and walk beside his badger friend.

"I haven't been around many fire callers in my long life," Banderbrock said, as they walked along in the shadow of the creaking wagon, "so I'm not yet adept at reading your expressions. But if I was to guess, I'd have to say you look very sad today, Max."

"You're right," Max said. "I do feel sad. In all my past adventures, I've never had to kill anyone before. Killing Lady Diana was the worst thing I've ever done."

"Who's Lady Diana?" Banderbrock said.

"The Cutter woman. I think that was her name. Actually, I'm pretty sure that was her name."

"How do you know?"

"I think her sword told me," Max said. "I'm not sure. It's not very clear yet, but I think her sword's been telling me things every time I've held it."

"Then you should quit holding it. That thing is evil."

"I'm not sure that's true. I wanted to know the name of the woman I killed and it told me. How can that be wrong?"

"For one thing," the badger said, "you didn't kill her. If that thing told you different, it lied."

"How can that be? We rolled down the hill together and I smashed her head against a rock. I absolutely killed her."

"Listen to me, my friend. I'll never know all of the amazing things you know how to do, making fire grow out of wood and solving mysteries and such, but I've been in the military long enough to have learned a thing or two about assigning proper credit—or blame—for a killing. By taking all of the blame on yourself for killing this woman, you're robbing credit from me and the bear. I did the most damage to the Cutter woman and therefore deserve most of the credit. Then Walden stepped in and broke a couple of her ribs, if I heard things correctly, and I'm sure I did. Afterward, while it's true you finished her off, from the way you describe it, that was more of an accident than anything.

"Sorry, kid, but at best you get the smallest portion of whatever blame or glory you think is deserved for this deed. Trying to take more than your fair share is a disservice to your friends."

"But, I . . ."

"The matter is closed," Banderbrock interrupted with a most badgerly growl. "You don't get to decide everything. Now get over it."

"It's not that easy," Max said.

"So? The first thing you learn in the Army is that the only easy day is yesterday. You bear the burdens you have to, but only a mad badger would fight to take on more than what was his due. And one burden you should dispose of right away is that woman's sword."

"Not until I work with it a bit longer. I believe there are clues within it that can unlock the big mystery we face, and possibly answer all of our questions. For example, do you remember how McTavish lost his tail?"

"Of course," Banderbrock said. "He told us that story the first night. Some dog bit it clean off years ago, back in his past life."

"But Banderbrock, that's not true. You saw him get his tail chopped off yesterday, in the fight with Diana. He still has the recent scab."

"How could he get a tail chopped off he doesn't have? He was a stub-tailed monster from the moment we met him."

"See what I mean?" Max said. "I talked with Paddy about it, late into the night. The sword changes things and somehow everyone goes along with the changes, even to the extent of remembering new events, except me. I think I can recall the real events because I have Diana's sword and access to the original information. If there's some way to save us from the Cutters, to protect us against their magic, the secret may be in the sword. So I can't just throw this one away, like the last one."

"I don't understand half of what you just said, but it makes me even more certain you should dispose of that thing."

"Paddy agrees with you. He won't even let me put it in the wagon, next to his eggs. He makes me tie it up on the roof when I'm not carrying it."

"I don't know that I trust this Eggman fellow," Banderbrock said. "There's too many odd things about him. He's the mystery you should be spending your time on."

"Oh, I've already solved that one. All the evidence points to the likelihood that he's clearly a madman. That's the reason the Blue Cutters were afraid of him. Many cultures treat the insane as persons to be feared, as if they're divinely touched and have special godlike powers, along with special protections from above. But notice that he didn't actually do anything to help Walden that a normal but learned person couldn't do? In fact, I'm the one who did all the actual work. Then look at his profession."

"He delivers eggs. What's crazy about that?"

"Nothing," Max said, "if that were true. But while

cleaning out his wagon to make room for Walden, I had a look at his so-called eggs, which aren't real eggs at all. They're just a bunch of colorful egg-shaped stones. Like many madmen, he needs props to help him construct and maintain his internal fantasy world; in this case stones as eggs, which were no doubt chosen because of their durability. His madness might lead to violent outbursts at times, and real eggs would suffer badly on those occasions. Since a lot of broken eggs might remind him of his own insanity, he substitutes stones, in order to better preserve his cherished fiction. It's pretty clever in its own way. Even a broken human mind can be complex."

"Do all fire callers talk like you? Sometimes I can't understand half of what you say, and wonder if we really are speaking the same language."

"No," said Max. "Most kids my age don't talk like I do, not even the ones in my Scout Troop. My Scoutmaster Mr. Barrow once said it was because I'm smarter than boys my age and that's why I'm able to solve so many mysteries."

"Smarter is good," Banderbrock said.

"Not always," Max said. "When Mr. Barrow told me that, he was scolding me for being impatient with some of the other boys in my patrol. Sometimes I forget that everyone doesn't think the same way I do. It makes me feel like an outsider, even among my own friends."

"Well, you're not an outsider here, among us," Banderbrock said. There was the hint of a smile in his voice. "A badger, a bear, the meanest cat ever created, and now a daft old man who delivers stone eggs? We're quite a collection of oddities, and you fit right in."

"A parade of weirdos," Max said, smiling for the first time in a long time.

"If the Eggman is crazy, then what do you think we should do about him?"

"Nothing for now, unless he does act out. We're safe from the Cutters while we're in the Eggman's company, so we should continue to take advantage of the rest he affords us. The more time we spend with him, the longer Walden has to recover, and at the rate this wagon moves along, that will be a long time indeed. Paddy told me he was going all the way to the Mysterly River, and since that's where we want to go, as long as the old man continues to be as harmless as he seems, we should stay with him."

"I agree for now," the badger said, "but I will continue to watch him carefully."

The wagon rolled on, with its strange collection of assorted passengers. When the sun hung low in the western sky, they camped along the side of the road. Walden seemed to have survived the first day's travel with little discomfort. The friends took turns keeping him company in the back of the wagon, and feeding him as much food and water as he would take. The next morning they packed up early again and rolled on.

Now that they were down in the lowlands, from time to time throughout the day they'd pass a roadside inn, or a farmstead. These were inhabited by very normal people and their nonspeaking animals. Everyone seemed to recognize the Eggman's brightly painted wagon. As it rolled up to the dwelling, jolly innkeepers or dour farmers' wives would come out to the road with baskets full of meats and vegetables and warm crunchy-crusted breads, dripping with melted butter, for the travelers. They also brought out oats for Incitatus and seed for Epiphany. They greeted Paddy with deference, calling him "sir" or "Mister Eggman, sir," asking no specific questions of him, but always wishing him a good day and safe journey.

Usually, when they saw that there were more passengers with the Eggman, they'd rush back into their home and return with more of whatever they had to offer. They never seemed to take special notice that some of the passengers were talking animals, but were polite to all who were aboard, and wished them well. Max however took special notice that no attempts were made on Paddy's part to act out any sort of egg deliveries to these kind and benevolent folk.

"Interesting," Max noted quietly to himself.

Days like that turned into more than a week. They continued to plod down the last part of the mountain road, to where it would eventually meet up with the eastern and river roads. When the frequent rains came, everyone would crowd into the wagon, except Incitatus of course, who seemed immune to the weather. They stopped at every possible opportunity, to fill up the water barrel from the many tributaries winding their way to the Mysterly, or pick blueberries, strawberries, cherries, or apples from the many fruit-laden trees and bushes, or just to let Incitatus roam free for an hour or two. No one seemed to be in a hurry, and no further sign was seen of the Cutters. After the fifth day of riding in the back, Walden felt good enough to walk on his own, outside of the wagon, for very short distances. His terrible wound seemed to be healing nicely.

On the afternoon of their ninth day on the road with the enigmatic Eggman, Max was riding up in front of the wagon when he heard Epiphany say, "We've come about as far west as we're going to on this road. This would be a good time to make the next Tharmas delivery." Paddy agreed and on instructions from him, Incitatus brought the wagon to a halt at the side of the road. Then Paddy got carefully down from the front bench and walked around to the back of the wagon, where Max helped him unlatch the short stepladder from one of the wagon's sides and hook it in place under the rear doorway, where the red-painted door was kept latched open, so that Walden could enjoy the fresh air.

Paddy climbed into the wagon and, stepping gingerly around the sleeping bear, went to the wall of small drawers. Once there he closely examined the label on each drawer until he found the one he was looking for, and extracted the polished and brightly colored stone from within. He brought the small egg-shaped stone out of the caravan compartment and carried it alone, out into the center of the roadway, about a dozen yards in front of the wagon.

Turning north, he held the stone out in front of him in both hands and said, "Urthona!" in a loud voice. Then he turned ninety degrees, until he was facing due east. Raising the stone again, he said, "Luvah!" Then he turned to face south and said, "Urizen!" And finally he faced due west and said, "Tharmas!"

Once this strange ritual was completed he looked at the stone and said, "Yes, it's for Tharmas, all right. Doesn't hurt to check twice and make sure you labeled it right. Always pays to be careful."

Paddy carried the stone back to the wagon and inserted it into the red velvet pouch hanging from Epiphany's neck. Once it was secure, Epiphany took off from her perch and flew high into the sky, circling to gain altitude with her burden. Then, when she was almost too high to still see, she headed due west and soon disappeared into the distance.

"That was an interesting thing to see," Max said, after Paddy had rejoined him on the wagon's driving bench. "What did it mean?"

"Just an egg delivery," the old man said. "Nothing special about it."

"Well, the egg seemed pretty special," Max said, carefully watching the old man, to see what his reaction might be. "I've never seen one like it."

"No, you wouldn't have, would you? Yes, sonny boy, my eggs are unique, because they're mundane eggs. Do you know what those are?"

"No, sir."

"They're the eggs that gods and worlds and sometimes entire universes hatch out of," Paddy said. "What do you think of that?" While Max searched for something to say, Paddy asked Incitatus to carry on, and the horse pulled the wagon back out onto the road.

"I find that astonishing," Max finally said.

"And well you should," Paddy said. "Mundane eggs are what gives birth to everything that isn't still part of chaos. All of it, including you. When that god you like so much first created the world, I delivered an egg to him to hatch it from. Then when he had his tantrum and flooded the thing, I brought him another one to start it over with."

"Wasn't it Noah in his ark that brought life back to the world after the flood?"

"Of course, boy, but what do you think the ark was? A bunch of pitch and gopher wood like those stories say? No boat made by the hand of mortal man could've held all the life needed to restart an entire world. Only one of my eggs can do that. The one essential thing that old boy's ark carried was one of my eggs. He didn't even know he had it. I slipped it into the boat while everyone was distracted, trying to push a pair of behemoths up the gangplank."

"So, in fact then you are the creator of everything? The whole wide world and everything that's in it?"

"Not at all," Paddy said. "Weren't you listening, boy? Am I talking to myself? I don't create. I'm just the deliveryman. And we're not talking about the World, but worlds, lots and lots of worlds; so many that I don't think even I could count them all anymore. There are bunches of creators starting new worlds all of the time, and each new world they create gives birth to another great bunch of creators who start making worlds of their own. My work just gets more and more piled up as time goes on. That's why I had to take a partner a few turns back. Too much work for me to do alone anymore.

"Epiphany's a good old bird, too. She'll probably work out okay. Cuckoos are adept at sneaking their eggs in foreign nests, and there's no nests more foreign than the four seas of chaos. She was born sterile, poor thing. Never had no eggs of her own to plant. It worked out well though, because she's taken to planting my mundane eggs as if they were her very own. I guess they are in a way, as much as they're mine."

"So how did the first egg get delivered then?" Max asked. "If we were all created from these eggs, who delivered them before you were hatched out of one of them?"

"I guess I wasn't clear in what I said before. It's been so long since we've carried passengers, I may be losing the art of conversation. I didn't mean to say all of *us* were created from the eggs, I meant all of *you* were. I delivered the first one and I'll be around to deliver the last, when the seas of chaos rise again to reclaim all the worlds that were born out of them."

"That's incredible," Max said.

"It sure is, but it's also the way of things. This Wizard Swift you're all going to see; what do you think he is?"

"I'm not sure."

"He's one of those creators I told you about," Paddy said. "And he was a real pain in my schedule before he retired, too. Oh, I liked him well enough at first, but not for a long time now. Most of those possessed of a creative mind were content to just make one new world, or maybe two, if they were really ambitious. But old Swift, he just went on and on, creating one new world after another. He used too many of my eggs, and hardly saved any for others. Gluttony, that's what it was. For a time it seemed every other delivery I had to make was for one of his projects, and they were scattered all over the place. That's just greed, plain and simple. The only reason he finally retired was that I threatened to cut him out of my schedule entirely."

"Will you be going by his sanctuary?" Max said.

"Not even on a bet," Paddy said, and then spit over the side of the wagon. "I don't talk to him anymore and he doesn't talk to me, and that suits both of us just fine. When we get to the crossroads, I'll be turning east, and you'll want to go south along the river, if you're still of a mind to go to his castle."

"That's still our plan."

"Good luck to you then. Once you leave me, the Cutters will be back on your trail. You can count on that."

"What do you know about them?" Max said. "And why are they afraid of you?"

"Maybe it's not really fear exactly. Then again it certainly isn't respect. But they leave me alone. They have to, because, without the eggs I deliver, they'd have nothing to corrupt, and soon enough they'd be out of a job. It's what hatches from the eggs, all the worlds and people and ideas that they want to change and change again, until they think they were the ones who made them. More important, they want to control all of it, not individually, but through huge committees, where no single vision is allowed to dominate. Like insects."

"They're powerful," Max said, not sure if he was asking a question, or making a statement.

"That they are," Paddy said. "And if they catch you, you can be sure they'll cut you up into something unrecognizable, and there won't be a thing you can do to stop them. But they're still not worthy of admiration for all of that. Don't buy all of that nonsense they like to spread around about their nobility. They aren't really grand lords and ladies, or noblemen of any stripe. They're no better than clerks, accountants, and office drones writ large."

Max continued to question Paddy about the Cutters. Even though he was convinced the old man wasn't entirely right in the head, and that he couldn't fully trust his answers about anything, Max needed to know everything about the cloaked hunters. How had their society started? Why did they do it?

He tried to question the old man further. But Paddy wouldn't cooperate.

"I'm tired of talking about them and their kind," Paddy said. "I realize they're looming pretty large in your lives at the moment, but they aren't consequential enough to me to let them disrupt the harmony of my life." After that he would say no more.

The road turned south and the wagon followed it. Early the next day they came up alongside the mighty Mysterly River, which Incitatus quietly insisted was actually so named by an old war horse friend of his called Traveler, who'd been through those lands some many years ago.

"Traveler named the river after his old master, who was a great hero in another life," Incitatus said. "But you're pronouncing it wrong. It's not called the Mysterly River. It's called the Mister Lee River."

Problems with Magical Eggmen
and Finicky Monsters

16 Less than an hour after they were driven from the mountain road by the unwelcome appearance of the Eggman, forced away from their quarry and back into the trees of the Heroes Wood, the Cutters found Diana's bloodied and broken body among the large boulders at the bottom of the hill. To no one's delight, that solved the immediate mystery of how the boy called Max the Wolf came into possession of one of their swords. Later that same afternoon, the Cutters held an impromptu war council around the freshly turned earth of Diana's grave.

"I don't understand the problem," Lord Hannan said. "There are nine of us and two score dogs besides. Why did we let them go?"

"Because they were with the Eggman," Patrick said.

"So? He's an old man. Why didn't we take him too?" Hannan was the most recent addition to this chapter of the Fellowship, having only recently passed through his trials before the Guarding Stone. His blue sword was new and never yet drawn in actual service.

"He's old all right," Lord Wilfred said, "maybe older than all of creation, if the tales are true." Wilfred's face was brown and creased with deep lines. He was the oldest member of the excursion force, having served in seven different chapterhouses. "Here's what I do know. When I was just a young pup I was apprenticed to Lord Berin. Anyone recall that name?"

There were a few low murmurs of assent. Hannan's voice wasn't among them.

"I hadn't even earned my sword yet and Berin was my final teacher," Wilfred continued. "He was always a brave one. Too brave. Foolish, some might say. One day a great host of us was out on the hunt and we came across the Eggman. He just sat up there in his wagon and watched us as we cornered our prey and began cutting him into a new man. Just a few preliminary cuts to keep him docile on the way back to our keep. Did the Eggman interfere? No, he didn't. I don't think he cares about individual people in all of the countless worlds he travels. How could he?

"But our target didn't go down easy. He was a fighter, and made another run for it, after we thought he was safely captured. Berin was obliged to shoot him down with his bow, but he missed. The arrow hit the Eggman's wagon instead. Another inch to one side and it would have hit the Eggman himself. So what did that old man do? He seemed content to tell Berin to be careful."

"Get to the point," Patrick said. "We can't tarry here all day."

"The point is this," Wilfred said. "Lord Berin was always a prickly sort of fellow, and sharp words were exchanged. He didn't like no one correcting him, not even the Eggman. So he starts to draw his blade against the old man and before he can even clear leather the Eggman just waved his hand, real casual like." Wilfred absently waved his hand to illustrate the gesture.

"And Berin burned. There was no smoke and no fire, but he burned just the same. His skin bubbled and cracked, and turned black as pitch. He screamed like no one ever did before, and then fell stone dead in the middle of the road. By the time we got to Berin, no more than ten paces, mind you, there was nothing left but ashes blowing away in the wind.

" 'Don't ever test me again,' the Eggman said to us and

then just drove away on his wagon, as if nothing bad had ever happened. That's how powerful he is, young lad, and that's why we leave him alone to this very day."

"I'm sorry," Hannan said, "but I find that story hard to believe. I've heard a dozen different versions of it, back in the Academy, and in each story it was someone else who was there to personally witness the incident, and some other famous old Cutter who was killed that day."

"You calling me a liar, boy?" Wilfred said. His voice was low and calm, but there was real menace in it, causing Hannan to flinch back a step.

"No," Hannan said. "I'm just saying that I think that's been a ghost story used for many years to scare new recruits, and maybe it's been told so often that everyone's started to believe it. What if it's all nonsense and that old man has no power at all, except what we've given him in our wild imaginations?"

Before Wilfred could speak again, Patrick stepped in. "I can't say if Wilfred's story is true," he said. "I wasn't there to witness it. But I do know what I saw today. My hounds wouldn't come near that old man. They were scared to death of him. And hounds don't know our stories and legends. They were responding to something more primal."

"If the Eggman doesn't care about the men and beasts we hunt," Lady Anne said, "then why did he welcome Max and his company into his care?"

"Who can say for certain?" Patrick said. "He doesn't exactly whisper all of his interests and concerns to us. Maybe Max the Wolf has powers beyond those that we know of. But I do know this. If the boy and his friends stay with the Eggman, we are undone. We won't be able to touch them until they scamper from the safety of the dreaded one's caravan, and through the gates of the Wizard Swift's sanctuary."

"Not necessarily so," Lady Anne cautioned. "There are reliable rumors that Swift and the Eggman will have no truck with each other. Though no one ever knows the Eggman's route save him, I'd wager there's a good chance he'll avoid taking the river road. If he turns onto the eastern road, then the fugitives will have to attempt to travel downriver on their own."

"If this turns out to be so," Patrick said, "and we prepare well, we'll be able to take them shortly after they leave the Eggman's wagon and start down the river road on their own."

"What are your orders then?" Lord Kelvin asked Patrick.

"I am master of the hounds," Patrick said, "and the hounds have to continue to follow the Eggman, in case the fugitives attempt to slip away from his wagon before they reach the river. Therefore I cannot continue to lead the main force of this party. Wallace, you will take command of all but Kelvin, Laura, and I. You will divert around the

Eggman's wagon tonight and hurry down the road in all good haste. When you rendezvous at the crossroads with Lord Robert and his riders, you will organize such preparations and traps as seems correct for you to do.

"I advise you to set watches over both the road and the river, and perhaps even in the woods of that area, in order to be sure to spot where they set out on their own. I must follow behind the wagon so that my hounds can pick up their trail, should they attempt to split off from the Eggman early. If past experience is any guide, he will go slow, and though that may frustrate me, it will ensure that you will have no danger of being overtaken, once you get on the road ahead of them tonight."

"In turn, I also advise you to exercise caution," Wallace said to Patrick. "These fugitives have proven themselves especially dangerous. One of our finest members is dead at their hands, and another swordless and mutilated for life. From now on, we should only approach them when we have overwhelming strength in numbers. Better to let the dogs have them than to risk losing another Cutter."

"Agreed," Patrick said. "Though they deserve as much as anyone to be saved, remade at our hands into better souls, I wouldn't regret simply killing this foul bunch if it became necessary."

Shortly after nightfall, Lord Wallace led his new command of five Cutters in a wide arc through the forest, until they came out onto the road well ahead of the Eggman's wagon, which was still parked where they'd first seen it, and wouldn't move until the following morning. Patrick, Kelvin, and Laura stayed behind with the dogs and most of the supplies. They made a camp nestled under the same boulders that had finished Diana's life, where the firelight would be well shielded from prying eyes.

Along the road, Wallace's force made good time, even though they were on foot. They bought food, and what other supplies they needed, from the same farmhouses and inns that would later serve and supply the Eggman for free. Even though they stayed in comfort in the inns on most nights, they easily kept well ahead of the Eggman and his fugitive guests. Sharp words of warning to each one they met on the way made certain that no one would tell the small company that the Cutters had preceded them.

Three full days before the wagon arrived behind them, Wallace's force met up with Robert's riders, encamped at the crossroads. They rested and worked out their strategies, and were well prepared by the time the Eggman's wagon was spotted.

The river road didn't officially begin at its northern-most end until the crossroads, even though the last stretch of the mountain road met up with and then paralleled the Mysterly River, leading down to the crossroads.

As the wagon creaked down that last bit of the mountain road, Paddy said to Max, "Young man, your company has been enjoyable, but our time of parting has come near. It's less than a day's journey to the crossroads, where I must turn east, and I would be surprised if we did not meet a strong force of Blue Cutters assembled there."

"I suspected that they would move ahead of us and wait where we will have to leave your safety," Max said.

"It seems the most logical choice," Paddy said. "If Epiphany had returned by now, I'd ask her to scout ahead and make certain. But, assuming they are there, I would suggest that you take another road, one they may not anticipate."

"Is there more than one road that follows the river south, to Swift's castle?"

"Yes, in a manner of speaking. I thought you might take the river itself. If things are as they normally are, just around this bend we'll be able to look down the embankment to a small dock—no more than a few logs lashed together actually—where a dairy farmer named Lundy Bugnail keeps his favorite fishing boat tied up. He seldom gets a chance to use the thing, so chances are excellent that it will be there, waiting to carry you downriver."

"I couldn't steal," Max said.

"I wouldn't consider this stealing," the Eggman said. "It's borrowing only, and in a good cause. Like most of the folk here, in their secret hearts, Bugnail would enjoy any chance to vex the Cutters, almost as much as I would. And he would certainly offer it if I asked. If you like, I can even send Bugnail a note to explain what I have arranged in his name. I'll do it a day or two after I set off along the eastern road, so you'll be well on your way by then. Epiphany can deliver a note to him from me."

"Okay," Max said, not quite convinced of the honor of the compromise. "Only because we're desperate, and I have your assurance he would allow it, if we were able to ask in advance. But Walden is awful big for a boat."

"It's not all that small. A boat large enough to carry four grown men and their gear should be big enough to carry one big bear, along with a boy and two smaller animals. Just keep him in the center of the craft and keep his center of gravity as low into the boat as he can get, and you should be fine.

"One warning though: The river is calm and easy to navigate for about three days' travel. Just keep yourself in the center of the current and the river will carry you along at a good pace. But as soon as you see the pillar of rock growing out of the middle of the water that looks like a giant crouching washerwoman, you'll have to pull over to this side of the river and continue the rest of the way on foot. A long set of rapids begins shortly after that marker, and your craft will not survive it. Be sure that you don't try to beach on the other bank of the river, and head south from there, or you'll eventually find yourself on the wrong side of a great river canyon, with Swift's castle unreachable on the other side. Once you leave the river, you'll be on foot, and in danger from the Cutters again, but that is the best I can advise you."

"We owe you our lives," Max said, and felt it wasn't enough, but could unlock no better words to convey the depth of his feelings.

"More than once," the old man said, "even if I can't recall the specific eggs each of your lives sprang from." His smile was wide as always, extra large to emphasize the secret, unspoken knowledge held back within it.

"I was glad to help you this time," he continued, "because I've come to enjoy confounding those Cutters and their designs. I shouldn't. A fellow like me shouldn't interfere with the lives he delivers. But I couldn't help myself. I took an instant liking to the bear and his wry sense of humor. I hope he makes it. I hope you all live long and happy lives. Probably won't, but who can say for sure?"

At that point they came out of the bend of the road, and Lundy Bugnail's boat was tied up right where Paddy expected to find it, bobbing sleepily at the end of a short rope. Incitatus stopped the wagon, and everyone helped Walden out of its back for the last time. He was much healed from his ordeal, and had been taking increasingly longer walks behind the wagon each day.

The company didn't take a long time saying good-bye to Paddy and Incitatus, only because they agreed it was best that the wagon spend as little time paused there as possible. They didn't want to alert any lurking Cutters, or other spying eyes, that the two groups were parting ways. Almost immediately the wagon continued on, with Paddy dozing in his usual spot where the driver might be, if a driver was needed.

Max and his friends crouched behind a big thorn-girdled oak tree, near the side of the road, until the enigmatic Professor Padraic Antipedes Hildemark, in his brightly painted wagon, was well on his way, en route to some other story. They all looked up and down the road, and all around, for any sign that someone had seen them.

When no such sign showed itself, the company left the cover of the oak, and slid on the steep, fern-covered embankment, down to the river and the moored boat. As he slid, Max fought to hold on to all of his possessions. He carried his wooden staff, Diana's sheathed sword, and the gray cloak, tied in a large bundle containing all manner of food generously donated from the old man's supplies.

Concealed within the tall bulrushes lining the river-bank, the man in green watched the odd collection of fugitives leave the Eggman's wagon and scramble down the bank toward the waiting boat. These must be the ones the Cutters were out in force to capture, the green man thought. They hardly look so impressive as to require such a large expedition.

Then again, this was the first time the green man had ever seen a new arrival in the Heroes Wood keep company with the Eggman. One or more of them might be more powerful than he looked to have such friends. He quietly strung his longbow as he watched Max and his companions. He also kept a wary eye on one of their enemies, who was nearby.

Several of the nonmounted Cutters had been spaced along the riverbank, just in case the fugitives attempted a river escape. Lady Anne was supposed to be farther up the river, but the sight of the tied fishing boat convinced her that this was the better spot to watch. She was seated comfortably, occasionally napping, at the base of a moss-draped hemlock tree, which drooped lazily out over the bulrushes of the river. Then she was jolted fully awake by the sound of the fugitives in their barely controlled scramble down the embankment from the roadway above.

Instantly she sprang to her feet and ran to intercept them, all the while shouting for Lord Edward, who was stationed on the other side of the fugitives, farther down the riverbank. She was under orders not to confront them alone. Her job, after spotting the fugitives, was to run for help. But she'd dozed at her post and let them get too close to the boat. It would be her fault alone if they escaped, so she drew her sword as she ran.

"Run for the boat!" Max called, as they all spotted the Cutter at the same time. It was quickly clear that she'd reach the boat at roughly the same moment they would. Having no time to consider the best course of action, Max threw his staff at the woman, like it was a javelin. It was the best of all possible throws, and the blunt end of the staff bonked squarely in the middle of the woman's forehead. At several times along the trail, Max had considered carving one end of his walking stick into a point, but he'd never quite gotten around to it. Had he done so, the staff would have split Anne's head open. As it was, it just stunned her, knocking her backward off her feet, onto her plump rear end.

"We'd better kill her!" McTavish shouted.

"Not this time!" Max barked back, almost savagely. "Never again! So let's get into the boat and get out of here." Max pulled on the end of the rope line, until the boat sighed against the edge of the shore. He held it as Walden carefully stepped aboard.

"Boat?" McTavish said. "Who said anything about a boat?" From downstream they could hear the sounds of another person crashing toward them, through the thickets of ferns and reeds along the riverbank.

"As usual, you were asleep when we made our plans," Banderbrock said. He didn't much look forward to river travel either, but knew when it was time to shut up and soldier on. He bounced up from the reeds, clawed his way over the gunwale, and flopped ungracefully into the bottom of the craft. The sounds of the other approaching Cutter got louder.

"I'm not getting in any boat," McTavish yowled at them.

"You don't have a choice," Max said. He looked back at the female Cutter to see that she was still dazed for the moment. He tossed his bundle and the scabbard of the blue sword into the boat. He held the naked blade ready to slice through the line securing the boat to the shore. Then he could push off from shore, jumping aboard at the same time.

"I'm not going out on all that water," McTavish said, frozen to his spot among the tall reeds.

"We don't have time for this," Max said. He cut through the mooring line and tossed the sword into the boat, well away from Walden and Banderbrock. He pushed the boat off from the shore with the biggest shove he could manage, which was not all that much, considering that he was still a relatively small boy, and that there was a heavy black bear in the boat. Then he jumped aboard. Turning around again to face McTavish, he said, "Now you can't waste time arguing any longer, or we'll be too far from shore for you to make it. Jump aboard now and I'll catch you. I promise."

"You haven't been listening to me, Max!" McTavish screamed back at him. "McTavish—does—not—get—wet!"

With that, the huge ugly barn cat turned his nub of a tail to his friends and dashed off through the ferns and reeds. "Good luck on the rest of your journey," he called to them from the concealment of the brush. "If you don't all drown, I'll meet you again at the wizard's castle. Unless I find a nice barn to rule first."

The boat was by that point too far out on the water to turn back. Max, Banderbrock, and Walden dumbly watched the intermittent flashes of yellow as their friend left them, darting in and out through the trees and underbrush.

"If you can't turn the boat around, I could swim back," Walden said.

"I don't think you could be of any help to him now," Banderbrock said. "You'd only provide the enemy with another, much bigger target."

"And you'd put too much strain on your wound," Max said. "It's still a long way from being fully healed."

"For better or worse McTavish is on his own," Banderbrock said. "But I'm not too worried. The wild old monster will lead them a merry chase and get away. I'm certain of it."

But the badger didn't sound certain.

Max used one of the boat's two long oars to pole the craft through the cloying bulrushes, out into the more open waters of the wide river. As he was doing so, another Cutter splashed his way, waist deep, out of a stand of the water reeds. He was almost to the boat before anyone spotted him.

"Cutter!" Walden shouted.

Already holding the oar, Max used it to fend off the man, who held his blue sword drawn in one hand. With a single deft move, the Cutter grabbed the end of the oar in his other hand and pulled hard. Max was jerked forward and had to let go of the oar, or fall out of the boat. The Cutter threw the oar behind him, into the reeds, and advanced with his sword. He had to walk through the clinging muck of the river bottom, which gave Max enough time to recover his own captured sword, which lay near his feet. He swung it in a quick slash at the Cutter's face, forcing him to step back. Then, before the Cutter could muster an attack of his own, Max aimed a stop-thrust at the man's sword hand.

Max had been forced, albeit enthusiastically, to take up the art of fencing during the Mystery of the Imaginary Swashbuckler. He knew that the stop-thrust was arguably the most difficult fencing move to succeed at, and no fencing master had perfected it. But he also knew the safest way to fight with swords was to stick your opponent in that part of him closest to you, which was most often his sword hand.

The Cutter came out of his protective crouch, with his sword out in front of him, ready to thrust as soon as it rose high enough to come on target against the boy. Max thrust his own blade out, off target, over the Cutter's blade. Then he let his wrist drop, bringing the point of his sword down onto the man's unprotected hand, cutting it only slightly—a successful, almost elegant example of the stop-thrust.

As the point set home in the Cutter's hand, Max concentrated with all his might. You have always been a fumble-fingered klutz, he thought furiously. You've never been able to hold on to anything.

The Cutter dropped his sword, and it immediately disappeared into the muddy brown water, with a single pronounced plop. "Not again!" the poor man cried, holding the tiny pinprick of his wound with his other hand.

After that it was an easy matter for Max to keep the unarmed man at bay with his blue sword, until the momentum of the boat carried them out into the swifter-flowing blue water of the river. As the current caught them, they saw the Cutter ducking into the water, over and over again, trying to recover his sword, which was lost in all the muck he'd churned up, trying to attack the boat. They saw the other one, the woman, splash out to join him, and say, "Hurry up and find the thing. You have to go warn the others, while I find us some more boats."

Finally, when they were so far out in the river that both shores seemed equally distant, they all thought they saw one last brief flash of yellow, which might possibly have been their friend, running south along the river.

"Good luck to you, old monster," Banderbrock said quietly.

River Travel and Unplanned Reunions

17 When the female Cutter moved to intercept the boy and the animals making for the boat, the man in green prepared to help them against the woman. He stood up in place, still well concealed by the bulrushes, set an arrow onto the bowstring, and drew back on the bow. But a remarkable thing happened just before he was about to loose the shot. The small boy threw his walking stick at the Cutter and knocked her senseless, right on her bottom.

Without pausing to puzzle over the extraordinary incident, the green man turned his bow on a second Cutter that had just arrived on the scene. This one was a young man who rushed headlong into the river to catch the boat that was starting to drift out into the middle of it. The second Cutter splashed about so much that the green man had to hold off for a moment, until he could be certain of a clear shot. If he missed he might hit one of the fugitives in the boat.

Before the man in green could make sure of his aim, the boy in the boat had saved himself again, by cutting the Cutter, making the villain drop his own sword into the water and the muck below it.

"Not again!" the Cutter cried.

The boy in the boat kept the unarmed Cutter at bay long enough for the boat to drift farther out into the river, until the current took them safely away. In a few minutes the female Cutter had recovered enough to help her companion frantically search the river bottom for his lost weapon.

The man in green was quietly astonished by what he'd just witnessed. It was unlikely enough that a small boy, an untrained new arrival to this land, could get the best of one Cutter. It seemed impossible that he might overcome two.

The man in green pondered what he should do next. He could easily kill the two Cutters now, recovering at least one blue sword, and possibly two. Recovering the blue swords was always a priority. But even though the risk to his own safety was slight, there was *some* risk, and he realized his most important duty was to make sure he lived to pass on the news of what he'd observed. Reluctantly he crouched in hiding again, set down his bow, and took his last precious piece of homing paper out of his kit. Quickly he wrote down everything he'd seen, including the fact that the fugitives had captured at least one of the blue swords. He also added his guess that they were headed toward the Wizard Swift's refuge. He would continue to shadow them, as best he could, and render what help he could to them. Finally he instructed the others of his order to meet up with him, as quickly and as best they could manage it, noting that he would leave signs for them along the way.

As soon as he signed his name to the note, the homing paper disappeared. It would instantly reappear in their order's way house deep within the wilder parts of the forest, where he hoped there'd be someone in residence to receive it.

When all that was done, the man in green picked up his bow again and set off down the banks of the river, hoping he could keep pace with the boat out on it. He spared one wistful glance back at the two Cutters, both of whom were armed with blue swords again. Too bad, he thought. Too bad.

* * *

Out on the river, Max fought to steer the boat. Missing one of the oars made controlling it difficult. It was long and fairly narrow, designed for four passengers to sit in a single row. In many ways it more resembled a very large, heavy canoe, with a squared stern, than a standard rowboat. The boat was too large, and the oar too unwieldy, to use it effectively as a single paddle. Eventually, with some hard work from his Scout knife, Max was able to gouge a setting in the middle of the stern board, to hold one of the oarlocks. Then, able to set the one oar in the middle of the back end of the boat, he used it as a steering rudder, and let the swift river current do the job of moving them along. By the second day of their river trip, Max had become quite adept at piloting the craft down the wide Mysterly River.

Walden, who'd never before been on a boat, found that he liked the experience. It was thoroughly exhilarating to move briskly along without having to expend any of his own energy. It seemed almost magical to travel nearly as fast as he could run, and be able to catch a nice nap at the same time. The extra rest also gave him more time to heal. His belly still hurt, but no longer so badly that he couldn't think of anything else. Life wasn't so bad when his only responsibility was to stay low in the boat, so as to not risk overturning them. The best way to stay low in the boat was to nap, and even when he felt in tip-top shape, Walden liked napping more than just about anything else.

On the other hand, Banderbrock hated the boat ride. He couldn't get used to the constant swaying motion under his four feet. It made him feel dizzy and nauseous. Max tried to explain seasickness to the poor badger, but being able to put a name to his troubles didn't help to raise his spirits. He spent his time lying in the bottom of the boat, grimly suffering each seemingly endless minute of undulating river travel, only rising every once in a while, to throw up over the side. It was slightly better at night, when the cool air made the experience a bit more bearable.

By the second full day on the river, Banderbrock had grown accustomed enough to the constant motion to try some conversation with Max.

"You're the only one of us doing all the work," he said. "How long have you been awake?"

"It's not so bad," Max said. "All I really have to do is sit in the back of the boat and keep us in the middle of the current. That doesn't take much effort. And last night I found a log sticking up out of the water to tie us to, while I slept for a few hours. Even now I can nod off for ten or fifteen minutes at a time, without fear of running aground. That's the advantage of being out on such a wide body of water."

"Still, I wish there was more I could do to help."

"You can talk to me, if you feel good enough. Boredom is the worst problem I have right now."

"Then tell me what you finally decided about the old man," Banderbrock said. "Is he insane?"

"I sure hope so. If I met him back in my own world, I wouldn't have any doubts. But in this strange land, who knows? I want him to be crazy, because if he isn't, the implications are too wild to consider. A detective isn't supposed to let his wishes influence the investigation, but I can't force myself to be impartial in this case. That's why I'm unable to come to a conclusion."

"Does it really matter anymore?"

"True," Max said, after pondering the badger's question for a while. "For better or worse we've probably seen the last of Paddy and his friends. Any impact he was going to have on our fates has already happened. Still, if I could finally decide about him one way or another, I could better judge what weight to give to his advice."

"His advice on what?"

Max didn't answer directly, but glanced down at the sheathed sword at his feet.

"Oh, that thing again," Banderbrock said. "Both the old man and I think you should get rid of it, but you disagree. In the end, it's not our choice to make, it's yours. So what's left to decide?"

"I did a very bad thing," Max said so softly it was almost inaudible. "In the last fight with the two Cutters at the riverside, I used the sword to change that man, the same way they use their swords to change others."

"How is that?"

"I made him drop his sword in the river."

"Of course you did," the badger said. "I saw the entire thing. You stabbed him in his hand and he dropped his weapon. There's no special blue sword magic involved in that. It's the simple cruel mechanics of tooth and claw."

"Maybe, but I'm not sure that was all there was to it. I tried to imagine him changing into someone who was always dropping things. If it worked, and I changed him into such a person, I'm as evil as any of them."

"And maybe you're just a big idiot with too much imagination," Banderbrock said, earning a surprised look from Max. "When I was no more than a young pup, with too much curiosity and too little sense, I used to sneak out of our family sett, to journey clear to the edge of the forest and watch a fire caller. He was building something out of planks of wood. I used to watch him all day, and was particularly fascinated when he would hammer nails into boards. Nails looked like claws to me, and claws are what give badgerkind most of our power. I was amazed at a tool that could wield so much power over those metal claws. I wanted to have that hammer and have power over all the claws of everyone in my world. So, every time the man left his workplace, I'd scamper in and sniff and paw at that hammer, trying to learn its secrets. How far do you think I got?"

"Not very far at all," Max ventured.

"Correct," Banderbrock said. "Do you know how to use a hammer?"

"Of course."

"And did you know how to use it the first time you picked one up?"

"No," Max said. "Not even close. I banged a lot of fingers before I learned how to use one effectively."

"So what makes you think you knew how to use the magic of this blue sword, the very first time you tried it? It seems much more complex a thing than a hammer. Didn't I hear you tell Walden that one should tend to believe the simplest of two or more possible explanations for a mystery, back when you were trying to give him detective lessons? Isn't that one of your big rules? So then, what's the most likely explanation for why that Cutter dropped his sword, some great magical thing, or the fact that he'd just gotten stabbed in his sword hand?"

The badger made sense and Max considered his words for a time. Finally he said, "Okay, I get your point. I'll quit moping about what I might possibly have done. Thanks, Banderbrock. I'm lucky to have your advice to guide me."

"I'm pleased to be able to help," Banderbrock said. "And I've got one other immediate bit of advice to give you."

"I know. I know. You want me to throw the sword away."

"Yes, that too, but for the moment I'm more of a mind that you should steer around that big rock in front of us."

"Oh!" Max said, looking away from his friend and back out in front of the boat. "Good idea."

Banderbrock insisted that Max get some sleep after that. For the rest of that day the badger kept lookout while Max dozed, waking him up each time the boat drifted so far out of the middle of the current that the boy would need to steer them back on course. It worked, more or less. Max got as much rest as regularly interrupted catnaps could provide, and Banderbrock had something to do, to take his mind off how miserable river travel made him feel.

While he slept, Max dreamed. He dreamed about being back home once more, with his parents and his baby sister. It was a happy dream, until Max realized he was holding the blue sword, and cut into his own father and mother with it. He made only tiny changes in his parents, just a few things to make their life better. His father often complained about the things his family couldn't afford, so he cut a bit more boldness into him, so that he would be more aggressive about asking his boss for raises. He also cut the persistent back pains out of his dad, which began when he'd fallen off a scaffolding at work one day, and flared up often in subsequent years. He cut his mother into someone who wasn't ever embarrassed anymore about how her sister was always considered the pretty one, owned her own wedding shop, and was generally considered more successful than she was. He only made one cut in his sister, just a small change so that she wouldn't keep chewing on his books every time she got away from Mom and into his room.

Just small cuts to make things better. What was so wrong with that?

Max woke with a start. He was covered with sweat, even though the evening air was cool. His stomach churned with approaching nausea, which never quite came, but left him unsettled just the same. For the first time since arriving here, he was happy to be in this strange land, rather than safe at home.

The next time he was able to sleep Max dreamed he was running through the woods, cutting deeply and wildly into every creature he could find. He could do things with the blue sword that no other Cutter had ever been able to accomplish. He could cut a great bear into a tiny mouse, with but a few quick strokes of his blade. He cut a sparrow into a giant fire-breathing dragon, on which Max would ride high into the sky, the master of everything he could see.

"Wake up, Max!" It was Banderbrock screaming into his ear.

"You're hurting me," Max said, as he woke. The badger had been shaking him and his long digger claws did indeed hurt, even through the protection of his thick cloak. "Why are you yelling?"

"Because you were crying in your sleep."

And it was true. Max brushed his face and there were tears on his cheek. "I was just having a bad dream," he said.

"Full of monsters?" Walden said. He'd also been woken by Banderbrock's shouts. "I'd get nightmares full of terrible monsters sometimes when I ate rotten fish. Did you eat rotten fish, Max? You shouldn't. I learned the hard way you should just walk away from rotten fish, even though it's such a shame to pass up a good meal."

"There was only one monster in my dream and it was me," Max said.

"I don't understand," Banderbrock said.

"Did you have horns and claws and a long tail?" Walden said. "Sometimes I wish bears had long tails like cougars do. Rake always had such a nice tail."

Max didn't answer. Instead he picked up the blue sword from the bottom of the boat and held it out over the water, almost desperately wanting to be rid of it.

"Good idea," Banderbrock said. "Throw that foul thing away."

"I should," Max said, "but I'm not sure. Some part of me still thinks there's some good this weapon can do, if only I learn how to make use of it."

"Does it still say things to you?" the badger said.

"I think so."

"Then toss it into the drink. The bottom of the river's the best place for it."

Max thought about it for a long time, but in the end he placed the blue sword back into the bottom of the boat.

"Not yet," he said. "I want to throw it away. I really do. But balanced against that is a small inner voice that's telling me this thing can help us."

"How?" Walden said.

"I wish I knew," Max said. "I think it's important to understand it though. Understand its power. In my past adventures, doing the easy comfortable thing was seldom the right thing to do. Most often the mystery was finally solved only after a difficult struggle. I've had so many past adventures I should be used to a few hardships by now. I think I'd best bear this burden just a little while longer."

Max rested again as they continued to drift in the current.

For the most part each bank of the great river was lined in the thick green forest that filled most of the Mysterly River valley, but once in a while they would spot a house, or an inn, or some other human structure along the left bank. By comparison, the right-hand riverbank remained unspoiled by any sign of human settlement. Twice they passed small villages clustered beside the water. Once in a while they spotted other boats out on the river, but those tended to stay close to the shore for the most part, and Max was easily able to give them a wide berth. At night they were serenaded by bullfrogs and cicadas and a hundred other types of singsong creatures. And once, just a few hours after the sun had set, Max heard the drifting strains of guitar music, accompanied by voices raised in song, and the delighted laughter of people gathered together safely, comfortable in the knowledge that they didn't have to live their lives on the run, hunted through a strange land by a band of fanatical cloaked swordsmen. Max wondered if he'd ever again be safe to enjoy such happy moments with his friends.

When he wasn't napping, Walden most often spent his time watching the left-hand riverbank, looking for any sign of McTavish.

"Do you think we'll ever see him again?" he asked.

"I wouldn't be surprised," Banderbrock said. "He's too mean to inflict on anyone else. I think a gang of desperate fugitives like us is the best chance he'll ever have at making true friends. Maybe he was our burden, like Max said, because we have to struggle before solving the mystery. Putting up with that ugly cat was a struggle every day. Still, for all of his infuriating ways, I liked him."

"Me too," Walden said. "And I think he liked us more than he would admit. Do you think that's true? I think it's true, even though he was so nasty all the time. Some of the things he said made me glad I have such dark fur, so no one could see me blush."

"We were sentenced to be McTavish's friend for our sins," Max said, with a small sad smile.

"What sins?" Walden said.

"It's just an expression," Max said. "I wasn't making a specific accusation."

"Oh good," Walden said, authentic relief in his voice. "I don't think I committed any sins. Well, not too many. Sure, I was never able to catch Rake, even though that was pretty much my only job. And I took too many naps back in the Grand Green, when I probably should have been on patrol. All things considered, I wasn't a very good sheriff, was I?"

"I'm sure you were fine," Banderbrock said.

"Do you think the Wizard Swift will make me a better sheriff when we get to his sanctuary? Maybe even give me real detective powers like you, Max?"

"I don't know," Banderbrock said. "Is that what you want most?"

"I think so. Or maybe a good stream filled with trout. Or a log full of endless grubs. Or a shady tree to nap under."

"I'll be happy with directions to the Great Sett," Banderbrock said. "If there are enough badgers living there, I think I might go into military service again and show those Blue Cutters what a real army in the field can do."

"Maybe the wizard can make you their general, or a colonel," Walden said. "Which one of those is the higher rank? I forget."

"It doesn't matter," Banderbrock said. "I wouldn't accept any rank I didn't earn for myself. What do you want the wizard to give you, Max?"

Max thought for some time before answering.

"I'm not sure," he finally said. "In the storybooks wizards tend to give you what they want you to have, not what you ask for. That doesn't always turn out so well for those who go off to see the wizard."

"Should we turn back then?" Walden said. "Go somewhere else?"

"No," Max said. "I think we should probably carry on. Those are just storybooks, after all."

Early the next morning they saw the mighty river split in half by a huge spire of rock that grew up from its center. Sure enough, from upriver, and with just a bit of squinting, it did look like a washerwoman bent over to wash her clothes in the river. After they passed the rocky outcropping, and both divisions of the river had rejoined into one, Max steered for the shore.

"Try to land as soon as you can," Walden said.

"Why?" Max said. "Are you finally getting seasick too?"

"No, but I can see two more boats far up the river, past the big rock, and they look like they may be full of Blue Cutters."

Max and Banderbrock turned to look back upriver, and saw the two boats that the bear had spotted. They were

still too far away to make out many details of their passengers, but none of the company wanted to let them come
close enough to make certain.

"Get out of the boat as soon as we touch the shore,"
Max said. "They're not likely to have hunting dogs with
them in their boats. So if we move out fast enough, we may
still lose them."

With some effort, Max was able to guide the boat to
shore in the middle of a wide clump of bulrushes. Once
they were among the reeds, they were hidden from anyone who wasn't close enough to touch them.

"If they can't see our boat, they may not be sure where
we landed," Max said. He jumped out of the boat, into the
knee-deep water, and pulled it farther toward the muddy
riverbank. Banderbrock jumped from the prow of the craft,
down into the slippery mud, which seemed blessedly solid
to him after three days on the water. Walden followed,
stepping more gingerly. Max lifted the food bundle, which
was much smaller after days of feeding Walden's fully recovered appetite. He also took the sheathed sword.

"Best if you leave that where it is," Banderbrock
growled.

"Not quite yet," Max said. "There are still secrets to
dig out of it."

The three of them fought their way through the thick
reeds, until they broke out onto a grassy field that sloped
gently up to the embankment of the river road, about two

hundred yards distant. There were only a few trees dotting the field here and there, not enough to conceal the surprising sight awaiting the small company as they broke out of the reeds. Up on the roadway, a large yellow cat sat casually grooming itself. He licked one of his forepaws and then ran it over his face. The white blazes of fur on his breast, one hind paw, and on the tip of his long tail shone pure and bright in the morning sunlight. The company ran forward to meet him.

"McTavish!" Max yelled in delight. "Is that really you?"

"What took you guys so long?" McTavish said, when they'd gotten closer. "I was beginning to wonder if you'd ever show up. But the good news is that it gave me plenty of time to scout the road ahead for a few miles, and it's all clear of the bad guys."

Max was in the lead, rushing up to reunite with a friend he'd feared he would never see again. Walden also lumbered along, but not nearly so fast as he used to run, before he was wounded. Oddly, Banderbrock hung back.

"I've never seen you look so clean," Max said. "Did you fall in the river after all, or did you finally decide that ratty matted coat wasn't a good look for you?"

"Max, stop!" Banderbrock screamed. "That isn't our friend!"

Max trusted Banderbrock enough to stop dead in his

tracks. He looked back at the badger in puzzlement. "Of course he's McTavish," he said. "There can't be two cats in this world that look like him."

Walden also paused and began sniffing the air.

"How many cats grow their tails back?" Banderbrock said. "He may still be McTavish, but he's no longer anyone we know. The Cutters caught him and changed him! I think we've just walked into a trap!"

For a moment, Max didn't know what to do. He looked between Banderbrock and McTavish a few times. It was true that the cat had gotten its tail back, smooth and silky. It wasn't even broken like it had been before. He felt his stomach turn over sickeningly, and his legs grow weak.

"Back to the boat!" he finally said. "Hurry!"

Walden and Banderbrock turned and began to run back the way they'd come. But before Max could follow, a Cutter stepped out from behind a tree, not more than twenty yards away, and put an arrow in him. The arrow hit Max in the center of his chest, but only after it passed through the food bundle he carried. Very little of the arrowhead poked through to his flesh, not more than half an inch. Max turned and ran after the others, almost giddy to find himself still alive. He let the food bundle fall open behind him, spilling its remaining contents on the grass, but managed to hold on to one end of the gray cloak that had surrounded it. As he ran, he whipped the large cloak back and forth behind him, hoping it might help to spoil the archer's aim, in the same way a bullfighter's cape confuses the bull. In his other hand he continued to hold on to Diana's sword and silently vowed he'd use it to protect his friends if one of the Cutters got too close to them.

More Cutters stepped out from behind the widely scattered trees. Only two of them were close enough to come between the three fugitives and the river. Without pausing, Walden barreled into the closer of the two, running on all fours. That Cutter flew aside like a rag doll tossed casually away by a bored child. The next one was better prepared and drew his blade. Walden had learned a hard lesson from his encounter with Diana, not to run onto the weapon. Instead he stood up on his hind legs and roared such a terrifying hot wet roar into the man's face that he was briefly frozen in place. That was all the time the bear needed to swat him with one huge paw. Walden's long claws drew four deep lines of crimson across the man's chest, but the man was no longer conscious to feel it.

The lone archer had nocked another arrow by that time, and looked for a target. The boy and the badger had already made it back into the reeds, but the bear was still visible, and still a viable target if he acted quickly.

Within the reeds, Max threw his cloak and sword into the boat and then picked up a surprised badger with both hands and tossed him in after them. Then he tucked his shoulder under the bow of the boat and ran it back into the water, with a strength born of fear. No sooner was the craft floating free again than the reeds parted with a mighty crash and Walden burst into view, running faster than ever before. He didn't have a hope of stopping before he reached the boat, so he leapt aboard at full speed. His momentum pushed the boat far out onto the river and nearly swamped it. More troubling though, it left Max stranded on the shore.

"Don't worry, I'm fine!" Max called to Walden, who looked miserably back at him, certain that he'd just betrayed his friend to the enemy. Without another word, Max ran a few splashing steps into the water, until he was deep enough to swim. Then he dove in and a few strong strokes were all it took to bring him alongside his friends. When he reached the boat, he didn't try to immediately climb aboard, but pushed against it as he kicked with his feet, adding his efforts to its bear-powered momentum. Only when it was safely back out in the swift current of the river did Max climb aboard.

"Is everyone okay?" Max said, between gasping breaths, after he landed in the boat like a pile of wet rags.

"No, I most certainly am not okay!" Walden said. "Look at what they did to me!" The bear carefully turned around in the wobbly craft, and showed the others his rear end, which had two long, colorfully feathered arrows sticking out of it.

"Ouch," Banderbrock said. "I bet those hurt."

Looking back at the shore, Max saw the new McTavish actually leap into one of the Cutters' arms, preening and squirming in pleasure, like a real domesticated cat, not at all like the feral monster of their past acquaintance. The sight made Max more angry than the ambush.

Then Max saw three more Cutters emerge from the obscuring bulrushes, quickly wading up to their chests. Max guessed that they would probably be of no further danger. The current had already carried them farther away from the landing place than even a powerful swimmer could cross, before they were carried downstream. Looking upriver though, he could see that the other boats, which had been following them, were now close enough to identify. They were two swift canoes and were indeed manned by Cutters, two in each boat. The Cutters were paddling furiously and their canoes were closing fast.

"Why am I always the one who gets shot or stabbed?" Walden said.

"Because you're the biggest target," Banderbrock said.

Max frantically used their single oar to steer them into the swiftest part of the current. "They don't look too bad," he said to Walden. "The shafts don't seem to be in very deep, and luckily this time, you weren't wounded in a vital spot."

"Not vital?" Walden cried. "How can you say my poor bum isn't vital? Try sitting down without one."

A quick glance upriver told Max the canoes were still

closing rapidly, as each Cutter paddled frantically. "I only meant I'm glad that there's no chance major organs may have been hit this time," he said to Walden, while keeping his eyes on the other boats. "I should be able to dig those out of you without too much trouble, but that will have to wait a bit. There are Cutters in those boats and they're gaining on us."

Walden and Banderbrock turned to look upriver. The two canoes were spaced about twenty yards abreast of each other, and getting closer to the slower craft by the moment.

"What do you plan to do?" Banderbrock asked.

"Continue going downriver," Max said.

"Weren't we warned against that?" Walden said. "Aren't there supposed to be dangerous rapids?"

"What choice do we have?" Max said. "The shore is closed off to us because of McTavish's trap, and we can't go back upriver because of the canoes behind us, and we don't have paddles enough to fight the current, even if they weren't there. The only other option I can see is to aim for the rapids and hope those Cutters aren't brave or foolish enough to follow."

"I hope they do follow," Banderbrock said. "I want an opportunity to pay them back for what they did to McTavish."

Even as the badger spoke, they could see the current was picking up speed, accelerating them ever faster downriver.

Max kept the boat centered in the fastest flow of water, hoping to outdistance their pursuers. But the canoes still came on behind them, steering to either side of their boat, so as to trap their prey between them. The distance between each shore had narrowed, forcing a huge volume of water into a steadily diminishing space. Each bank rose higher out of the waterline the farther they were swept downriver. There was no longer a place to land the boat, even if the rushing water weren't forcing them along toward unseen rapids ahead.

"Try to hang on as best you can, without sitting down," Max said to Walden.

"Not that I could," Walden answered, forlornly.

Judging by the sounds ahead of them, the rapids were close.

Cutting Lessons

18 The day after McTavish left his friends on the riverbank, he found a large and sprawling farm along the road south. The farm had a big old barn and the barn was home to a number of barn cats.

"Who's the current reigning king here?" McTavish asked loudly, to no one in particular, as he swaggered into the barn. No one answered, not the horse in its stall, or the two milk cows in their pens, not the chickens or the geese, and not one of the six or seven cats he could see.

"Oh no! Are you all just dumb animals like Max said?"

Possibly for the first time in his life, McTavish was unsure what to do next. What he'd planned to do was quickly kill whoever was running the barn, establish himself as the new monarch, and then leave as soon as he was certain he'd secured his dominance, to see if he could find Max and Walden, and even that annoying Banderbrock. He wanted to bring them all back here where they could be safe and happy under his wise and benevolent rule. But how does one communicate all of this to a barn full of nonspeaking animals?

McTavish thought about it for a moment and had almost concluded that he should just kill two or three creatures at random and see if that would do the trick of showing them who was the new boss around here. While he was still thinking it over, sizing up the other animals, he heard an almost musical twang behind him. At the same time he felt an arrow pierce him from his hind end to his chest.

McTavish yowled in agony and tried to roll away, but the wickedly barbed arrowhead had gone on to bury itself in the earth after it exited his chest. He was helpless, pinned by the arrow's long shaft to the barn's dirt floor.

"Good shot, Michael," Lord Robert said, stepping through the open barn door. He walked up quickly behind the feral cat, who was bleeding dark blood into the ' and moldy old straw. He leaned down to examine vish, who hissed and spat at him, and tried to turn over to rake the man with his claws, but the arrow passing through more than half of his body prevented him doing it.

"I'll kill you dead!" McTavish spat. "And then I'll kill your children and then dig them up and make them have children of their own, so I can kill them too!"

"I can begin to see why poor Ander so hated this creature," Robert said. "He's a mean one, to be sure. Then again, the fouler the beast, the more grace we earn by redeeming it." Robert stood up and turned to Michael, still standing in the doorway, with a second arrow ready in his bow. "He won't last long like this. Your shot was too deadly. No time to get him back to Cutters Keep to do the work of changing him, so we'll have to do the best we can here and now. Who's the best Cutter we have with us?"

"That would be Lord Stephen, I would think," Michael said. "At least he's the most inventive."

"Fetch him quick," Robert said, "before this ugly thing dies."

The man in green moved quickly through field and forest, along the banks of the majestic river. Most of the time he was able to keep sight of the boat out on the water, with the boy, the bear, and the badger in it. Sometimes, when he had to rest, or divert around farmsteads, small riverside towns, or Cutter patrols, he'd lose sight of the boat. But he knew the river well and could guess the boat's speed and progress with some accuracy. He was always able to catch up and spot it again.

As he traveled, he left signs and markings that the others of his order could read, should there be any of them close enough to answer his call.

"Hold him still," Lord Stephen said to the other Cutters helping him. They'd moved the dying cat outside of the barn, to take advantage of the better light. Two of the Cutters had entered the farmhouse, rudely commandeering the farm wife's kitchen table, dragging it outside, despite her strongly voiced objections.

"You men! You terrible men!" the farmer's wife screamed at them. "Wait until my own good husband gets home. He'll teach you lot not to come uninvited into a poor woman's house, taking her tables, and bossing her around so ungentlemanly!"

"Be quiet, old woman," Robert had responded, "or I'll order one of my men to cut you quiet."

"You can't do that to me," the woman shouted back, no softer than before. "I know the law. I was born in this world, so you people have no right to change me. You can only cut the new ones, the talking beasts and such! I know the law!"

"That's true," Robert said. "We can't cut you to change you. But I can order your throat cut in the normal way, and then you'll be just as quiet and peaceful as I'd like you to be, wouldn't you now?"

After that the woman shut up and went meekly back into her house, and never a peep was heard from her for the rest of the day.

"I told you to hold the beast still," Stephen said again, as he prepared to make his first cut. Four Cutters held the cat, belly up, on the farm wife's table. One held each paw. Even while dying, McTavish squirmed and howled and dug his claws into the hands gripping him.

"He keeps trying to scratch me," Lady Ruth said. She was one of the four riders drafted into service.

"Of course," Stephen said. "Any subject of a cutting is going to fight you at first, if he can. That's one of the things you'll need to expect, and find ways to overcome. I selected each of you to help me because you're the least experienced in cutting a creature. But someday any one of you might find yourself in the position of having to take the lead in some creature's redemption. Pay attention and this can be a valuable learning moment for you."

"I'll give you a valuable learning lesson, when I eat your eyeballs and your liver," McTavish hissed up at Stephen, but there was no power behind it. The old cat was not long for this life, and fading fast.

Stephen moved quickly now, snapping the arrowhead off where it extruded from the cat's chest, just below his neck. Then with a single deft motion he pulled the remaining shaft out the other way. This caused McTavish nearly unbearable pain, but by now he hadn't enough strength left to do anything but quietly moan his displeasure.

"When treating a subject who's already wounded," Stephen said, "the first thing you must do is extract any obstructions, dirt, and foreign material from the wounds, such as Michael's perfectly placed arrow in this case. If you don't do this, then any cuts you make with your blue blade will only occur on the physical level, causing more injury to your subject, rather than on the superphysical level where the real changes need to happen."

Stephen made one quick cut, deep into the cat's chest wound, followed by another. Bright blood welled out of the cuts, mixing with the darker blood that had been flowing.

"There'll be blood at first, even with a healthy subject. The first cuts always work on both levels, creating the transition from one state to the other. That's why we call them the bridge cuts. Work fast during this phase. Your subject's life often depends on it. Always proceed with confidence. Remember, 'The timid hand cuts no one any good.' Once the transition has been established, prioritize your first changes. In this case we want to turn this poor beast from a wounded, dying cat to an unwounded, healthy one. That's all we're concerned about now. The redemptive cuts can wait."

"What if he escapes after you've made him hale and well again, but have yet to cut any of his villainous ways out of him?" Lord Jonas asked.

"Then we have to hunt him down again and start all over," Stephen said, "after we chastise the Cutter who should've been holding him better." He smiled to take some of the sting out of the small rebuke. "First we'll save his body, so that he can survive long enough to receive our other blessings. Then we'll cut a better mind and heart into this monster, gentling his spirit. And only then, if we have time, I think we'll make him pretty again, the way a proper house cat ought to look."

Stephen worked for hours, taking no breaks.

Near the end of his second full day following the boat, the man in green had to hide quickly as a host of riders came thundering down the road, headed in the same direction he was going. There were eight of them and they were Cutters all. They seemed in a terrible hurry, which made the green man increase his pace as well. Whatever was about to happen would be happening soon.

He ran as fast as he could, taking chances he normally wouldn't take, but ultimately he arrived too late. He crested a rise along one of the riverbanks just in time to see the boat with the fugitives leave a shoreline full of the same Blue Cutters that had passed him earlier. The boat headed into the strong currents, past the washerwoman rock, and raced headlong toward the river rapids. It was closely followed by two canoes, paddled by more Blue Cutters.

The Dragon's Roar

19
To the unlikely question "How many Cutters are foolhardy enough to follow their prey into dangerous rapids?" the answer seemed to be, "Exactly half of the available number."

Max, Banderbrock, and Walden watched one of the canoes turn around at the last moment. Its two passengers paddled madly against the current, to fight their way inch by inch back upstream. The other canoe came on, though, accelerating so quickly that it seemed to fly over the surface of the rushing crystal water. In little time the remaining two Cutters were but a few feet behind the fugitives' much heavier craft.

"Stupid, stupid men," Walden said, "to attempt these rapids without even a boat."

"But they're in a boat," Max said, sounding confused.

"You think so? Watch."

In another moment the canoe came alongside, lightly bumping its pointed bow against the rowboat's starboard planks, as both boats picked up speed together. The Cutter in the front of the birchbark canoe reached out to grab the rowboat's gunwale, then flinched back as Walden rose up before him on his hind legs, then fell forward onto the canoe's high prow with his full weight. Three times the bear bounced up and down, his front end on the canoe and his back end planted securely in the heavier, more stable rowboat. The colorful arrows sticking from his rear waved back and forth in the sunlight, like festive holiday pennants.

On the first bounce, the Cutter in back was launched into the sky, as his part of the canoe flew violently upward. It took two additional bounces to spill the one in front, only because he held on hysterically to both sides of his craft, and the relative leverage wasn't as much in Walden's favor with the man being closer.

The canoe became much less stable after the weight of the two Cutters was removed, and Walden had a difficult time getting both of his ends back in the same place, almost swamping their own boat in the process. But the bear worked it out, if somewhat ungracefully, and soon found himself entirely back in a single vessel.

"That was magnificent!" Banderbrock said, after their boat steadied enough to convince him he wouldn't immediately join the Cutters in the water.

"That should teach them not to shoot arrows at me," Walden said.

"Well, to be fair, neither of those two were the Cutter that shot you," Banderbrock said.

"As an honorable peace officer, I cannot in good conscience subscribe to the concept of guilt by association," Walden replied. "But even the most humble bear of law has to admit that every rule has its exceptions. Did anyone see if they've popped up again?"

"I haven't had time to look!" Max said. "We've made it to the rapids, and you'd both better get as low in the boat as you can, and hang on!"

While everyone but Max had been distracted by Walden's impromptu acrobatics, they'd been carried along into a boulder-infested part of the river, where great funnels of water turned snowy white as it dropped rapidly in elevation, pouring between huge polished rocks. The heavier boat gave the rushing juggernaut of water more surface to push against, so their craft dashed away from the empty canoe, which bobbed and danced uncontrolled behind them. Banderbrock and Walden ducked low, hugging the bottom of the boat with their bellies. But Max couldn't do that. In order to have any leverage on his makeshift rudder, he had to remain standing in the back of the boat.

He set his feet wide, wedged his toes under the bench struts in front of him for extra traction, and threw his full weight against the steering oar, fighting to keep the prow of their boat centered in the monstrous, unforgiving water flow. He also prayed. He prayed as he'd never prayed before. If you allow that the average Boy Scout is sufficiently reverent, in accordance to their laws, then you'd also have to allow that the same Boy Scout, riding such rapids as these, struggling alone to pilot a vessel never designed for such punishment, is by comparison devout nearly to the point of sainthood.

The boat flew forward and ever down, as the rushing river dropped rapidly in elevation. At times they were fully airborne, moving faster than Max had believed any watercraft could go. It bucked and tossed and careened off boulders, with sickening smacks of splintering, weakening boards that always threatened to shatter but amazingly held time and again. Max was certain he was screaming out his fear at the top of his voice. But the only sound he could hear was the roaring of the savage river as it tried to kill him and his friends with perfect, undiluted indifference.

He was blinded by curtains of white spray that impacted on his face and body like ten thousand shotgun pellets. Most times he simply had to guess in which direction he should try to steer the boat. Often he guessed wrong and they smashed against another unseen boulder. It seemed to go on forever.

And then, suddenly, they were dumped out into a vast area of calm water, where they slowed and then drifted gently into a tiny safe harbor, formed by a pocket of boulders and captured driftwood. They were able to tie the boat in place and rest.

"Did you think we were doomed?" Walden said, after they'd been there for some hours. "Personally, I thought we were doomed."

"Dragons," Max said.

"What about them?" Banderbrock said.

"Why is there any need to invent dragons, and other mythological beasts, when there are terrible forces like this in nature?"

"Because they exist too," Banderbrock said softly, and refused to elaborate further.

Once he'd rested enough to steady his hands, Max cut the arrows out of Walden's rear end. They were only short stumps by then, both shafts having snapped off and disappeared sometime during their chaotic tumble down the rapids. As Max guessed, neither arrowhead was in very deep. Both were lodged relatively safely within the fatty parts of Walden's well-padded hind end.

"They'll hurt coming out," Max said, while running a

candle flame back and forth under the open blade of his Scout knife. "And you'll be sore for a while back there, but you're in no mortal danger from these wounds."

"Unlike the last time, you mean," Walden said.

"Yes. Unlike then."

"Well, I suppose now's the best time to do this," Walden said, "because I'm so happy to have survived the boat ride, a little more pain isn't going to bother me."

After Max tossed the second bloody arrowhead in the drink, he got out the needle and thread from his Lost Kit.

"When Scoutmaster Barrow told us what to put in our Lost Kits, he never mentioned the needle and thread would be needed to constantly sew up wounded bears."

"Hardy har har," Walden said, sarcastically, but not unkindly.

The calm pool was deep in the shadow of twin canyon walls, of ancient sandstone that climbed so high above them the sky above was a single thin ribbon of blue, paralleling the river course. When Max finished sewing the bear's rump, he suggested they all sleep, and the other two gratefully agreed, knowing they were in about as safe a place as possible; at least where visits from any more Blue Cutters were concerned.

When they woke up late in the afternoon, they talked of doom and dragons, and other things. None of them was in any particular hurry to continue on to the next set of rapids, which they could hear in the distance. Eventually the talk turned to the subject of their lost friend.

"Maybe we acted too quickly," Max said. "We shouldn't have left him behind. I was so close, I might have been able to grab him."

"Nonsense," Banderbrock said. "I don't mean to brag, boy, but I'm about as tough a critter as ever prowled these lands. I could kill you with just a whisper. But even I would think twice before laying paws on that monster. With the changes they made in him, there's no telling what he would have done to you, but I know what he could have done to you, and it's not a pretty thing to imagine."

"Banderbrock is right," Walden said. "If we hadn't turned around and ran just when we did, we'd never have gotten away. We'd all have been killed, or changed into different creatures from the Cutters' long knives by now." He spoke in a halting, almost tear-choked voice, whether from his wounds or grief over the lost friend it was impossible to tell.

"In matters of strategy and long-term planning, and just about everything else, I'm content to defer to you," Banderbrock told Max. "But any time we get caught in a fight, or a situation that could become one, you'd best take direction from me. You've got as good a heart as the Great Creator ever put in any creature, Max, but it isn't a warrior's heart. Those take a bit longer to grow.

"McTavish is lost to us," the badger continued.

"For now, maybe," Walden said. "Not forever."

"True enough," Banderbrock said. "But it's up to us to go on now."

"Yeah, I know," Max said. "I just wish things had turned out better. In the past I was always able to keep my friends from any real harm by just solving the mystery in time. Once I did that, the danger always went away. The Cutters don't seem to care what gets solved or figured out. They still keep coming after us, over and over again."

"Find a way to get us out of here," Walden said, looking high and low, all about them. "It must be one of your mysteries, because I sure can't think of a way."

"We can't climb these walls," Max said, "and we can't go back up the way we came, so the only way out is to go down through the next set of rapids."

"That wasn't the solution I was hoping for," Walden said.

"Sorry," Max said. "But the good news is that we won't be trying it soon. It's too late in the day and I don't want to risk making the next run in the dark. So we'll take advantage of this safe spot to get more sleep tonight, and worry about it in the morning. We have all the fresh drinking water that we could ever want. I wish I hadn't lost the last of our food."

"Oh, we won't be going hungry tonight, if that's your worry," Walden said. "Look down in the water. There's fish everywhere."

"Can you catch them from our boat?" Max asked.

"Maybe not, but these rocks we're tied to look solid enough to support one little bear," Walden said. "And except for napping, fishing is what I do best."

True to his word, Walden caught more fish than the three of them could eat. Max was able to break up and cut off enough of the piled-up driftwood to make a warm fire on the crown of the biggest rock. He used the fire to dry all of his soaked clothes, and cook big steaks from one of the huge salmon Walden caught. With no other fare available, Banderbrock overcame his dislike of fish, and even found it less objectionable when Max cooked some of his share.

They slept warm and toasty in the bottom of their boat, snuggled together, Max wrapped in his newly dried cloak. In the morning, Walden and Banderbrock silently agreed not to mention all the things Max cried out in the night, as he tossed and turned in the grip of another terrible nightmare. Having nothing else to do to prepare or improve their chances through the next series of rapids, they decided to leave as soon as it was light enough to do so.

This time Max did all of the things he didn't have time to do before the first rapids. He made sure his knife and Lost Kit were in button-down pockets. Then he attached the sword's scabbard onto his belt, and tied the sword into its sheath with some of his heavy twine.

"You're working awful hard not to lose that thing," Banderbrock said.

"That's right," Max said. "This has become our most valuable possession. It saved our lives yesterday."

"What makes you think that?" the badger said.

"You made me halt because you realized McTavish had grown his tail back, and we were able to escape. But how did you remember he'd ever lost his tail? The things those Cutters do not only change the animal they cut, they also change everyone's memory, so that we all believe they were always that way."

"So you've said," Banderbrock said. "Then why did I know he'd been changed?"

"I think the Cutters are able to recall the changes they make, and now I believe that power also comes from these swords. We knew McTavish had been altered because we'd all spent several days in the boat, in direct proximity to this sword. I think its power has been gradually seeping into us, giving us some small degree of immunity to what the Cutters do."

"I don't want anything from that sword seeping into me," Banderbrock said. "It's evil."

"No, my friend, I don't think so. Though it's obviously very powerful, this is just a tool, and tools can't be good or evil, any more than they can be happy or sad. It's only those who use them that can use them for good or evil."

"I'm happy to see that you're detecting again," Walden said. "I could never have figured all of that out. It makes me hopeful we'll all get through the other rapids and the rest of this day okay, because you can always figure stuff out."

But they didn't get through okay. The next set of rapids made the first set look gentle by comparison. The first funnel of rushing water slammed their boat against the rock wall like the irresistible hand of a vengeful god, tearing it apart in an instant. Each of them was pitched into the rolling, crushing waters, and swept helplessly downriver.

The last thing Max saw, before he was dragged under for the final time, was a vision of Banderbrock tumbling over and over in the surging foam.

The Dragon Had a Daughter

 Max hung in dark space, suspended between a thousand intercanceling gravities. Distantly he remembered the warm embrace of God's hand, the comforting feeling as His cyclopean fingers wrapped around him, and lifted him up into the heavens. But that dream had detached itself. It was far away now, and he was cold again. When the cold got colder, and then became wet freezing, he reluctantly agreed to open his eyes.

It was nighttime and he lay in a bed of ferns, below

giant trees. He was still in his Cutter's cloak and Boy Scout uniform. They were wet and lay heavy on him. He was lying against the base of a large pillar of some smooth and intricately decorated material that stretched up into the shadows, farther than he could see in the darkness. Then the pillar moved. It stretched and uncoiled, becoming something else. Something from the realm of nightmare. The top of the pillar languidly bent over him, coming closer into his field of vision, until Max could see a dragon's head on the end of it.

"You're alive then," the dragon said, in a voice like the most soft and lovely music that Max had ever heard.

"Not for much longer," Max answered. He wasn't overly afraid of the hallucination, other than it emphasized how far he'd gone; how much danger he was in. He'd been immersed for some time in freezing water, and was now somehow lying in the cold night, in wet clothes, shivering profoundly. Hypothermia—some part of his numbed mind provided the name of the deadly peril he faced. "I have to make a fire or I'll die."

"I can't help you with that," the musical dragon said. "But I'll guard you while you do it."

"You can help me by talking to me and by keeping me talking," Max told the hallucination. "If I fall asleep again I won't wake up."

Max considered that this might be the reason people close to death so often hallucinate. Such manifestations

might be needed to engage a mind that wants to surrender
and shut down. Their very weirdness helps to wake a mind
back up and get it working toward survival again. They
help it fight off the attractions of giving in to comforting
oblivion. Maybe it's another wonderful part of a complex
and brilliant design, one more of a thousand different survival mechanisms built into the amazing human machine.
He'd been talking about dragons earlier, so he conjured
one up to save him. Basic psychology.

"Tell me your life story, or what you like to do with
your free time, or how you found me," he said. "Tell me
anything."

Max sat up, and with fumbling fingers, slowly managed to untie, unbutton, and unzip, stripping himself out
of his clothes. Wet as they were, they added to his danger.
Everything came off, until he was completely naked. He
hardly needed modesty in front of imaginary creatures.

"I found you in the river," the undulating dragon said.
"At first I planned to gobble you up for dinner, but then I
saw the cloak and sword that identifies your kind. I saved
you so that I might further work off my obligation to the
men of the Fellowship."

"You pulled me from the river?" Max said, dimly remembering something, the feeling of being enfolded;
wrapped in . . . what? Coils? He couldn't recall more
than a foggy image. Naked but still wet and shivering, he
looked all about him. This was a third-stage forest area,

or was it called second stage? Or fourth stage? He couldn't remember, because his mind was barely functioning. In any case it was the kind of forest where the high tree canopy blocks out so much sunlight to the forest floor that very little underbrush could grow. It would be difficult to find the right things to burn here.

"Yes," the dragon said. "And because I recognized you, I took your captive out as well, but lost it to the forest men."

"Um, okay, sure," Max said. "Look, if you really want to help me, I need lots of firewood, very fast. Nothing living. It needs to be dry, dead wood, or it won't burn well. And I need moss and lichens to start it going. As much as you can find."

That's it, he told himself. If I must hallucinate, get them working for me. So what if it really means I went out and found the wood and mosses myself, while I think I'm actually doing other things? As long as it gets found and gathered in time.

"I'll try to do that, great lord," the dragon said, and moved off into the night. Max watched it go. Giant ropes of coils unstacked and unfolded, trailing after its head, which had lowered to just a few feet off the ground. His imaginary dragon was a long serpent, like a python or anaconda, but multiplied many times over, to gigantic dimensions, as any proper myth creature should be. Max also moved off to gather what he could find. He ran mostly, not only because he had a limited time before hypothermia claimed him, but to let his exertions aid in warming him.

When he returned—after how long he couldn't say—his dragon was back and had brought a great load of wood and moss, compared to his paltry finds. Of course I really gathered it all, he told himself, but you'd think I'd have given my real self some credit and at least imagined the two piles a bit more even.

Max built his fire, lighted it, and then continued building it, and built it higher still, until it was as big as he could make it. He crouched and stood and danced as close as he could get to the leaping flames, constantly having to dodge flying embers. When he finally began to feel warm, he started drying his clothes, holding each piece up to the flames, until it steamed too hot to hold on to. As he worked, he noticed that his imaginary dragon didn't fade or diminish, as it should have, once he was assured of surviving. It stayed at a distance from the fire, coiled in a great pile, watching him from the near shadows.

"I think I'm going to have to reevaluate you," he said.

"Sir?" the dragon said, silky and enticing.

"You're real, aren't you?"

"Of course."

If it was real, the serpent was so large that grown men could be part of its diet. Hadn't it already admitted to that? Maybe even larger things fed it too. It looked big enough to swallow small horses.

"And you really saved me, because you owe some services to the . . . to my people? My organization. The Blue Cutters."

"Yes," the dragon said. "The Fellowship. I'm required to serve you, until my debt is paid. How is it you don't know this?" Its head swayed hypnotically back and forth, about seven feet above the earth.

"We're a big organization, and I have my own responsibilities," Max said. "Which Cutter do you most deal with? Who . . . ah, recruited you?"

"He is called Lord Stephen."

"Oh, yes, Lord Stephen. He's a good man. Fine fellow. Always gets his work done." Max looked to reassure himself that the cloak and sword were still present, realizing that they'd been the sole reason this thing—this self-confessed servant of the Cutters—made the mistake of saving his life, rather than ending it. All the Cutters wore the blue sword and gray cloak. "What's your name?"

The beast made a long musical sound that Max couldn't begin to try to duplicate. After he stared dumbly at the giant serpent for a few seconds, it said, "Lord Stephen couldn't pronounce it either, and called me Lady Slider, and sometimes just Slider."

"I'll call you the same, then," Max said. As each piece

of clothing finally dried, he began to dress as he talked. "Tell me, Miss . . . ah, Lady Slider, what are your duties toward us? Did Stephen give you specific tasks to accomplish?"

"I hunt the animals that talk like men. Those who haven't yet been saved. Just as he hunted and saved me."

"Oh, of course. That makes sense. And you don't eat them, right? You bring them to us, for cutting?"

"Yes," Slider said. "If they're like me, if they talk like men, I don't eat or kill them, but bring them to Lord Stephen, or another lord or lady of your kind. That is why I saved the bear as well, but then I heard the forest men coming. Lord Stephen commands me never to let the men of this land see me, so I had to leave, with time to take only one of you with me. I chose to save you."

"You mean Walden . . . uh, the bear, was still alive too?" Max hardly dared to get his hopes up.

"Yes," she said. "At least up until the forest men found it. I heard some talk about the rewards they could get, and about how they should build a cage to hold it, but soon I'd gotten too far away to hear more. I thought it best to get you far enough away to ensure your safety from the forest men. They are a band of thieves and cutthroats, and are always to be found in numbers."

Max could hardly believe his good fortune. Alone, nearly frozen to death, and half drowned, he nevertheless felt like it was Christmas and Santa Claus had granted all of his wishes. Then he remembered Banderbrock, and his fears returned.

"Was there a badger too?" Max said, dreading the answer he knew would come. "Did you rescue him?"

"I saw no such creature," she said, and Max's heart fell. "Perhaps Mother River took him. She eats many of those who venture upon her, as her rightful tithe."

As bad as he felt just then, Max could almost hear what Banderbrock would command him to do, in his gruff badgerly voice. Weep for the dead later, he would say. But save the living first.

"What happens once your debt to us is paid?" Max asked the giant serpent.

"Then Lord Stephen has promised to free me. He will cut freedom back into me and I will no longer serve anyone."

"Well, Lady Slider, how would you like to work off the rest of your debt to us, all at once?"

"What must I do, great lord?"

"Oh, you can call me Max . . . uh, better make that Lord Max. Now here's what we're going to do."

Max outlined his plan to Lady Slider.

Sando and Breck liked teasing their new captive, poking sticks through the stout wooden bars of the cage, until they provoked a fierce cry of rage from the beast.

"Cut that out!" Mike Fen finally growled from his seat by the campfire. "You want to bring every kind of bad thing down on us here?"

As the leader of a small army of woodsmen thieves, Mike didn't fear much. But he knew cries of despair in the night, from any creature, could attract evil ghosts and spirits, and he had no power to defend himself against those. He ordered Three Finger Tuck to put more wood on the fire, to build it up against such visitations. He didn't mind the sort of thing that a large and open flame would attract. In fact he'd sent most of his men out to find just that sort of fellow, leaving him, Tuck, Sando, and Breck to guard their treasure. Any Cutter in the area would likely come to investigate the source of the fire, and they were what he wanted now. They always had gold to trade for such oddities as this talking bear.

"Stop that!" the bear said, after Breck poked him again.

"That's it!" Mike Fen said. "I'm through telling you!" He began to get to his feet, but as soon as he started to do so, both of the others relented. They backed away from the cage, retreating to the far side of the fire. They knew they could get away with just about anything, until Mike got mad enough to actually stand up. Then they'd better back off immediately, or risk losing a finger, or an ear, as punishment for making their large and fearsome leader angry.

Three Finger Tuck was a living reminder of Mike's unforgiving policies. Mike knew they'd mind now, and started to settle back onto his log bench beside the fire. But before he could do so, one of the gray-cloaked Cutters suddenly appeared out from the shadowed forest surrounding them. Mike shot to his feet again, and found himself mildly surprised to be so much taller than his new visitor.

"I've come to take the bear," Max said from under his hood. He tried for a commanding voice but wasn't sure he'd succeeded.

Sando and Breck edged closer, to get a better look at their visitor. They'd never seen a Cutter before and wanted to get a good look at so famous and fearsome a figure. Tuck had seen one twice before, and edged backward, because he knew some of what strange powers they had.

"Aren't you a bit puny to be a Cutter?" Mike said. "And you sound like you're no more than a young boy."

"Our strength doesn't come from our physical stature, but from the powers in our swords," Max said, and set one hand on the hilt of his sheathed sword to underscore his statement. "Now open the cage and turn that creature over to me." Max pointed at Walden in the tightly lashed cage.

"Not until you show us some gold, boy," Mike said. "That's always been the deal."

"I don't have gold with me at the moment, but I promise another will return with your reward."

"That won't do," Mike said. "And now I wonder if you're really what you pretend to be. I never met no child

Cutter before, and I certainly never met one that didn't always have a fat purse hanging from his belt."

Mike stepped forward, fingering the long knife in his own belt. "Maybe that ain't no real blue sword you got tied to you. Maybe you're no more than another thief in the night, hoping to bluff us out of our goods."

"And maybe I'll cut you in two parts, if you keep coming forward," Max said. He drew the sword out of its sheath with a dramatic flourish, and held it high, turning it slowly back and forth, so the firelight could reflect off its polished blue blade.

Mike paused. He'd seen a Cutter's weapon before and knew the boy's was authentic.

"I won't ask you again," Max said. "Release the bear or face the power of my sword."

"You think you can cut all of us before we slit your skinny throat?" Mike said.

"You're a fool if you think the only power in this blade is its ability to cut," Max said. "And since you've been properly warned, and still refuse to obey, I now call upon the powers of my blade to conjure a terrible dragon to come feast upon your thieving bones!"

On cue, Lady Slider whispered into the campsite, like a great serpentine ghost. She raised her head until it towered several feet over the tallest of the forest thieves. Every one of them stepped back in terror at the sudden appearance of the monster.

"You are commanded to breathe your poisonous breath on these wretched men, and gobble them all down!" Max shouted.

Slider opened her massive tooth-filled mouth wide and reared her head back, loudly drawing in breath as she did so. That was all it took to break the already trembling spirits of each one of the thieves. They turned and ran screaming into the night, rushing off in four different directions.

Walden had watched the entire performance from his cage, as terrified as the others, but unable to flee. When Max turned his back on the horrible dragon, showing no fear at all, to walk up to his cage, Walden said, "Oh no, Max. They got you too?"

"Hardly," Max whispered to him, when he'd reached the cage. "But don't say that out loud. My new friend over there is only a friend as long as she believes I really am a Cutter. So shush, and don't speak for a while, okay?"

Walden agreed, but only with reluctance and wariness. He kept whispering frightened questions to Max, until Max finally told him that it was all complex detective business, which he couldn't explain right then. Then Walden was comforted, because, though he didn't personally understand detective stuff, he knew Max was an expert at it, and so things were well in hand, no matter how strange or frightening they seemed. He had never suspected before that detecting involved bossing giant dragons around, and became even more excited about the profession, and more determined than ever to learn all about it from his friend.

Once Max had cut Walden free of the cage, he turned to the giant snake and said, "Your duty to me is almost finished. I need to take this creature away to where I can work on him in peace. I want you to stay behind and search around, and make sure none of the forest men try to follow us."

"That will be easy enough," Slider said. "I'll simply track them down, one by one, and swallow them."

"Um . . . well, I'd rather you didn't do that unless you have to," Max said. "But once you are certain they'll all leave me and the bear alone, you have my permission to go north, to the crossroads, where Lord Stephen will finally cut you free of us."

"Thank you, Lord Max," she said, her voice as soothing as a string orchestra. Then she turned away from them and slid almost silently into the darkness. It took nearly a full minute for all of her long body to follow where her front end had led the way.

"I'm still confused," Walden said, after the dragon had gone. "Did you really join the Cutters, or not?"

"Only temporarily," Max said, and explained the concept of undercover work to his friend as they walked together, in the direction Lady Slider had assured them was south.

The Cost of Calling a Wolf's Bluff

Max and Walden walked south for two days, remaining inside the narrow forest of giant redwoods that separated the river from the road that followed it. Max examined the bear's wounds and saw that the ones in his rump were fine, but the old wound in his belly had bled again. It hadn't bled much, and had already scabbed over, but Max was still worried about it. He told Walden of Banderbrock's death, and they stopped on the morning of the third day to have a private service in his honor, where they each tried to hold back their tears as they shared their fondest memories of their beloved friend.

"He was the bravest of us all," Walden said. "At least McTavish is alive somewhere. Maybe someday we'll get to see him again and make him all better. But Banderbrock—" The bear was too choked up to continue.

"Two of us gone now and just two of us left," Max said. Tears were in his eyes and he didn't try to hide them. "We should move on now and try to reach the Wizard Swift's castle. Both of our lost friends would have wanted us to be safe."

Just then they heard a soft rustling of ferns and dried needles. They looked back to see the giant serpent named Lady Slider approaching them, curling and bending around rocks and trees.

"I ordered you to stay behind," Max said, as boldly as he could manage. By daylight the giant snake was even more frightening than at night. She was green and blue and black, in an elaborate three-rowed diamond pattern along her back. Her under-scales were of an ocher tan color.

"Yes, you did, and yet here I am," she said. "And you also ordered me not to eat the forest men, if I could avoid it. But I found myself able to swallow them down without any anxiety or pain from disobeying you. And when I'd made sure that there were no enemies left to follow you, I discovered no compulsion to go north to the crossroads, even though you commanded me to do so. I've always had to obey the orders of any Cutter in the past, but not now, it seems. Why do you suppose that is?"

"I'm certain I can explain," Max said, without much confidence.

"I hope so," Lady Slider said, "because I can only think of two possibilities. One is that I am already free from the Cutters, and finally able do as I choose, in which case I am free to eat you. The other possibility is that the forest man was right, and you aren't really a Cutter, in which case I am also free to eat you."

"Those are both good options," Max said. "Except that I don't think you'd enjoy your meal, if you swallowed this." He drew out the blue sword and held it pointed between him and the dragon. Lady Slider reared back, raising her fearsome head nine or ten feet off the ground. She hissed out a deadly warning to the boy and his bear.

"Get behind me, Walden," Max said, "so she can't attack you either. Once she strikes at me, you run as fast as possible, while I hold her off."

"I don't think so," Walden said. "Your job's to do the thinking, and now that Banderbrock isn't here anymore, I think it's my job to do the fighting."

Slider's head raised and lowered, and darted this way and that, looking for an opening through which to strike. With four grown men inside her—making her lovely sleek body look fat and lumpy—she felt full, dull, and a bit lethargic, but she was still fast enough to kill one small boy and his fat, slow-moving bear. The first time the tiny blue sword was slow to follow her movements, she'd have the boy.

"That's nonsense," Max said to Walden. "You wouldn't stand a chance against her, but at least she's wary of my sword."

"And I thought I told both of you to leave the battle plans to me," a familiar voice said. From behind them, a small brown, black, and gray form shot toward the giant serpent, and collided with its massive coiled body. Then, still mostly a blur, the furry thing scampered up the snake's long twisting neck, leaving a number of tiny blood spots behind it, everywhere its digger claws punctured the beast's tough hide.

"Banderbrock!" both Max and Walden shouted in unison.

"You're alive!" Max went on to say.

Slider's wide jaws bit at where the badger had to pause for an instant, hanging on while her coils whipped and thrashed, but Banderbrock dodged at the last moment, and the snake bit deep into her own body instead. Her scream of pain and rage was so musical as to be almost spiritual. When the badger had nearly reached her head, she thrashed her neck against the trunk of a mighty redwood tree, forcing him to let go of her or be crushed.

"See?" Banderbrock said, after hitting the ground and

instantly rolling back onto his feet. "The trick is to make her beat herself up."

Then the snake's huge jaws shot toward the earth, engulfing the tiny badger completely. Almost as quickly her head flew back into the sky, her jaws still open and trailing a number of twisting streams of blood.

Banderbrock was left behind where he'd been, down on the ground. His snout and two forepaws were painted red. "Bet she doesn't try that again soon," he said. Then he scampered back in among her wildly thrashing coils.

One of the snake's whipping coils passed close enough to Max and Walden that they were forced to retreat by several paces.

"Should we help him?" Walden said.

"Only if there's an obvious opening," Max said. "But I think we'd probably just get in his way."

The battle between the giant serpent and the furry little badger continued to rage on. Every once in a while Max or Walden caught a glimpse of their small friend clawing his way toward Slider's head again. Then a twist or tuck of writhing coils would cause him to vanish once more. The serpent tumbled wildly through the forest as they fought. Several times Max and Walden lost sight of them for long minutes, and had to follow the sound of raging battle to find them again. Then Max and Walden lost them for a much longer time, and became gravely worried when the battle sounds suddenly ceased.

Frantically they searched the woods together, trying to follow the path of destruction the fight had caused, but it had been too chaotic to leave a clear trail. Eventually they found their friend alone, lying on a low rounded rock, contentedly licking blood and snakey goo off itself.

"I finally got one of her eyes," Banderbrock said, in lieu of a greeting. "She seemed to lose interest in the fight after that, and slithered off in an awful big hurry. Too bad. I'm pretty sure I could've got the other eye, if she'd stayed just a bit longer."

"I can't believe you're still alive!" Max said.

"What do you mean? I told you I could beat at least two of anything. I have to confess though, I'm glad there was only one of her, but never repeat that to anyone else, or I'll call you a liar."

"That's not what I meant," Max howled in delight. "I meant I thought you drowned in the river. Oh, it doesn't matter now, just as long as you're back with us!"

"I agree," Walden said. "But I think we should leave here quickly, in case that thing returns with her Cutter friends."

"That we should do," Banderbrock said. "According to Prince Aspen's directions, we shouldn't be more than a few days north of the Wizard Swift's sanctuary by now. I think it's about time we finished up this journey, but there's only one small problem."

"What's that?" Max said.

"One of you is going to have to carry me. I think that snake broke both of my hind legs."

That was when Max noticed the badger's completely crushed hind end for the first time.

Banderbrock rode on Walden's back when they could afford to go slow, or more painfully in a makeshift papoose pack Max had fashioned from his cloak if they needed to move faster. They diverted around most of the farms and inns, and the few small towns that were spread out along the roadway. This close to the sanctuary they didn't want to take chances on who the people might be loyal to. Best just to avoid everyone rather than find out too late who was a friend to the Blue Cutters. Except sometimes Max would leave Walden and Banderbrock alone in the woods while he sneaked into a barn or empty farmhouse to steal food. He always felt guilty when he did that, but Banderbrock was in need of medical care and needed to reach Swift's stronghold as soon as possible, so they could no longer afford the time to hunt and forage on their own.

One night they spotted a horse and wagon parked outside of an inn, from which music and laughter and loud voices could be heard. When a drunken fellow left the public house hours later, he found both horse and buggy had disappeared. The horse returned alone the next day, walking peacefully into his accustomed stall in the puzzled man's stable. Two days after that he learned that someone had found his abandoned wagon many miles down the river road.

"So how did you escape the river, and then find us again?" Max asked Banderbrock on one of the days when the badger seemed more alert than he'd been of late. They'd made good time on the stolen wagon a few nights back, but mutually decided that it would be too risky to continue using it after daybreak. With the sunrise they'd taken to the woods again, paralleling the road.

"I was tossed around in the water for a long time, until I was able to catch a ride on a passing vehicle," Banderbrock said.

"The empty canoe!" Max said. "Of course! I'd forgotten about that."

"Yeah, me too," Banderbrock said, "but that wasn't the vehicle I meant. I never saw the canoe again, after we left it behind us. But one of the dead Cutters floated by, his clothes all puffed up with trapped air, and he didn't seem to mind when I crawled on board."

"Oh dear," Walden said.

"I got aboard him in time to watch that big snake grab up you two, so I rode him down the river a ways, and hopped off as soon as I found a place in the cliffs that I had a chance of climbing. Then it was just a matter of doubling back until I picked up the snake's trail."

"And you arrived just in time to save us," Walden said. "That's what I want to do, after I learn how to be a detective. I want to learn how to be the hero that arrives just in time."

"Well, I actually arrived a bit before that," Banderbrock said. "But you two were so busy saying such nice things about me, it didn't seem polite to interrupt you."

They walked slowly and slept little. Banderbrock murmured the pain in his sleep that he'd never admit to while he was awake. The farther south they came, the more and more depressed Max seemed. Walden assumed at first that he was just sad about Banderbrock, but it continued to grow worse. Max talked less often each day, until one day when he never spoke at all, so Walden finally decided he had to ask him about it.

"Yes, I'm sad about Banderbrock," Max said, "but he's a tough one, and I don't think he'll die before we can make it to the wizard's castle. We have to be very close by now. And if he's a real wizard, he should be able to help him."

"Then why have you stopped talking?" Walden pressed. "Are you mad at me?"

"Oh, heavens no," Max said. "You're one of the three best friends a boy can have. I guess I'm acting this way because I've finally solved the mystery."

DOWN THE MYSTERLY RIVER

"The big mystery?" Walden said. "Everything about how we came here, and why?"

"Yes."

"And why the Blue Cutters hunt us?"

"Yes, everything," Max said. "There were several good clues. The fact that none of you could remember the details of your early childhood, or you couldn't recall your own parents. There were large gaps in my own memory too. In fact my only clear memories before showing up in this world are when I was solving a big mystery in the previous one.

"And, I'm sorry to say this, but talking animals just aren't possible. The serpent Lady Slider provided the last clue I needed; though, looking back, I can now see that the evidence was all around us the whole time. I just refused to recognize it. It was all so obvious actually. I guess she just put the final cherry on the sundae."

"So, what's the answer?" Walden said.

"I don't want to say yet," Max answered, softly. "It's not very good news, and I think we should wait until we get to the Wizard Swift's castle, in case there's the slightest chance I'm wrong."

"Do you think you might be wrong?" Walden said.

"No," Max said.

"Not even a teensy little possibility?"

"Shhh," Max said. "Banderbrock's asleep and I don't want to wake him."

* * *

Two long days later, the three of them topped the rise of a small wooded hill and looked down, across the river road to the arched entrance of what had to be the Wizard Swift's lands. A low ivy-covered stone wall spread out from the open archway in each direction along the road, enclosing wooded lands and gardens and orchards, as far as the eye could see. Far back from the entrance, peeking over the tops of oaks and ash and beechnut and every other kind of tree, they could see the top spires of the castle's many towers. Bright pennants of every color fluttered from the top of each pointed roof.

"We made it," Walden said.

"Maybe not yet," Banderbrock said. "Look up the road. Those horsemen are coming fast."

"Cutters," Max said. "And there are dogs with them."

Sure enough a half-dozen mounted riders, each wearing their identifying gray Cutter cloak, were trotting down the river road from the north. A number of barking dogs ran along with them, weaving in and out of the horses.

"With the dogs, we can't even hide up here until they pass, or get tired of waiting for us and go home. They'll be on our trail soon enough, and they're too close to run from this time," Max said.

"No, we can run from them, and maybe beat them, to one place," Banderbrock said.

"Where?" Walden said.

"To where we were going all along," Banderbrock

said from the papoose pouch tied to Max's chest. "We'll make a run for that stone arch, and pray it really is a sanctuary they can't enter, and also hope that the barrier starts there, and not all the way back at the actual castle."

"We can't count on that," Max said.

"True, but all of life is a risk," Banderbrock said. "Better to dare and maybe fail than to sit here afraid to do anything and let them find us anyway."

"Okay," Max said. "I'm ready to try it, before they get closer. How do you feel, Walden? Are you able to run?"

"Faster than you," Walden said.

"He's right," Banderbrock said. "We stand a better chance of all making it if he carries me instead."

"You'd never be able to hang on to his back at a full run," Max said.

"I don't plan to try," Banderbrock said. "Walden is going to carry me in his mouth, hanging in this sack you've made."

"Okay," Walden said.

"You'll bounce around too much," Max said. "The pain will be horrible."

"The pain may get a bit tough," Banderbrock agreed, "but all the damage down there has been done. I'll manage. Just wrap me up as tight as you can get me, and then, Walden, you get a good grip on the cloth and don't let go."

"I promise I won't," Walden said.

"Okay," Max finally agreed, "but let's work quickly."

Lord Robert rode in the lead of the small force. Stephen, the master of horses, rode close behind, and Patrick, the kennel master, brought up the rear, trying to keep order among his hounds from the back of a horse. Anne, Kelvin, and Wallace were the other riders. This time, each rider carried a bow and arrows. If it came to a choice between killing the fugitives or allowing them to enter this hated place they approached, they'd decided they had to kill them. Robert knew their prey had to be close. Lord Stephen's pet serpent—now short one eye—found them and reported as much. When all at once the dogs scrambled up into the low wooded hills, across the road from the wizard's estate, howling and baying, he knew they had one last chance to capture or kill these creatures that had already cost them so much in blood and treasure.

But, surprisingly, at the same time the dogs ran up into the woods, the fugitives ran out of them, crossing the road just a few feet in front of the horses, in a mad dash for the stone archway that marked the Wizard Swift's lands. Robert had to choose immediately between trying to ride them down or shooting them dead. He wouldn't have time to do one, if the other failed.

"Your bows! Your bows!" he cried, reaching for his own, while his mount bucked and reared beneath him, probably nervous from the sight or scent of the bear.

Max ran for all he was worth, holding one hand down

on the sword sheath to keep it from slapping against his legs. His lungs burned as he fought for air that wouldn't come fast enough to help him. He couldn't risk a sideways glance at the Cutters, who were all so close to them now. He only looked at the stone arch, and how slowly it seemed to get closer.

He heard the *wicker-snick, wicker-snick* sound of a number of arrows being loosed. He saw a blurred image of one passing within an inch of his face, and felt another tug at the back of his red jacket that puffed out behind him. He saw Walden pass him, going fast. Banderbrock bounced madly up and down in the bear's mouth. It had to feel like torture to the badger, but he made no sound. *Wicker-snick,* another arrow passed close.

Then he was finally past the archway, and let himself stumble to a halt, as Walden did in front of him. There was no barrier to hide behind so that the Cutters couldn't get to them, if they still intended to. Either the sanctuary started here, and was absolute, even against arrow shots, or they were already as good as dead.

Max bent over, bracing his hands on his knees, and pulled ragged gulps of air into his lungs, and waited to see which it would be. He saw Walden gently set Banderbrock down on the ground so that he too could breathe easier. There were no arrows in him this time. In fact, Max couldn't recall any arrow coming close to the bear. They all seemed to have been aimed at him. But eventually, Max realized that no horses had thundered in at them, and no more arrows seemed to be flying their way. He looked up.

All six riders had their bows drawn and all six arrows were aimed directly at Max.

"They're past the gate," Stephen said. "Remember the treaty."

"Damn the treaty," Robert said. "These criminals killed and mutilated my men. They need to die!"

"Any Cutter who lets fly with his bow will die before his arrow finds its target," another voice said, surprising them all.

As Max watched, still huffing air into his tortured lungs, a man dressed all in green walked out of the forest, behind the riders. He had his own bow drawn and was aiming it at the riders. Lord Kelvin turned in his saddle and tried to bring his bow to bear on the newcomer, but the man in green let his arrow fly. Kelvin dropped lifeless out of his saddle, the green man's arrow buried deep in his chest.

Before any of the other riders could bring his weapon to bear, the man in green already had another arrow nocked and ready.

"Kill him!" Robert cried. "He's all alone!"

"Do you think so?" the man in green said. "Then where do you imagine your dogs got off to? Why haven't they charged out of the woods and mobbed me?"

Lord Patrick became especially worried then. Lowering his bow he whistled for his hounds to come. But no dogs appeared out of the woods. Instead three other figures stepped out from the trees. They were two men and a woman and they all wore muted forest colors, similar to the man in green. Each one carried a longbow of yew.

"We got them all, Jack," one of the newcomers said.

"Thank you, Tom," the man in green said. "Well done."

"You killed my dogs?" Patrick said. It was something between an accusation and a whimper.

"You didn't give us much choice," the woman from the forest said. "You should have called them off the moment you saw that you were too late."

"They don't seem to believe they were too late," said the man in green. "They were just about to violate the treaty by shooting these fellows down, even though they'd fairly reached the Wizard Swift's sanctuary. If you were to do that, if you'd loosed a single arrow past the wizard's gate, then we'd have open war again. Are you ready for that, Robert?"

"I remember you, Jack," Lord Robert said. "I know you and I'll mark this day. Jack in the Green. That's a name people won't dare to speak after today, for fear of earning my wrath."

"Withdraw, Robert, or we'll shoot you down," Jack said. "Our aim from steady ground will easily best yours from the back of those shifting, turning horses. You can't win here. Withdraw."

The Cutter called Robert was red of face, coldly furious, but he didn't try to shoot after that, nor did he say anything further for a long time. Then he simply said, "Let's go," to his fellows, while putting a spur to his mount. The mounted riders followed him. Lord Stephen was last, having dismounted long enough to recover the dead Cutter's sword before he rode off after the others.

"Go on in," the man named Jack called to Max and his friends. "You're safe at last. We'll follow the Cutters for a while to make sure they're really gone." And with that the four strangers slipped back into the forest.

The Wizard

22 For a few minutes Max watched the Cutters ride away. The feeling of grave danger they'd inspired for so long vanished with them, crumbling away in the wind, like dry leaves in autumn.

Then Max turned back to his winded friend Walden, and his broken friend Banderbrock. Carefully he gathered the badger up in his arms and carried him up the gravel and dirt pathway to the great stone castle beyond the trees. Walden walked at his side.

There was no longer any hurry, so they walked slowly, savoring these final steps to the end of their long and difficult journey. Max was extra careful not to make any jarring misstep that might further harm Banderbrock.

The path was in no more hurry than they were to get where it was going. It wove this way and that, around the trees, which were all well on their way toward dressing themselves in the glorious golds, browns, and reds of the swiftly approaching fall. Birds sang in the treetops, and some of them, if Max listened very carefully, seemed to be singing in a language he could understand. Colorful butterflies fluttered here and there. His mother used to call them tiny splashes of spilled paint from when they were still building Heaven. Golden bumblebees darted about, which made Walden hope that there might be honey to be found there.

A final turn in the path, as it came out of the trees and onto a wide green lawn, revealed the castle to them. It wasn't grim enough to be a fortress, nor quite elegant enough to be a palace, but it was large, solid, and stately, like a manor house. It stood several stories tall, and had many high towers and wings attached to it. And there were other outbuildings that weren't directly attached, but clustered attentively around the main building, as if they wanted to stay close so as not to miss out on any good stories or gossip.

There were many windows in the buildings, some

wide and tall and arched, hinting at large and important rooms within, while other windows were small and square, promising more intimate and comfortable spaces. At least one of the larger outbuildings had tall, colorful stained-glass windows, and looked as though it might be the estate's chapel. In the center of the main building, up a wide flight of stone steps, was a large doorway, at least fifteen feet tall and nearly as wide. In the doorway, the two huge and heavy wooden doors were carved with elaborate decorations and stood fully open, as though inviting anyone at all to simply walk in.

"What should we do?" Walden asked, when they'd reached the steps leading to the open doorway. "Should we wait for someone?"

"No one seems to be about," Max said, "and open doors imply that they expect folks to walk in."

"What do you think we'll find inside?" Walden said. He was nervous. In all his life, he'd ever only seen buildings from a distance, and he'd never entered one, or ever contemplated doing so.

"Books," Max said sadly. "We'll find lots of books."

"Is that part of the mystery?"

"No," Max said. "It's part of the solution."

They walked up the steps. At the doorway, under the watchful eyes of many carven statues, they paused for a moment, to see if anyone would appear, and then entered. They found themselves in a great hall and, exactly as Max had predicted, each vertical surface was covered in book-shelves that reached from the polished stone floor to the top of the walls, which must have been two or more stories high.

Each shelf was packed full of books of every shape, size, and color—thousands of books in all, or more likely tens of thousands. Warm beams of afternoon sunlight shone down at an angle through the high, narrow windows, evenly spaced between the bookshelves along the western wall. Motes of dust drifted lazily in the sunbeams. Three huge chandeliers hung from the arched ceiling on long chains. They were spaced in a row along the length of the great hall. Walden's claws made soft clicks against the floor's polished flagstones as he walked.

"I wonder where we'll find your Grand Green," Max said, looking around the great hall. He spoke almost in a whisper. The room seemed to inspire hushed conversation.

"It's a long way away," Walden said, not sure why Max chose to bring it up then.

"No, it's here," Max said. "Somewhere in this room, I'd guess."

"You sound like you know something we don't," Banderbrock said, in a strained voice. He'd kept silent since the run across the road, to keep from revealing the terrible pain that it had caused him.

"What I know is, we've got to get you some help right

now," Max said. "Hello?" he called loudly. "Is anyone here?"

"You shouldn't yell like that," a faint, small voice said from far away and high up. "It's quite rude."

They looked in the direction of the voice. Far down the western wall, almost obscured by the many intervening beams of sunlight, they saw a high ladder on rollers and wheels, leaning against the bookshelves. Almost at the top of the ladder, at least a dozen feet overhead, a fluffy black and gray ringtailed raccoon looked down at them. He was holding a small feather duster in one of his tiny hands, and wore a formal black frock coat with a proper inch of white shirt collar showing above it.

"We're sorry," Walden said. "We're new here and don't know the rules yet."

"It's not so much a matter of rules as good manners," the raccoon said. "If you've only recently arrived, you'll need to see the wizard."

Max and Walden continued across the floor, toward the raccoon's ladder, until they stood near the bottom of it, and had to crane their necks to look up at him.

"If he can help our injured friend, then that's what we want to do right away," Max said. "But if someone else is the doctor here—if you even have a doctor here—we want to see him first."

"Oh dear," the raccoon said. "Oh my. How badly hurt is he?" He set his feather duster down on one of the ladder's wide steps and began to climb down, pausing on each step to make sure he'd safely made it that far, before continuing on to the next one.

"Bad enough that I fear he's in danger of dying, if he doesn't get attention soon," Max said.

"Well, we don't want that," the raccoon said. "We don't want that at all." He stopped while still a couple of steps up the ladder, putting him at eye level with Max and just above Walden—as long as the large black bear continued to stand on four legs. Now that he was closer, they could see that the dignified raccoon wore a small set of spectacles clipped around his narrow snout, the end of which had begun to turn silver-white with age. He tsk-tsked while peering at Banderbrock, who was still carried in Max's arms. He said "Oh my" many times over. Then, completely ignoring his recent lecture on manners, he raised his head and shouted out, "Martin!" at the top of his voice, which turned out to be quite impressive, despite his small size. He shouted the name again, drawing it out. "Maaaaaaaarrrrtin."

In a short while, a very large, very black raven flew into the room from a connecting hallway, and landed with a flurry of his wings, perched above the raccoon's head, on one of the ladder's steps. "You called, Major?" he said, after he'd fully settled.

"Martin," the raccoon said, "I want you to hurry to the infirmary and have them send a wheeled gurney here, right away. Then I want you to go find Doctor Nicky, or Doctor Mary, or maybe it would be best if you get both. Tell them they have a patient in need of immediate care."

"You got it, Major," the glossy black raven named Martin said. With another short flurry of wings, he flew off, disappearing in the direction he'd come.

"Is Major your name, or rank, or title?" Banderbrock asked weakly, while they all waited for the bossy little raccoon's instructions to be carried out.

"My name is Mr. Wunkleblunt," the raccoon said, pronouncing it as if it were the very best name ever imagined, "but nobody here seems to want to take the time to use it. Since I am the majordomo of this estate, they tend to call me Major. And since it is at least a title of respect, I reluctantly allow it."

"Oh, so you weren't a military man, then," Banderbrock said, in such a way that it seemed to imply that the gravely injured badger felt superior to the raccoon. But that seemed hardly possible to Major, since he controlled the daily functioning of a great estate, while this badger was obviously nothing more than another ruffian from out of the wilderness.

If Banderbrock's first impression of the superior-acting Major wasn't all that wonderful, Walden's sure was. The black bear took an instant liking to the raccoon, who reminded him of his dear old friend and faithful deputy Dudley, back in the Grand Green. Major even talked in the same fussy, disapproving tone of voice that Dudley had always used when speaking to him.

After a while, a small but sturdy gurney was wheeled into the room by a polite and deferential otter in hospital whites. It was just the right size for an injured badger. It was well padded on top, and had wooden rails all around to keep a patient from falling off.

"Are you the doctor?" Max asked the otter, in a voice that hinted he desperately hoped it wasn't so.

"Oh no," the otter replied, looking embarrassed. "I'm Mrs. Landerhoven, the nurse. Only one of the nurses, actually. I didn't mean to imply that I was the only nurse, or even the most important one. Doctor Nicky is being summoned to the infirmary now."

Max helped Mrs. Landerhoven lay Banderbrock on the gurney, and while they did so, he explained how Walden had also suffered many injuries on their journey, though they weren't as recent as the badger's. He asked if the bear couldn't follow along, both to keep their friend company and also be seen by the doctor, when he'd finished with Banderbrock. Mrs. Landerhoven agreed that it would be fine for Walden to come along, and in a short time, all three of them—the otter, the badger, and the bear—had disappeared from the room, but not entirely from the rest of our story.

"I think it's time for you to meet the Wizard Swift," Major said, once the others had left.

"Yes," Max said. "I think so too."

"He's usually in the east garden, at this time of day," Major said. "Follow me."

Major led the way through one of the many exits in the back wall of the great hall. Rather than walking on all fours, like a raccoon is designed to do, he walked upright on his hind legs, very much like a raccoon isn't at all designed to do. He didn't seem to be very good at it either, which made for slow going, but he seemed determined to do it that way, perhaps because it wasn't dignified for a majordomo of a great estate to walk on all fours. Max had trouble walking slowly enough to stay behind, and not overtake the fellow. But before too long—at least as trees and continents measure such things—Major had finally escorted Max down several hallways, past many rooms, most of which were as filled with books and bookshelves as the first one, and out a more modestly sized side door with leaded windows in it, into the east garden.

They passed a sculpted hedge maze, dotted with a light brown dandruff of early fallen leaves, and then rosebushes, whose blossoms had already grown sleepy in the waning months of the year. Following that they arrived at the edge of a vast rolling green lawn. Major stopped there and pointed Max onward. A few feet out on the lawn, there was a statue of a woodland faun pipe player. One of its arms was missing, broken off long ago. The statue's pedestal, as well as most of the statue itself, was covered in vines of green ivy, bent on world conquest. In the shade of the slowly drowning faun, Max saw a man sitting in a wicker chair, chatting to a tawny yellow cougar sprawled lazily at his feet.

The man was portly—not nearly fat, but something beyond stout—and looked a bit older than middle-aged. He had black and gray hair where he wasn't going bald. He had large eyes and a strong nose, and a double chin that mostly only showed when he tucked his head to look down at his companion. He wore a heavy tan sweater, unbuttoned over a white shirt, and dark brown slacks. A wide-brimmed yellow straw hat was lying in his lap. A violin and bow were propped against one side of his chair.

The man looked up and saw Max at the edge of the lawn, and waved for him to come closer. As Max approached, the man whispered something to the cougar, who stretched languidly and then stood up and padded off toward the woods bordering the far end of the lawn. When Max stood beside his chair, the man looked up at him with a broad smile. He shaded his eyes with one hand and offered the other to shake hands with Max, who felt suddenly awkward taking it. He was tired and dirty from life on the trail, and wore clothes that hadn't been washed since being dunked in the river, many days past. He realized he must look and smell awful.

"You're Max the Wolf," the man said, not as a question. "I'm very pleased to finally meet you, even though

I've known you so well for so long. I'm the Wizard Lawrence Swift, though I like to keep things informal around here, so just Swift will do fine from now on. That's what everyone's come to call me."

Max in turn simply looked dumbfounded at the man, and couldn't think of what to say.

"I'll bet you're surprised to discover a wizard that looks so ordinary," Swift said, "but you're too polite to say so, leaving you not knowing what to say."

"Well, yes," Max admitted. "I'm not sure what I expected, but . . ."

"Oh, I have the long robes covered in arcane symbols," Swift said. "You can't enter the wizard trade without having all sorts of such nonsense thrust upon you, but I keep them stashed away in the attic, or in a trunk somewhere. I've never been much of one for playing dress-up."

"I'm also surprised that you seem to have been expecting me," Max said.

"Not exactly expecting, but let's call it hoping for," Swift said. "I imagine there are other wizards in the other sanctuaries wondering if you might show up there. But in this case, there were no magic powers involved. A few minutes ago, Martin flew out here and dragged Doctor Nicky away to tend to your badger friend. He told me you'd arrived."

"Is Doctor Nicky a good doctor?" Max said. "Will he be able to help Banderbrock?"

"I imagine so," Swift said. "He's the finest surgeon I've known, and I've known a few in my time. And he's also conversant in most of the shamanistic arts."

"He's both a medical doctor and a witch doctor?" Max said.

"He's every sort of doctor one can be," Swift said. "Your friend is in good hands. In a little while we'll go see how he's doing, but for now it's best to stay out of the way and let the doctor work. In the meantime, I'll bet you have any number of questions you're dying to ask me."

"Yes," Max said, "I do. But first, if you don't mind, I think I'd like to see the books. My books, I mean. The ones I'm in."

"What an astonishing young man," Swift said. "I believe you're the first new guest to have figured that out in advance. How did you do it?"

"I only worked it out a few days ago," Max said. "The final clue was when I met a person—well, a creature—that couldn't possibly have existed outside of a storybook. I should have guessed much earlier, when I'd landed in a place where animals talk, but by the time I'd given up thinking this was all a dream, I'd gotten so used to them that it slipped by me for a while. I guess it turns out I'm not as good a detective as I thought I was, or I'd been written to be."

"Let's go into my study," Swift said. "I had your books, and those of your friends, delivered there when

I thought I'd have to be the one to break the news to you. I'll have refreshments sent to us there, and you and I can have a long talk."

Swift pulled himself up from the large wicker armchair. He placed his straw hat on his head and bent down to pick up his violin and bow.

"Don't worry," he said. "I'm just bringing these inside, in case it rains. I don't plan to inflict my playing on you. I'm no sadist."

Together they walked back into the wizard's castle.

The Many Stories of Max the Wolf

23 Max looked at the pile of thin hardback books, spread out on a giant oaken table that had been polished to a mirror finish. He recognized every one of the titles. Here was *The Mystery of the Imaginary Swashbuckler.* Underneath the main title it read, *A new Max the Wolf adventure, by Lawrence Swift.* On the dust jacket there was a painting of Max in a fencing uniform, holding up a foil in his right hand and with his fencing mask under his left arm. It was a very good likeness of him, perfect in every detail. Next to that book was one titled *The Mystery of the Missing Star,* with its painting of an aging John Wayne on the night he gave his famous speech describing what each phrase of the Boy Scout Oath personally meant to him. The artist had painted Max, in full Scout uniform, seated at the closest table to the main dais and the famous American seated there. In all, there were thirty-seven volumes in the popular Max the Wolf series, and each one was laid out before him.

"Lawrence Swift," Max said. "That's your name."

"Yes, it is," Swift said.

"You wrote me." There was a catch in Max's voice. "The Eggman was right. You created me and the world I lived in. They were just stories. But each one of these stories are like real memories to me. I feel like I actually lived these events."

"They are real memories," Swift said, kindly. "You did actually live those events."

"That's nonsense," Max said. While they spoke he'd been thumbing through one volume after another and now held up the final one in the series. "Look at the publication dates. These books were written over a span of more than twenty years. But here I am in my first book, as an eleven-year-old Tenderfoot Scout, and two decades later, here I am in the last book, barely having achieved the rank of Star Scout, and still only twelve or thirteen years old. That's not possible! That's not real! I'm not real, and neither is Banderbrock, or Walden, or McTavish, or anyone else I ever loved or cared about! We're just made-up characters in somebody's stories. Nothing we did matters, because it was all fictional!"

Tears came unbidden to Max's eyes, though he tried to fight them back. This was the terrible secret he'd deduced days ago in the woods, and then kept from his two friends, trying to spare them as long as possible from the unbearable truth that none of them actually existed.

"Oh dear," Swift said. "Is that what you think? No wonder you came in here looking so miserable. You've figured everything out, but still managed to come to all the wrong conclusions. You and your friends exist. You're as real as anyone or anything ever was."

"How is that possible?" Max said, wiping away the tears that Swift pretended not to notice.

"It's not possible; it's impossible, and that's the trick of it all," Swift said. "It would take me years to teach you enough higher-order physics to explain how it all works, but let me try it this way: Didn't you mention you met the Eggman, and traveled with him for a few days?"

Max nodded.

"Why do you think the most magical things that ever existed, the eggs that hatch out entire worlds and universes, are called mundane? It's because every act of creation is impossible, in the sense that it involves the employment of miracles from the most mundane sources. A man in one world sits down at a battered old typewriter and starts tapping out words, until an amazing new world is formed. That, or rather some variation of that, is how everything was ever created, or will be created in the future."

"You mean all writers and storytellers are gods?" Max said.

"I guess you could argue that theory," Swift said, "but most of us in the world-making business settle for the slightly less extravagant title of wizard, and then only after we retire to become caretakers of one of the booklands, like this one. The important thing for you to know is this: You are real. You were real when you lived in your former world, where you were a Boy Scout who had adventures and solved mysteries, and you're still real now that you passed on to this world."

"That's just it," Max said, still miserable—or miserable again. "Maybe you could argue that I actually had the adventures, but I didn't solve any mysteries. Not one!"

"How can you say that?" Swift said. "You solved at least one huge mystery in every book, along with any number of smaller ones."

"No, sir. You were the one who created the mysteries and then worked out how to solve them. I just acted out the part. I did the things you had me do, said the things you told me to say, and ever only had the ideas and insights and moments of inspiration that you wrote into me. I never deduced anything on my own. I don't know what I am, but I certainly know I'm not a detective."

"Except that you are," Swift said, an impish look in his eyes.

"How can you say that?"

"Easy. You may not have legitimately solved all those mysteries in your books, but you solved the big one. I haven't been allowed or able to write a single word of your life since you entered these lands, and yet you still put it all together. You figured out everything about this world and your new dilemma all on your own. The important facts, anyway. Try telling me that isn't a first-rate bit of detective work."

Max couldn't think of anything to say to that, and so he said nothing for a long time. Gradually his tears dried up and the feelings of uselessness and his dizzying sense of panic began to fade.

After a time he said, "How did I get here?"

"There are many reasons a character travels to a world like this. Pardon me for calling you a character, but it is the best word available for purposes of our discussion. In this world it's not an insult. Far from it. In most cases a character's author dies, freeing him up to enter this land, where he finally gets to control his own destiny. His creator no longer gets to run his life. That's what happened to you, Max. I died a dozen years ago."

"But I only arrived here a few weeks ago," Max said.

"Yes, sorry about that," Swift said. "Sometimes clerks make errors. You should have been here long ago. Well, not here, exactly. This wasn't the bookland you were supposed to go to, but errors do creep in. Papers get placed in the wrong file. Things happen."

"I'm free now?" Max said. "You no longer control me?" There was a disapproving tone to Max's voice, and the wizard couldn't help but pick up on it.

"There's a lot of politics involved where there're so many creators running about, building worlds and characters," Swift said, "like a Boy Scout detective in America's Pacific Northwest. Or a mean old barn cat on a Midwestern farm. We had to strike a balance between the needs of the authors to craft the stories they wanted, and the rights of the characters created. We finally agreed that characters would be set free upon the death of their creator. They would come to a new world, far away from anyplace their author goes to, where they would finally enjoy free will, and be able to chart their own course in life, as best they can.

"That's why you find me here, caretaking a world designed for talking beast characters, far removed from the types of stories I told and the lands where my characters went after my death. It distances me from the temptations of continuing to run their lives."

"But I came here anyway," Max said.

"Not by design, young man. You were supposed to go to one of the human booklands, but someone must have been confused by your Wolf title and sent you to one of the beast lands. We might be able to correct that, once—"

"You died?" Max said, remembering what Swift had said earlier. "So Banderbrock was right. This is an afterlife?"

"Among other things," Swift said. "Banderbrock did come here because he died in the story in which he appeared. Our various laws and treaties also require that characters come to these lands when their creator is through with them, so they won't have to unfairly wait in limbo for their creator to die."

"Then, if you're the caretaker of this world—"

"One of them," Swift interrupted.

"Okay," Max continued, "if you're one of the caretakers of this world, and you're here to watch out for us, why do you just sit behind these walls doing nothing, while we have to fight our way here, risking death and injury on the way? And why do you let those Cutters run all over the place, destroying everyone they can catch?"

"Those are fair questions," Swift said, "and I fear that the answers I have to give you won't be very satisfying. First you have to understand that all of the agreements I spoke of, all of the treaties and laws we established, were the products of negotiated compromises among many factions, every one of which had their own desires and beliefs and agendas. There were many conflicts to settle. So the best possible results we could come up with would still be messy and full of disappointments, and ultimately ⟨...⟩ying to no one.

"In this particular case, some argued that, if we really intended to grant characters free will, then we should stay out of their lives completely, and provide them no help whatsoever. You'd have the perfect freedom to live or die according only to the law of the jungle.

"But others believed equally strongly that we should be out in the world, using our great powers to keep all of you safe from any harm, even though that meant you'd be less free to whatever extent we looked after you. That was the gist of it. Freedom is risk. Safety requires control.

"In the end, as always, we compromised. We established a policy of providing these safe havens, here and there throughout all the booklands. Places of absolute safety, where any of you can come to rest for a while, or stay for the remainder of your lives. It's up to you. Within the sanctuaries, our power is near enough to absolute. But outside, you're on your own."

"So you just allow the Blue Cutters to run all over out there and do any bad thing they want?" Max said.

"Yes."

"Even though they capture and ruin most of us who end up in this world?"

"Sadly so, the answer is also yes," Swift said. "As I said, it was difficult to reach an agreement where we were allowed to even do this much. You have more questions, I see, but let's order dinner first, so that they can prepare it while we continue to talk."

Dinner Conversation

24 Swift didn't call out, or pull a cord, or ring a bell, or do anything else to summon anyone that Max could discern, but a moment later Major appeared in the doorway of the wizard's study.

"Yes, sir?" the raccoon said.

"How are this young man's friends doing?" Swift said.

"The badger is still in surgery. Doctor Mary has examined the bear and has scheduled treatment for tomorrow.

I believe she gave him something to help him sleep in the meantime."

"I've never known Walden to need help sleeping," Max said.

"I understand he was anxious to remain awake so that he could continue to look after the badger," Major said, "but Doctor Nicky thought it best not to have him in the surgical theater."

"As soon as Doctor Nicky is finished, or has anything to report, I want you to bring the news directly here," Swift said.

"Yes, sir."

"In the meantime," Swift said, "we'd like dinner prepared and served to us here. Is there anything you'd prefer, Max? Some treat you've missed since leaving your accustomed home? I'll bet I could name a few."

"Oh boy, is there ever!" Max said. "I'd like cheeseburgers and french fries, and root beer, and maybe even pizza. But I don't suppose you have those."

"You'd be surprised," Swift said.

"We take pride in the ability of our kitchens to supply meals to match the most diverse tastes," Major said with obvious pride. "From the cuisines of Paris to Pelucidar, no challenge is beyond our chefs' talent. Your requested menu will present nary a problem."

"After you see to that, arrange rooms for Max," Swift

said. "I imagine he'll also want a hot bath, and laundry service."

Once Major had left, clearing away the teacups and cake dishes from earlier on his way out, Swift invited Max to continue asking his questions.

"Since I ended up in the wrong world, can you send me to the place I was supposed to go?" Max said.

"No," Swift said, "because that would require violating my pledge not to extend my powers beyond this estate. But you can go there, if you like. It's a hard journey and much more dangerous than finding your way here, but it's possible. Do you want to go?"

"I don't know yet," Max said, "but I'd like the option. How is it done?"

"Oh, there are many ways," Swift said. "The Eggman can travel freely through all of the worlds. So, if you're lucky enough to find him again, and he's going in the right direction, and of a mind to take you, that would be the safest way to go."

"What are some of the unsafe ways?"

"At the edges of every bookland, there are huge dragons, called bookwyrms. They constantly eat holes through the natural barriers between worlds, and those holes take a while to heal themselves. So, if you can find a bookwyrm—which is difficult, because they're imaginary until you get close enough—and it doesn't gobble you up, you can follow one of them through their wyrmholes, into another land."

"You're pulling my leg, right?" Max said.

"Not at all," Swift said. "Many a character has become adept at traveling from one world to another by wyrmhole. How do you suppose Robin Hood showed up in the novel *Ivanhoe,* as well as in his own stories? It was a short trip through only one wyrmhole, as those two booklands were bordered on each other, and eventually merged completely."

"That's amazing," Max said.

"Exactly."

"And I could travel through wyrmholes until I found the world I was supposed to go to?"

"Yes," Swift said. "Or you could go to any bookland that suited your fancy. You could even travel far and wide."

"Am I allowed to stay here?" Max said. "Even though you created me?"

"Of course," Swift said. "It isn't allowed for me and my kind to seek out our characters. But nothing was said about you and your kind. You're free to do as you wish from now on. We separate ourselves from our own creations partly to discourage that sort of thing, but 'discouraged' is a far cry from 'forbidden.' Many of the characters I created in my long writing career have found their way here, over the years. I tended to write the sort of characters who couldn't resist such a challenge, much like you. Once you get the scent of a new mystery, you can't rest until you solve it. Some of my characters came to thank me, or ask the questions anyone wants to ask of his creator, while others came to punch me in the nose, or worse."

"What did you do with the second kind?" Max asked.

"Though I have the power to stop them, I usually let them—punch me in the nose, I mean, not the 'or worse' option. I figured I owe them at least that much. If I had known what I was really creating when I set down to write my innocent little adventure stories, I'd have been kinder to most of my characters. Would you like to punch me in my snout, Max?"

"No, sir. At least I don't think so."

"Any more questions?"

"Plenty. Hundreds," Max said. "Who are the Cutters really and why do they do what they do? And are they just in this world?"

"No," Swift said sadly. "In one form or another, the Cutters inhabit every world. Some wield the blue sword, and others blue pistols, and even worse weapons in other lands. They're many different types of people, but in one way they're all of a kind. They're the frustrated people that inhabit every sort of world. Some of them are failed creators. Others just have a hunger to control others, and seek places where they can become the authorities."

"They're like you?" Max said.

"I hope not. But they sure want to be like me and the other wizards. Cutters are the ones who might not have the talents to become creators in their own rights, but wish they did. They're the ones all too common in every world who equate leadership with force and have allowed the various frustrations in their lives to corrupt them.

"It's scant surprise then that they band together in groups and companies and secret societies of their own kind and try to capture and control the things others have created. Once empowered by the blue swords, they change characters to suit their own whims, or the fashion of the moment, or try to reforge them into whatever interesting thing or idea they'd most recently heard of from a friend, or some passing stranger, or out of another book. Perhaps by changing another creator's character, they fool themselves into believing they're also creative."

"Do they realize how evil they are?" Max said.

"Most think of themselves as crusaders, spiritual shepherds, and warriors in the cause of justice. Some simply want to keep everyone and everything safe, despite themselves, for their own good. Adventurous types then, like those who tend to people the truly fun stories, become intolerable to them, and have to be changed. Tamed.

"Fashions and laws, and the basic concepts of what's good and right, change over time. And each time such a change comes along, the Cutters rush out to make every character in all the worlds conform to the new standards of the moment. They're constantly cutting and recutting characters over and over again, so their lives become whatever a Cutter wants them to be at any given time. Other Cutters have their own personal causes and try to cut those into everyone they can find. So it isn't uncommon for the ones who fall into their hands to be cut over and over, even daily, nevermore to be allowed to be what they were to begin with, or even who they've been changed into, for any length of time."

"That's horrible," Max said. "Can't you get rid of them?"

"No," Swift said. "The ones who can't create worlds on their own always outnumber the ones who can. Individually they're not as powerful as a successful world-maker of course, but they're strong because they've banded together. And to fight them openly would require violating our own laws, as I've explained. So, the best we can do is resist them."

"What about us? About me?" Max said. "You said we were free to do as we want, right? Am I allowed to fight them?"

"Yes," Swift said, "and because you asked that on your own, I'm allowed to give you what aid and advice I can. Now that you're free of my stories, you have the option of finally getting older and growing up if you want. You can become a man, and once you do, you can join the Rangers, as many of my characters have done."

"The Rangers? I think I may have met some of those," Max said, "right outside of your gates. What are they?"

"They call themselves the Free Company, or the Wardens, and also the Rangers, as I've mentioned. They're the warriors who travel the booklands, fighting the Cutters."

"Who are they? Who becomes a Ranger?"

"Some of them are characters from books, like yourself," Swift said, "or like Jack in the Green, who you encountered earlier today. But most of them, surprisingly enough, are Cutters."

"What?"

"No, don't be alarmed. They're not Blue Cutters any longer, but some start out that way. Just like the Cutters, they're story lovers who, for one reason or another, never could or never got around to creating their own worlds. So they do the next best thing by trying to help the characters from other stories find their way in this world. In one sense that's the same thing the Cutters are trying to do, but their ways aren't so pleasant. You could say they're two sides of the same coin, really. On one side you have the Rangers, trying to help characters find their way in these dangerous worlds. They want to help characters live their best possible lives, without taking away one jot of their freedom. On the other side you have the Cutters, who believe force is a perfectly acceptable method of improving the lives of every created soul they encounter."

"And you can help me become one of these Rangers?" Max said.

"Yes, I'm allowed to do that much," Swift said, "provided your training takes place on my lands. You'll find as you grow, the longer you stay here, you'll gradually become more and more immune to the Cutters and their powers. Their swords will lose the ability to cut unwanted changes into you."

"Then that's what I think I want to do," Max said.

"I'm pleased to hear that," Swift said, "but you've plenty of time to make such decisions. I don't want to encourage you to rush into anything, and make lifetime commitments after only your first few days of real freedom."

"I'll think it over," Max said, "of course. But I don't think the rest of my life can be just about what I want. It also has to be about what I should do. In this case my duty seems pretty clear. The Cutters nearly killed every one of us, and it's only by a sliver of luck that we survived to reach your sanctuary. And what they did to McTavish . . ." The anger showed clearly on Max's face.

"Revenge isn't a good motive for any important decision," Swift said.

"No, of course not. But they can't be allowed to continue." Max thought about the limited times he made use of the blue sword he'd captured. Even in the very limited way he was able to employ it, he felt deeply shamed by the experience.

"I had a tiny taste of using one of their swords," Max continued, "and it's a filthy, evil thing they do."

"I can't argue with that," Swift said. "But wait at least until your friend Banderbrock is healthy enough to leave."

"Leave?" Max said. "Why would he want to leave? He's going to stay here with his friends."

"I'm sorry," Swift said. "I thought you knew. He told the doctor he'd be going as soon as he was able."

"You need to stop him," Max said. "He needs to rest and be safe."

"How could I possibly do that?" Swift said. "He's the only one who can decide the course of his own story now. If I tried to force him to stay, even for his own good, I'd be no better than a Cutter."

"But we all made it here together," Max said. "We have to stay together!"

"I'm sorry," Swift said, "but I think you know that isn't so."

Then their dinner arrived, wheeled in on an antique cart with a white tablecloth, and served under trays of real silver. Every kind of food he'd dearly missed was brought to him, but Max found he'd lost his appetite.

Swordbreaker

25 Max stood out on the south lawn, next to the large flat stone that seemed to grow up from the grass like a single tooth of some buried ogre. The Wizard Swift stood to one side and a little behind him. All around them were gathered strange and myriad residents of the sanctuary. Max was surprised to discover that there were so many.

Animals of every kind were in the gathering. Some wore clothes, or spectacles, or carried some other human-like thing. There was a dashing cat, much more hand-some than McTavish, who wore a musketeer's hat, cape, and sword, and stood in a pair of buccaneer boots. Most, though, looked like standard animals.

There were also other people in the crowd. Swift said some of his own characters—children of his many creations—had chosen to stay with him. Max decided to make sure to talk to some of them later. In one sense they were brothers and sisters. Max was surprised to learn that Lawrence Swift was a prolific writer who'd created many more books than his boy detective series.

As tired as he was, Max had trouble sleeping on his first night in the sanctuary. He couldn't help but think of many more questions he needed answered by the odd but gentle old man who'd created him.

"Why did Danny Underbrink have to die in *The Mystery of the Lopsided Mountain*?" he'd asked.

"I didn't know at the time I was creating anything more than thrilling fictional stories," Swift said. "I didn't know then that I was playing with real lives."

"Why did you make me like Taffy Clark so much, but then make her be Joe Wilke's girlfriend?"

"Because that made you sad, and that conflict made for a better story," Swift said.

"Do you regret some of the decisions you made, just for a more interesting dramatic result? Are you ever sorry?"

"Every day, Max. Every day."

"Will I ever see my family again? Are they free too, now that you died?"

"Yes, Max, they passed on to one of the booklands too, but years ago and far away from here. There are places where secondary characters go."

So many questions Max had, and more every day. Finally Swift had to put a stop to it for a while. "You've got things you need to do, Max, and some of them need doing sooner, rather than later. We've years to get to all of your questions."

One of those necessary things brought Max out here on the lawn one morning.

Walden was there, standing humbly among the others. Wide white bandages were wrapped completely around his huge belly. The shy Mrs. Landerhoven stood attentively close to him. Noble Banderbrock was still confined to his bed, after coming through many hours of surgery and other treatments, and couldn't attend. Max recognized the Ranger named Jack, and made a mental note to be sure to talk to him before the day was out. But first the ceremony. The morning's rain had finally stopped and the sun was out again, allowing the solemn ceremony to proceed on schedule. Everyone watched Max expectantly.

He was dressed in his full Scout uniform, freshly laundered and pressed, making him look appropriately distinguished and formal for the occasion. Only the sword and leather sheath attached to his belt was nonregulation, but the sword was the reason for this gathering, and so Max, as the one who captured it, was obligated to wear it one last time. The crowd had been quieted and Swift whispered to him that he could proceed. Max didn't know if he was supposed to say anything, and looked at Swift for advice.

"Go ahead now. It's your honor and no one else's," was all the wizard said.

So Max pulled the sword out of its sheath one last time and held it up for all to see. Sunlight danced off the dazzling blue metal. Many in the crowd were awed by the thing, amazed at its terrible power, and by the young boy who'd been able to take it from a real live Cutter. Some showed their hate of the thing by mouthing soft boos and hisses, but then were quick to reassure Max the catcalls weren't directed at him. After all that were gathered there had time to see it, Max laid it down flat across the surface of the stone, still holding its grip, but with his left hand this time. Swift stepped up then and placed a short-handled sledgehammer in his right hand. It was heavy, but not too heavy for the boy to lift. He raised the hammer high over the blade, and paused.

"One strike should do it," Swift encouraged him. "These things lose their power after enough time within my lands. It will break easy enough now."

Max let the hammer fall on the blade, with too light a tap, he worried at the last instant. But the blade shattered easily, into several large fragments. Then those too began to crumble into smaller shards, until the entire blade dissolved into a dry blue powder that quickly disappeared in the breeze.

As soon as the hammer blow was struck, Max felt all of the power go out of the thing. More important, he felt everything this sword had done, since it was first made, come undone. Every person or creature it had changed into some other thing was restored to its original form and mind with the sword's unmaking. Max felt his recent friend Prince Aspen of the hidden grove suddenly recover his old self—the self Max had briefly encountered, before Diana had discovered him and recut him into another identity. He felt a serene and placid yellow-bellied marmot named Jackpaw recover his fiercely independent ways, and sarcastic wit. And he felt the incredible release of so many others, hundreds of creatures, who were suddenly, joyously remade into their original selves.

Max felt dizzy and started to stumble backward, but Swift was there to catch him.

"Feels good, doesn't it?" Swift asked with a large smile.

"Yes," Max said. "Very much so. Have you done this before?"

"Once or twice."

"And this is what the Rangers do?"

"When they can."

"Then I'm even more determined to do it also," Max said. "I'm going to join the Rangers, find the blade that cut McTavish, and break that one too."

"I believe you will," Swift said. "I do believe you will."

Okay, this next story is about how McTavish decided he was going to steal Old Farmer McDonald's tractor and use it to conquer the next farm over," Max said.

He was sitting in a chair, next to Banderbrock's hospital bed, which was so huge for him that the small creature looked lost in a vast sea of clean white bedsheets. Max was reading from one of the three McDonald's farm storybooks that featured the crazy exploits of their dear old friend McTavish the Monster.

"I can't believe these stories were written for kids," Max went on, "because, even though I dearly love the old beast, he's just so mean."

He'd also brought the single large old book called *Grand Green Tales,* to read from later. After their first publication in a single volume, the stories were later split up and published as a number of smaller books, which all featured Rake the Cougar prominently in each title, because it turned out Rake, rather than Walden, was the main character in most of the tales. Max was worried about how to break the news to Walden, but he needn't have fretted. Walden was overjoyed to find out he was mentioned in any book, for any reason at all, much less in over half of the stories about his old home.

The affable bear made Max read him each story about himself, many times over, all the while saying things like, "Yes, that's right, that's exactly what I did!" and at other times, "Oh yeah, it happened just the way that book says! That old Rake really tricked me good that time!"

But mostly Max spent his reading time sitting next to Banderbrock, as he continued to improve every day. He'd read the McTavish stories, or talk about their adventures on the trail together, or Max would just sit back and listen to the fruggerdly old badger complain about how much it itched under the rigid plaster cast that covered the entire lower half of his body. Several times the frustrated doctors complained to Max about how often they'd had to replace his cast, after finding it mysteriously clawed to pieces in the night. The claw marks always exactly matched Banderbrock's own front claws, but he always claimed to have been sound asleep all night, and had no idea how the destruction had happened.

"Why don't we save the next story for a bit later," Banderbrock said. "I'd like to talk about serious matters for a little while."

"Okay, sure," Max said. "Anything specific?"

"The doctor says I'll be out of this cast for good in a

few days," Banderbrock said. "And shortly after that, I'm going to leave here. And that's fine, because out there is where I belong, even though I'll miss you and Walden."

"I know," Max said, "and Walden and I have been talking about it, and—"

"Yeah, I heard about that," the badger interrupted. "And that's what I want to talk to you about. When I leave here, I'm leaving alone. You and the bear are not going with me. Don't look at me like that, I've known for two weeks what you two were planning. Walden is a wonderful fellow, but he can't keep a secret to save his life. I'm going, because that's what's best for me. I'm a soldier. Always will be. Too much soft living would be poisonous to me. But you two are staying, and that's that."

"But we're friends," Max said. "We belong together."

"We're friends all right, and that will never change," Banderbrock said. "But we don't belong together. If all three of us leave, then what was accomplished by coming here in the first place? You need to stay safe, long enough to grow up from a smart young pup to an adult warrior, like me. And Walden? Do you see how happy he is here? He has his pick of four different trout streams to fish on the property, and an endless number of good trees to nap under. That's all he ever wanted in life, and I'm not going to be part of dragging him away from his dreamland."

"But—"

"I'm not finished yet," Banderbrock said. "Who taught you to interrupt your elders like that?"

Max didn't argue the point, even though he could've pointed out that he was the eldest, since his books had been in print for over thirty years, whereas the badger's story had only just been published a few years ago.

"Maybe you should take lessons in manners from that fussy old raccoon, Mr. Wendel Wunkleblunt," Banderbrock said. He steadfastly refused to use the raccoon's common nickname, Major, ever since learning it wasn't a properly earned military rank.

"One other thing you should consider. If you two insist on going along with me, you're going to put me in all kinds of added danger. I'm small and can hide as easy as anything, but both of you stand out real obvious like. No offense, kid, but you attract too many Cutters in too many numbers for my comfort."

"I hadn't thought about it like that," Max said.

"Well, start. I'm safer on my own, and that's final."

"Then what do you plan to do when you leave here?" Max said.

"I've been thinking about what you told me about breaking that Cutter's sword," Banderbrock said. "And how it made everything it had ever cut change back to the way it was. Well, it seems to me what I need to do is start hunting down them Cutters one by one, and breaking their swords, until I find the one that can restore McTavish to his original, annoying, miserable old self."

"I had the same thought," Max said. "That could be dangerous."

"It will be, but I'm a cunning old soldier who knows when to duck. Who knows? I may find the right one the first time, or it may take a while. And soon enough, you'll be a Ranger and out there helping me."

"I will be," Max said, "as soon as I can. I promise. But you be careful in the meantime."

"Don't worry about me, kid. As I always say . . ."

"You can beat two of anything."

"You got that right, kid. End of story."

Epilogue

Walden the Bear never did learn how to be a detective or how to be the hero that arrives just in time. In fact he never again left the comfortable confines of Swift's protected lands. For his remaining years he spent most of his time looking for sweet honey to borrow from the grumpy bees, or nice grubs and beetles hiding under rotted old logs, or fat, tasty trout in the cold streams, or, best of all, a nice shady tree to nap under. From time to time he'd visit with his old friend Max, during his frequent returns to Swift's lands, or one or another of the many new friends he'd met in the sanctuary.

Once, after a few seasons had come and gone, Swift overheard the gentle black bear mention how sometimes he missed being sheriff of the Grand Green. So the kindly wizard asked him if he wouldn't mind helping him out by agreeing to be the sheriff of all the forests and orchards contained within the walls of his estate. From that day on Sheriff Walden would daily make a patrol of the vast estate, carefully making sure that all the trees were safe to nap under, the rotted logs were safely emptied of tasty grubs and beetles, the streams weren't too full of trout, since they're so slippery someone could step on one and suffer an accident. He also made sure that too much honey wasn't allowed to pile up in the many honey trees. He'd cheerfully admonish each friend he encountered not to turn to a life of crime, and since no one living there ever did, Walden was generally acknowledged to be a very effective sheriff indeed.

One day, when one of Mrs. Lippersong's newly hatched chicks fell out of their nest, after trying to learn to fly too soon, Walden picked the bold young robin up in his jaws and climbed high into their homey elm tree, to carefully deposit him back in the nest. Hardly a feather was ruffled on the tiny adventurer, and for days afterward Mrs. Lippersong sang Walden's praises to all who would listen. Eventually word of the brave deed got back to the castle and the Wizard Swift commanded all within his walls to assemble in the main hall, where after much pomp and ceremony, he presented the sheriff with a gold medal that said Walden was officially a Hero of the Realm.

The wizard tied the gold medal around Walden's furry neck on a bright blue ribbon, which stood out quite nicely against his reddish brown fur. Swift said that he was the best and bravest sheriff his estate had ever had, which was literally true. The kindly wizard never mentioned that Walden was the only sheriff they'd ever had.

Walden proudly wore his medal all the rest of his days, wearing out any number of bright blue ribbons in the process, until the cold and snowy winter two years after he first arrived at the sanctuary. The bear settled down under a cozy cedar tree for a quick nap, and quietly died in the night. His old wound from the long-ago battle with the Blue Cutter, which had never completely healed, and which always gave him trouble when it was cold, had finally gotten the better of him.

Hundreds turned out for his funeral, from many lands far and wide, including Max and old Banderbrock.

Walden was buried with his gold medal, under the very same elm tree where he'd become the Hero of the Realm. His many friends visited it often and kept it well tended.

And then one night, in the warmth of the following

summer, a tawny yellow shape slipped silently over the low stone wall surrounding the wizard's estate, and padded through the dark, until it arrived at the bear's grave.

"Walden," the visitor called down into the earth, while scratching at the grassy mound with his claws. "Walden, wake up."

"Who's there?"

"Who do you think? Time to wake up, old bear. Are you planning to sleep the rest of your days away? You've been snoring away down there for six months, lazybones."

"But I thought my days were done."

"No one's days are ever done. We go on and on. Only this one story is done, but others are waiting for us, old friend. Hurry up. Let's go find other fields to play in, where more adventures await."

"Okay, if you're sure we're allowed to. I don't want to break any laws."

"Don't worry, Sheriff. Breaking laws is my job. Now hurry up, before someone comes."

"How?"

"Just follow my voice."

And Walden did, rising up through the warm earth, without disturbing a blade of the achingly green grass that covered his grave-mound. When he arrived up above, he saw the yellow fur and feline shape of his visitor.

"You look familiar," Walden said, "but I can't seem to

recall your name. Are you Rake, or McTavish? I can't remember."

"Does it matter?"

"I guess not. But we were friends, right?"

"The very best of friends, and fine adversaries too. Come on now. The night won't last forever, and we have to be long gone before sunrise."

"Where to?"

"There's vasty worlds out there, Sheriff. Let's go conquer a few."

The big yellow cat sprang silently off into the darkness, and Walden followed him, fast and silent, like he'd never been before. When they reached the old stone wall surrounding his old world, Walden leapt over it easily and kept going into the endless new stories that awaited him.

MAX'S FIVE MOST IMPORTANT
RULES OF DETECTION

1) At the beginning of the mystery, the best way to isolate what you don't know is to first take stock of everything you do know.
2) Most detection is simply a process of elimination.
3) One should tend to believe the simplest of two or more possible explanations for a mystery.
4) A detective can't solve a mystery simply by picking and choosing the evidence that suits him.
5) Figure out enough of the small details, and the big mystery will solve itself.

THE BOOKS OF LAWRENCE SWIFT

The Max the Wolf Series: Thirty-seven books in print for over thirty years

1. *The Mystery of the Tardy Tenderfoot*
2. *The Mystery of the Spotted Dog*
3. *The Mystery of the Silver Moon*
4. *The Mystery of the Gruesome Grizzly*
5. *The Mystery of the Leaking Tent*
6. *The Mystery of the Mad Scoutmaster*
7. *The Mystery of the Curious Cowboy*
8. *The Mystery of the Imaginary Swashbuckler*
9. *The Mystery of the Missing Star* (featuring John Wayne)
10. *The Mystery of the Forgotten Forest*
11. *The Mystery of the Cautious Kidnappers*
12. *The Mystery of the Minor Samurai*
13. *The Mystery of the Lost Jamboree*
14. *The Mystery of the Broken Arrow*
15. *The Mystery of the Distant Campfire*
16. *The Mystery of the Frightened Fox*

17. *The Mystery of the Bad Deed*
18. *The Mystery of the Worst Girl Scout*
19. *The Mystery of the Lazy Stag*
20. *The Mystery of the Reluctant Ghost*
21. *The Mystery of the Lopsided Mountain*
22. *The Mystery of the Fearless Forest Ranger*
23. *The Mystery of the Third Skunk*
24. *The Mystery of the Broken Compass*
25. *The Mystery of the Unlucky Rabbit's Foot*
26. *The Mystery of the Troubled Troop*
27. *The Mystery of the Untied Knots*
28. *The Mystery of the Flash Flood*
29. *The Mystery of the Twice-Haunted House*
30. *The Mystery of the Twelve Bells*
31. *The Mystery of the Flying Tiger*
32. *The Mystery of the Stolen Canoe*
33. *The Mystery of the Broken Badge*
34. *The Mystery of the Twisting Trail*
35. *The Mystery of the Walking Snowman*
36. *The Mystery of the Fifty-Mile Hike*
37. *The Mystery of the Fallen Eagle*

Select other novels and book series by Lawrence Swift

The Gunfighter on Mars Series (Featuring the
   adventures of Eli Cross, a western gun-for-hire

transported to an alien world full of romance and adventure. There were seven books in this series.)

The Arcadia Series (Also called the Brona Cross Series, after its heroine, a direct descendant of Eli Cross. There were fourteen books in this series.)

The Ryan Grady Detective Series (An adult mystery series that was rumored to take place in the same fictional world as the Max the Wolf books, though never addressed in any of the stories. There were eighteen books in this series.)

How to Get Away with Murder (A nonfiction stand-alone book about how to write mystery novels.)

And the other storybooks involved in this story

The Three McDonald's Farm storybooks, by Felix Carol Brume:
1. *A Family Vacation on the McDonald's Farm*
2. *Lazy Days on the McDonald's Farm*
3. *Hard Times on the McDonald's Farm*

Grand Green Tales, by Caroline Weir

An Island Called Miranda, by Daniel Moffat (the novel that Banderbrock appears in, published just a few years ago).

ACKNOWLEDGMENTS

I am deeply indebted to friend and agent, Ken Levin, who thought there was enough life in this book, after a few years of dust had been brushed away, to think it worth sprucing up and shopping around. Also to my lit agent, Seth Fishman, who so deftly knows how to navigate the ins and outs of the book-publishing world. Susan Chang at Tor knew all the right questions to ask in order to move this story out of the sow's ear end of the spectrum and nudge it closer into the silk purse end. She has my gratitude and continuing astonishment at seeing a natural-born editor ply her trade. I am also indebted to the lady and gentlemen of the Clockwork Storybook writers group, the second best writing group in the history of English Letters, for their critiques, comments, and insights on the early version of this tale. Mark Buckingham also read and commented helpfully on this story, long before we drafted him to illustrate it.

Starscape

*Award-Winning
Science Fiction and Fantasy
for Ages 10 and up*

STARSCAPE

www.tor-forge.com/starscape